MADISON WRIGHT

Copyright © 2025 by Madison Wright.

All rights reserved.

No portion of this book may be reproduced in any form without written permission from the publisher or author, except as permitted by U.S. copyright law.

Cover Design: Sam Palencia at Ink and Laurel

Editing: Beth Lawson at V.B. Edits

Instagram: @authormadisonwright

To my baby girl,
I can't wait to be your mom.

READER NOTE

THIS BOOK CONTAINS DISCUSSIONS of an off-page miscarriage, panic attacks, parental neglect, and body image insecurity. It is my hope that I have handled these topics with the care they deserve.

ONE

ELSIE

JANUARY

I'm not supposed to be single. Of course, no one gets married thinking they'll eventually end up single again. But I've never really been single. I met the love of my life at sixteen. And now here I am at twenty-eight, a faint tan line still haunting my ring finger, being hit on by a man who's pretending he doesn't notice it.

"What are you drinking?"

That's the best he could come up with?

I fight to keep my eyes from rolling as he examines me from the barstool next to mine. The one that was blissfully empty until just moments ago. Until he slid into it, a thick thigh bumping against mine. I was hoping that would be the last of our interactions for the night, but unfortunately, I was wrong.

Swiveling my lightly spinning head in his direction, I let my gaze rove over his features. He's blond with eyes as blue as the icy lake outside. A haircut that probably costs more than I'll make in a week at my new job as a dance teacher. He screams *trust fund*, which means he's a tourist, likely here to ski on the slopes that this area of Montana is known for. We usually don't get tourists this far out, in my sleepy little hometown, but I can envision him in his hotel room searching Yelp for where the locals like to drink.

There's not a single bone in my body itching to speak to this man, but I'm too tired to explain to him that yes, in fact, I am going to be the first woman he's encountered to ignore his advances. I may be lonely, but I'm not desperate.

"Tequila," I answer.

His brows shoot up, a disbelieving smirk that he probably assumes is charming playing at his lips. "Straight?"

I motion to the bartender that I want another. She's been shooting me dirty looks all night because this is the smallest town in the world and she knows *exactly* why I'm here drinking tonight. But even she eyes the man next me, looking hesitant to serve me more. When I give her a slight shake of my head, she seems to deem me clear-headed enough and refills my glass without making eye contact.

That's what it's been like the last few months—no outright hostility, just cold indifference. I think I'd rather they chewed me out.

I shake the thought away and turn back to the man beside me. "Straight," I confirm. I tip back the shot, loving the way it feels as it burns down my throat. It hurts, but that, at least, is *something* when I've spent months feeling *nothing*. I can sense the guy's gaze on me as I swallow, and I let my eyes slide over to him. "It's been a rough few months."

His expression softens with empathy, and for a moment, I consider that maybe I judged him too harshly. "I'm sorry to hear that."

I shrug and grip the edge of the sticky wooden counter as the tequila moves its way through my body. It makes the edges of my vision pleasantly soft, and the tension that's held on to my shoulders for dear life for the last nine months begins to loosen its grip.

"Want to talk about it?" the guy asks, his gaze never straying from me. I hate that it feels good to have him look at me like that, to feel the warmth of his attention and know he likes what he sees. I hate how good it feels to feel interesting again.

I really, really *don't* want to talk about it, but the alcohol is loosening my tongue and my inhibitions, so I shrug again and lean in until our shoulders are brushing, my knee bumping his beneath the bar top.

"I was a ballerina—a good one."

He leans into me too then, icy blue eyes suddenly looking warmer with interest. The edges of his full lips curl into what is a rather good-looking smile. "I feel like this is going to be a long story."

A sigh slips out of me, ruffling the fringe of my bangs, the poorly planned ones I got the day after I told my husband to move out. They're longer now, an awkward length somewhere in between purposeful and hack job. The feeling of them against my temples makes that familiar weight settle in my stomach once more, heavy and unwelcome. "It's not short."

"Maybe," he says, and the word feels fraught with meaning, "we should go somewhere more comfortable to talk."

I blink, the last of the pleasurable alcohol haze clearing enough for his words to settle in. Warm, sticky air from the jumble of bodies cramped into this too-small bar rushes between us as I back up, head spinning. A sick feeling settles in the pit of my stomach, and nausea claws at my insides. The way he's looking at me no longer feels nice at all.

I'm just about to firmly tell him *no, thank you,* when an achingly familiar scent surrounds me. Leather and sunshine and freshly fallen snow.

"I don't think so," a deep, raspy voice says. One I've heard millions of times—yelled over the applause at the end of a ballet performance, whispered in my ear as our bodies tangled in sheets that stuck to our skin, murmured directly to me like no one else was watching as we recited our wedding vows.

A hand falls to my waist, heavy and easily recognizable, finding the same place it always has, right where my hip flares, landing dangerously close to the curve of my ass. Even now, the touch doesn't fail to send a thrill down my spine, landing in the place right behind my belly button.

"My *wife* will be coming home with me."

The last vestiges of the tequila buzz wear off the second Beau pulls me outside, the bitter cold slicing through my thin coat. It's dark outside and has been for hours. A dim streetlamp flickers overhead, illuminating the wintry wonderland beyond us as he stops in the middle of the sidewalk and spins to face me, dark messy hair catching in the chilly wind. His eyes, a familiar chocolate brown, a color I've never been able to keep myself from getting lost in, spark with anger. It's an emotion I've rarely seen from him. It feels so much better than the hurt I've seen there in the last few months. But beneath the anger, I see that familiar hurt, and it slices me to the core. The kind of pain that leaves me breathless.

Everything inside of me itches to push back that stray wave that always falls over his forehead, to press a kiss to his cheek, and to tell him that everything is okay.

But everything is not okay. In fact, everything is very, very wrong, and the weight of it crushes me. The yawning emptiness I was trying to avoid by braving the cold to come out tonight threatens to consume me once more.

Letting out a sigh heavy enough to pull me under, I say, "I wasn't going to leave with him, Beau."

His eyes hold on mine, examining my face for answers he won't find. I see the moment he gives up, hurt and anger warring for dominance in his expression. Right now, he looks like he's at the end of his rope. "Are you serious right now, Elsie?"

For a moment, all I can do is blink. I think maybe I imagined it in my tequila haze, the harsh tone of his voice, but when I see the ticking of his jaw, the way his body is coiled tight like one single press of his buttons would make him erupt, I know I didn't.

Maybe it should frighten me, but it doesn't. This is Beau, my *husband*, and even if we've been apart for the last few months, there's still no one I trust more.

I hate that I've hurt him again, that after all this time, I don't know how to stop. It feels like another piece of my soul shrivels and dies. Even to my own ears, my voice sounds dull, lifeless. "I just told you I wasn't leaving with him. What else do you want from me?"

The words and my tone only seem to anger him more. "I want you to use your head, Elsie," he says, voice low, breath puffing in the cold air around us. He's practically pleading, and something about it stokes a fire deep in my belly, in a place that has gone unnoticed for much too long. The feeling sustains me, makes me want to keep standing here forever in the freezing night air, with snow dancing all around us.

"I can take care of myself, Beau." I say.

His jaw tenses further, hard enough to crack a tooth. "Of course you can," he says with a tired laugh, looking into the black sky above us as if he's asking God for patience.

His disbelief pulls my spine straighter. "What's that supposed to mean?"

Concern edges past the anger in his eyes. "You couldn't even sit up straight in your chair. How were you supposed to drive yourself home? You didn't even notice when I walked in."

My gaze narrows on his. There are snowflakes in his eyelashes. I'm not sure how they're not burning up on contact with the angry heat pouring off him. His hair is tousled by the night air, and his skin looks flushed from the cold, the tips of his ears and nose red beneath the streetlight. He's always had stubble, but sometime in the last two months, he's grown a mustache too, and it looks good on him. I don't want to notice these things about him, but I've never been able to ignore him. Even when we were in high school, my eyes would somehow always find him in a crowd, like he was a homing device made just for me.

It's why I notice exactly the way his nostrils flare and his shoulders straighten when I say, "So that's what this is about, then?"

"What?" he asks, breath puffing in the cold.

"You're mad I didn't notice you," I say. It's the truth. I feel it deep in my bones. It makes that ache inside me yawn a little wider.

His jaw ticks, drawing my attention. I want to put my thumb there, feel it flicker against my skin. It's been so long since I've touched him, and suddenly, I need to do it again. To banish the aching guilt bubbling beneath my skin. I want him to take that anger and turn it into passion. Direct it right at me.

I don't expect his honesty, not when I haven't been with him, so the words feel like a slap. "What if I am?"

Then he steps closer, and I instinctively step back, my back bumping into the cold brick wall behind me. He doesn't stop until there's only a breath between us. "You asked for space, and I gave it to you." His jaw, still tight, dips as he nods toward the door to the bar. Hurt flashes behind his eyes again, and I feel it deep inside my chest. "I didn't agree to *that*."

"Didn't agree to what?" I have to know what he thinks I was doing, if he really thinks I'd betray him in this way too.

He leans impossibly closer, his breath tickling my neck, his lips brushing against the shell of my ear. "I'll give you all the space you want, Elsie, but if anyone is taking you home tonight, or any night, it's me."

His words slice through me, cleaving my heart in two. I want—no, I need—him to know that despite everything, he's the only person I've ever wanted. That there's not enough space in the world that could make me consider someone else.

It's not a good idea, I know that, but right now, it feels like the best idea I've ever had. "Take me home, then."

The truck smells just like it always has, like Beau and sunbaked interior. The seats feel the same. Soft, supple leather cracked with age. This truck is as familiar to me as its owner. Unconsciously, my eyes flit to the back seat. I've had sex in this truck. With my *husband*, who is sliding into the driver's seat beside me. My husband, who I've hardly seen in months, who, using all the strength I had left in my heart, I asked to leave, to give me space, to give me time.

I guess the clock has run out.

I can't make myself feel upset about it. Not when he looks this good, his cheeks flushed from anger and cold. Not when he smells like home, like all my favorite memories. Not when I know that he's going to stay when I ask him too. That we will both feel good for the first time in so long.

We're silent the entire way home. *My* home, I guess I should say. He's lived in a cabin at his parents' ranch since Thanksgiving, and I've lived alone in our house. He hasn't stepped over our threshold since then, but I hope he will tonight.

I may have been the one to ask for space. I might not be any closer to knowing how to fix our future. But I know what I want right now.

And it's Beau.

The truck comes to a stop at the end of the driveway, and a thick silence hangs heavy between us. Electricity crackles in the air, steel to flint, waiting to catch fire.

My eyes slide over to him. His hands are still tight on the wheel, knuckles white. The sight of it makes my mouth dry. I don't know that he's ever looked this raw to me, barely hanging on to his sanity, or maybe his self-control. I want to press it and see what happens when it snaps.

He clears his throat, loosening his grip. "I'll walk you to the door."

I should say I'm fine, that it's just a few feet away, that the snowfall is thick enough that I won't slip, even if I'm still a little tipsy. But I don't, and his relieved sigh rends the still air in the cab between us.

We're quiet as we climb out of the truck and walk the short distance to the door, the silence hanging heavy between us. The porch light has died since he left, and I've been too lazy to replace it, so we're bathed in darkness. It makes the moment feel more intimate, the air between us more electric, the reasons I asked him to leave more hazy.

It's too dark to see him, but I feel his stare all the same. We've always been opposing magnets, drawn to each other in a way that feels instinctual. Twelve years together, and I know him more than myself. I know that he won't ask to come inside. He'll wait for my decision, test that patience he's been hanging on to by a thread while I've been trying to figure things out these past few months.

I know I shouldn't ask him inside. I know what will happen if I do. But suddenly that doesn't seem like the deterrent it should be. My skin hums in a way that I haven't felt in so long, longer than the few months he's been gone, and electricity sparks in my veins. Need and want settle low in my stomach.

Years' worth of memories flash through my mind. I know how he will feel. I know how he will make *me* feel. And I want it. I want him.

"Beau…" I trail off, and I can feel him tense as he waits. I can't help it, I lean into him, and I tell myself it's to escape the cold. But it's not, and we both know it. His hands find my waist and grip *hard*. Hard enough that sparks prick behind my vision in the most delicious of ways. A gasp rips out of me when he presses my back against the door, the movement causing his chest to brush against mine. I can feel every line of his hardness against my curves.

I am on fire.

His breath is warm on my neck as he leans in, lips brushing the delicate skin there, mustache scraping. I know it's going to leave a mark, but I don't care. Everything feels like *too much* right now, in the best sort of way, making my knees weak enough that I have to grip his forearms to keep myself steady. But he doesn't go any further, and it has my patience wearing thin.

"What do you want, Elsie baby?"

I know what he's doing. He wants me to say the words, to ask him. I'm ready to beg.

"Come inside?"

That's all it takes for his lips to crash into mine, stealing what little breath I had left. *Nothing* feels like this. Like Beau. Like us. My hands find his hair and his find my ass, lifting, pulling my hips against his until stars dot my vision. We line up perfectly, always have, and my body moves on its own, rolling against his in a way that has us both groaning.

I don't know how the door gets open, but suddenly we're stumbling into the living room and Beau is kicking the door shut behind us, leading me to the bedroom like he has hundreds of times. When we lived in Utah, we stumbled through our living room of our apartment too many times to count, ending up on the floor or pressed against whatever piece of furniture we could find. But this is the first time we've woven through the maze of this particular house. We never felt this kind of frenzy here, and the thought makes a pang slice through my chest.

It's swiftly doused the moment Beau walks through our bedroom door, however. All rational thought leaves me when he drops me onto the edge of the bed. He's breathing hard. We both are. His hair is mussed from my hands, and his chest rises and falls with deep breaths. It's all I can make out of him in the darkness. I want to turn on all the lights and strip him bare and watch him as he falls apart, but there's no time. So I just drag him down on top of me and sigh into the familiar slide of his lips. His tongue tangles with mine, and my breath hitches when his hand finds the bare skin of my thigh beneath my skirt. This is the first time I've gotten dressed up in months, and I'm suddenly grateful for it. Grateful that he doesn't have to rid me of pants to touch me. Grateful that I can feel his calluses on my skin for the first time in far too long. Grateful for the way his eyes flare at the first touch of soft lace.

"I've missed you," he whispers into my neck.

It feels like a hit right to my solar plexus. The way he doesn't say he missed *this*, that he said he missed *me*. Because I feel the same, even though it was me who asked him to leave. Sure, I've lain awake at night, the sheets sticking to my overly warm skin, missing the way his hands and mouth and body feel on mine, but I've missed him more. His presence. His laugh. His ability to make the dark days seem brighter.

And there have been so many dark days.

But I don't want to think about that now. Not when his hands are wandering, when he's saying "arms up, Elsie baby" while pushing my shirt over my head and dipping his mouth to the skin exposed. Not when I'm desperate for more, for everything, for *him*.

So I push the thoughts down and reach for the hem of his shirt and then the button of his jeans. I drag my hands over skin that's always so much warmer than mine. I move my palms over the hard planes of his chest, feeling his heart hammering against my hand. I love that he's as affected by this as I am.

His lips find my neck again, and a strangled sound slips out of me when he bites down there, hard enough to leave a mark that will have me blushing into the mirror when I discover it in the morning. My fingers tighten on his biceps, pulling him harder against me, loving the way his body molds with mine, his mouth trailing down my neck, over the swell of my chest, tongue leaving a trail of wetness.

When his eyes connect with mine in the darkness from where he's halfway down my body, I think I might pass out. Nothing has ever felt this good before. Nothing has felt like having him here with me right now.

I'm frantic then, hands moving fast and gripping hard. I touch the places that make him gasp and groan, loving the sound of it, memorizing it, like I've ever forgotten. His skin is hot enough to burn, warm like he's been baking in the summer sunshine all day instead of bundled in winter coats to ward off the bitter cold. He feels like sunshine and tastes like something decadent.

I want to devour him.

But it seems like he's going to beat me to the punch, his mouth slipping lower. I want to fight him, to have my turn first, but his strong hands pin me down, fingers tightening on my thighs. I hope there's fingerprint-sized bruises there in the morning, another memento to remind me this actually happened, that it wasn't another desperate dream I woke up from in the middle of the night, alone in our bed again.

His teeth bite lightly into my hip, and I feel him smiling against it at my gasp. There's no use fighting him now, so I sink into my mattress that doesn't feel cold and empty for the first time in months, hands gripping the sheets, the only thing tethering me to reality.

I'm weightless and burning, feeling too much all at once. Starlight and moonlight pour in through the windows, making everything feel that much more magical, but I hardly notice any of it. I'm lost to sensation. To feeling. To skin and sweat and heat and Beau. To shattering apart for him, the sounds of my gasps and moans filling the quiet of our bedroom.

I shiver when he whispers that he loves me as he settles his body over mine, fingertips pressing into the skin on my hips, hoping he doesn't notice that I can't work past the lump in my throat to say the same. Even though it feels as if the words are clawing to break out of me.

For tonight, I make myself forget. The gnawing emptiness that's been spreading through me for the last nine months. The nights I've spent alone in our bed since I asked him to leave. The tears I wish I could shed. The way my heart has broken over and over and over again.

I forget it all and disappear into need and want and desperation and *Beau*.

TWO

BEAU
JANUARY

My phone buzzing on the nightstand is what wakes me up. I'm in my own bed for the first time in two months, worn flannel sheets soft against my skin. Soft, muted early morning light pushes past the sheer curtains of our bedroom, and just beyond it, I can see the mountain in the distance, covered in a thick layer of snow. Our house is on a small stretch of land ten miles down the road from Lucky Stars Ranch, the ranch that's been in my family for four generations, with views of the mountains rising in the distance. The closest neighbors are far behind a copse of trees, making it feel secluded, and although the view isn't as good as the one from my cabin at the ranch, I'd give up that perfect view to wake up in this bed every morning again.

For the first time in two months, everything is right again.

I reach for the phone on the nightstand, eyes still blurry with sleep. I have several missed notifications, all texts from my twin brother, Cooper.

Cooper: Where are you?

Cooper: Did you leave?

Cooper: I'm assuming you left.

Cooper: We shared a womb and you couldn't even say goodbye. Smh.

Then another that just came in.

Cooper: Seriously, are you alive?

I let out a sigh and rub a hand down my face. God, he's exhausting.

Beau: I'm with Elsie.

A text bubble pops up as he types, then disappears, then pops up again.

I chew my lip. I probably shouldn't have told him that, but I blame my sleep- and sex-addled brain. It's been far too long since I've had a good night of either.

Cooper: You sure that's a good idea?

I let my head slide across the pillow, eyes landing on Elsie, who's still sound asleep next to me. Just the sight of her makes the breath catch in my lungs. She's so stunning in the mornings, when she's messy and sleepy and carefree. She's so rarely carefree. She's a planner, and she likes everything to go the way she envisioned. She likes order.

And this last year has been anything but orderly.

It's been so long since I've seen her like this. For the last year, even while she slept, her brow was wrinkled, her face pinched. In pain. In worry. In grief, most of all.

A matching grief pricks at my chest, but I push it down. I don't want to let it in right now. Not when I finally have my wife in our bed again.

My fingers move over the keyboard.

Beau: Best idea I've had in months.

The entire town knows that Elsie and I have been split up for months, but Cooper is the only person I've really confided in. He alone has experienced my grief, has kept me busy, and he hasn't allowed me to slow down enough to crash out. I know he's going to have opinions about me hopping back into bed with Elsie without trying to work through our issues, but I can't bring myself to care just yet.

To him, this might seem like a mistake. To me, it's the first step forward.

Discarding my phone on the nightstand, I let my eyes trail over her for another moment.

Plaid flannel sheets pool over creamy skin, and I itch to pull them away, to explore her again like I did last night. Last night was perfect, and a rush of heat slams through me when I notice the mustache burn on her neck, the fingerprint-sized marks on her hips where I lifted her to meet my thrusts.

I'm just caveman enough to want to take her back to that bar like this and show that blond city boy with the brand-new six-hundred-dollar boots and perfectly gelled hair who she belongs to. I've never felt overly possessive before, but when I saw him touching her last night, something in me snapped.

Just the memory of what happened between us almost makes me wake her up in my favorite way, but I hold myself back. As much as I want a repeat of last night, I want to take care of her more. She's spent so much of her life taking care of herself, and taking over that job has always been my favorite way of showing her how much she means to me.

So as much as I want to stay in this bed with her for the rest of the day, I force myself to push the blankets off and slide off the mattress. I'm determined to make this the perfect first morning back at home. I have to hold back a hiss when my feet hit the icy wood floors. My clothes got discarded somewhere, my pants in a pile at the foot of the bed, my shirt hanging from the bedside lamp.

I tug my shirt over my head and allow myself one last glance at Elsie, pale blond hair draped over both our pillows, thick, barely visible lashes fanning over her rosy cheeks. She looks so small and fragile in our bed. I always used to think she was so strong, so unbreakable. I was wrong. I was so, so wrong. Beneath her strength and resilience is a fragility, one I should have done a better job of protecting. It makes that ache return to my chest. I have to physically rub it away, feeling my heart pound beneath the pads of my fingers.

I'm so focused on her that I almost don't notice how vacant the wall above our bed is. Before, there were two paintings. Portraits we did of each other at one of those paint and sip parties back when we lived in our tiny apartment in Utah. Neither were masterpieces, but Elsie's portrait of me was especially bad. I remember her face scrunched up, brows knit together as she tried to paint me, her wine sitting untouched beside her. Mine was gone, and the buzz from it made my hands sloppy. Still, my portrait of her somehow came out better. It wasn't that surprising, since I've always been artistic, and to that point, all of Elsie's creativity had been channeled into dance. But still, we took them home that evening, had a few more glasses of wine, and hung them up on the wall, which caused our grumpy neighbor to pound on the door of our apartment and threaten to call the cops if we didn't stop that "wretched banging."

It was a different scene hanging them on the wall in this house. I'd stood on the bed, adjusting them to make sure they were straight while Elsie stood at the other end of the room, shaking her head because I wouldn't allow her to help. Even now, I can still hear what she said.

I'm pregnant, not an invalid, Beau.

She was smiling, hands propped on her hips—ones she swore were already expanding—looking so radiant that I'd ended up putting the paintings down and lifting her against the wall and showing her that I knew exactly how much she could take.

The absence of the paintings now, memories haunting me everywhere I look, makes that ache in my chest spread, threatening to consume me. But I shove it down, spin on my heel, and leave the bedroom and the memories behind.

I've always loved this house. Even as a kid, when someone else owned it, and even more so since we bought it and started making improvements. It's a cabin that used to be much more rustic than it is now, with a wraparound porch and a metal roof that sounds hypnotic when it rains. In the summer, you can look out the windows and see the wildflowers growing up in every direction in the tall grasses. In the winter, you can see snow for miles. And no matter the season, you can stand on the porch and look at the wide blue sky stretching out as far as the eye can see.

Right now, the house is cold, so I start by building a fire in the fireplace, making a mental note to chop more wood to fill the rack beside the hearth. I may not have been home in months, but it hasn't stopped me from leaving piles of wood on the porch so Elsie never gets cold.

I warm my chilled hands over the cracking fire before heading into the kitchen. I'm not surprised to find that it isn't well-stocked. Elsie has always been the healthier of the two of us, dedicated to fueling her body for the hours of ballet she'd practice every day. After her injury, the one that ended her dance career, she'd stopped eating except for when I was home to make her. She started wasting away. The light dimming from her eyes, the pallor seeping from her skin. Until she got pregnant and had a reason to take care of herself again.

When we lost the baby, she lost herself once more. The eating stopped, and so did the sleeping.

I'm happy to see leftovers in the fridge and fresh produce on the counter. It may not be the well-stocked kitchen it used to be, but it's something. It's evidence that she's healing. Even if it's without me.

I shove the thought away and get to work fixing breakfast. There are eggs and yogurt, so I decide to make scrambled eggs and parfaits. I'm finished with the eggs and cutting strawberries for the parfaits when Elsie pads into the kitchen, the blanket from our bed wrapped around her shoulders and her feet covered in fuzzy slippers.

It's such a normal scene—me in the kitchen making breakfast, her walking in looking sleepy, her long hair a mess and eyes still bleary—that it almost makes me want to cry. A thick lump forms in my throat, and every bone in my body quakes to be closer to her, to feel her again, remind myself that she's real and I'm here, not back in my too-quiet cabin, alone and dreaming.

Without even realizing I'm doing it, I'm moving toward her, eating up the distance between us.

But then I notice the look on her face, and it stops me in my tracks. Bottom lip tucked between her teeth, eyes shuttered, and brows knit together. That look is regret. And guilt. And it feels like lead sinking in my gut, threatening to pull me under.

"I'm sorry, Beau," she says, her voice barely above a whisper. "We—" she cuts herself off, looking for the words, eyes trained on the ceiling before they finally lower back to mine. Her shaking hands tighten on where she's gripping the blanket beneath her chin. "That shouldn't have happened."

A rough exhale escapes me without my permission. I search her face, silently begging her to take it back. "You don't mean that."

Pain slashes over her features, like she knows she's hurting me and it physically hurts her. I want nothing more than to erase it from her face. She's felt enough pain in her lifetime, and I never want her to feel it again. It's why I've stayed away when everything in my body rebels against it. If my leaving could keep her from hurting even a little, it was worth it.

"It shouldn't have happened," she says, sounding strangled. "I'm not ready for...us again."

I swallow against the lump rising in my throat, my chest actually aching like she struck me there. Her words from two months ago come back to haunt me.

I need time. I don't know who I am without dance. Or after...after losing the baby. I don't know who I am at all. I need to figure myself out, get better. I can't do that with you here.

Leaving was the hardest thing I've ever done, but I always thought after time, she would still want *me*.

Scrubbing a hand down my face, I search for the right words. I feel like I'm being strangled. Frustration claws at me, and time feels like it's slipping through my fingers. I can't leave again. She might need time, but I need *her*.

"Elsie—I—" A breath heaves out of me. "It's been two months."

Her eyes connect with mine, the blue of the summer Montana sky. "Sixty-three days."

The fact that she's been counting soothes some of the hurt roaring in my chest, but it still lingers. I need to touch her, feel her, beg her not to make me leave again. I dare to take a step closer. She looks so small, wrapped in our comforter, shivering either from cold or pain or nerves or a mixture of all three.

"Els, please," I beg, not caring how my voice breaks, how desperate I sound. "Don't make me leave again. We can figure this out together."

For a moment, she almost looks like she might give in, like she might let me stay, but I see the moment the shutters drop over her eyes, and I know I've lost.

Her head shakes ever so slightly, looking like the movement is taking all her strength. "I can't." The words sound rough, like she's forcing them out.

I want to protest, to tell her I'm not leaving. I want to push like I did last night, see if it makes her come alive again. But I don't want to risk it having the opposite effect. I've never been able to stand seeing her hurting. So I force myself to nod, even though everything inside me is screaming to do the opposite. "Okay."

Her shoulders slump and relief colors her features. I think we both know she would have caved if I'd pressed her, but I don't want to. I want to come back when she's ready, when she wants me to, even if every minute apart is ripping me to shreds.

It doesn't keep me from drawing closer, from wrapping my arms around her, breathing in the achingly familiar scent of her—amber and vanilla, leftover perfume that I can imagine her spraying onto her neck last night. She sinks into me, inhaling the way I just did, digging her face into the crook of my neck.

We've always fit together so perfectly, like we were made with each other in mind.

"I made breakfast," I say into her hair, the soft strands feeling like silk against my lips. "I can stay, if you want. Just to eat."

She shakes her head, causing strands of her hair to get stuck in my mustache. Her voice is muffled by my neck when she says, "I have to go to work."

I pull back, looking down at her, taking in all the familiar curves of her face—the pert nose tipped up to the sky, the blue eyes framed by lashes light enough to be almost invisible, the freckles covering her cheeks and forehead and nose, the berry-pink lips I love so much. Her eyes connect with mine. "You got a job?"

Warring emotions fight inside me. On one hand, I'm thrilled for her. Elsie is the most driven person I know, and being without a job has been difficult for her. On the other hand, I hate that I didn't know. That I didn't get to celebrate with her. That her life is happening without me.

"Yeah," she says, a hand coming up from inside the blanket to tuck a strand of hair behind her ear. "At the dance studio. Ballet instructor."

My brow wrinkles. "Are you going to be okay? You're not going to aggravate your injury?" The tear to her Achilles that permanently ended her dance career. The one that required two surgeries and months of recovery.

She shakes her head, and when she speaks, there's sadness tingeing her voice. "No, I won't be dancing. Just teaching."

I want to ask more questions, like if throwing herself back into this world is going to be a good thing or a bad thing for her, but she said she wants to figure things out on her own, and I don't want to get in the way.

So I just nod and release her, even though my hands protest at the movement, itching to return to her hips. "I'm proud of you, Els."

A sheen coats her eyes, but she blinks it away. "Thank you, Beau."

The ache in my chest spreads because I know I need to leave now, that I need to go back to my cabin at the ranch. Alone. When all I want is to stay here where I belong. Keep my vows to love and cherish and protect her.

But I know that's not what she needs or wants right now, and I'm trying my hardest to do what she asks. Even though every cell in my body rebels at it.

"I guess I'll be going, then." My voice sounds rough, emotion clogging my throat, and I know Elsie hears it.

"Okay," she says softly, head dipping down.

Before I can talk myself out of it, I tip her chin up so her eyes meet mine once more. They're wide and sad and so heartbreaking to look at that I almost wish I hadn't done it. But I force myself to hold her gaze as I say, "Elsie, I know you need time, and I'm fighting myself every day to give it to you, but I want you to know that no matter how long you take, I'll be waiting for you at the end of it. I know what I want, and no amount of time is going to change that."

I don't give her a chance to respond before I turn on my heel and stride out the door of my own house, forcing myself to leave my wife for the second time.

THREE
ELSIE
JANUARY

"You look like shit," Tonya, my current boss and former dance teacher, says the second I walk into her office at the studio.

To some people, this might seem offensive, and sure, it kind of is. But in the dance world, commenting on someone's appearance isn't abnormal. I once had a dance teacher tell me he could see my lunch through my leotard, so this is nothing.

Still, I level her with a flat glare. "Gee, thanks."

"No, seriously," the older woman says, steepling her fingers beneath her chin. "You really look like shit."

I slump down in the chair across from her desk, using posture that, years ago at the barre, she would have yelled at me for. My eyes connect with hers, and I debate whether to tell her what's been eating at me since I woke up with Beau in bed this morning. But Tonya is like another mother to me—more of a mother to me than my own mother, truthfully—so I just say it.

"I slept with Beau last night."

At this, she perks up, brown eyes twinkling, leaning across the desk like closer proximity will make the gossip reach her ears faster.

"Good for you. You know that boy has a truly fine ass. It's a damn shame he was never put in dance classes as a kid," she says. "I'm glad you guys worked things out. You're both too beautiful to be single."

I press my fingertips into my eyes, pushing hard enough that I see stars behind my lids. I don't want to tell her the rest, but I know she will find out soon enough.

"We're not," I mumble, and when I open my eyes, she's staring at me.

"You're not what?" she asks, but she knows the answer. You don't spend your life teaching preschool to teenaged children, the majority of them girls, without being able to read between the lines.

A sigh escapes me. "We're not back together. I...asked him to leave again."

"Why the hell would you do that?"

After the injury that ended my dance career, when Beau and I moved from Utah back to our hometown in Montana, I isolated myself from pretty much everyone. I was in a dark place. It only started to lighten when I found out I was pregnant. And then we lost the baby at eight weeks, and I was plunged back into the blackness.

I'd only just begun to start crawling my way out of it. It wasn't until a few weeks ago, well over a month after I asked Beau to leave, that I finally agreed to meet with Tonya. I could tell she had questions about me and Beau. She even asked some of them, but I only gave her the *Reader's Digest* version. That I needed space to figure out who I was after losing dance and the baby. That I needed time.

She told me I was stupid and that one of her teachers had just quit and that she expected me at the studio to teach a ballet class in the morning. I wasn't going to go, but I knew she'd just show up at my house and drag me.

So I went. And, to my surprise, it helped. So I kept going. And after a week, she gave me a paycheck. And I felt like a functioning member of society for the first time in months.

It was my first step to putting myself back together, one of the reasons I finally felt ready to go out to a bar in a pretty skirt last night. But even though I'm healing, I'm not fixed enough for Beau yet.

I just don't know how to tell Tonya that.

"Can we talk about something else? Literally *anything* else?" I finally ask.

She holds my gaze for so long that I think she's not going to agree. "Fine."

A relieved sigh breaks through my lips.

"Someone wants to buy the studio," she says, and my breath catches in my throat, my heart stopping in my chest.

"What?"

She looks up from where she went back to flipping through papers on her desk. "You said you wanted to talk about something else."

"Like the weather," I sputter.

She rolls her eyes. "Wow, we got another shit ton of snow. What a huge surprise."

"Someone wants to buy the studio?" I ask, voice shaky.

She nods, pulling up an email on her desktop. "An out-of-towner."

That's not that surprising, seeing as how *she* is an out-of-towner. Tonya grew up in LA and then danced for a company in Boston until she retired. After she retired, she said she had no desire to see traffic or large groups of people ever again. She looked for the tiniest town she could find on a map, one that was in the middle of nowhere, and moved there.

It was Larkspur, Montana.

She'd been here for a few years by the time my parents started researching studios outside the metropolitan areas. They, too, wanted somewhere quieter. And when my mom saw that

Tonya Ballard, a dancer she'd admired for years, had started a studio in a small mountain town in Montana, she told my dad that it was where we were moving.

The studio exploded over the years, drawing in locals and others who, like my parents, were looking for good dance studios in small towns. I'm not surprised it drew the attention of a buyer. It has before.

I am surprised that she's bringing it up now.

"Are you considering selling?" I ask the question, unsure whether I truly want to know the answer.

Tonya fixes her gaze on mine. "I don't know. I wasn't, but traveling has its appeal."

"Traveling," I echo.

She shrugs. "Owning a business doesn't allow for much of it, and I miss it. Plus, it would be nice to travel when it's not for ballet and I can get drunk on wine and not worry about getting yelled at for it. I deserve to be fat and happy."

My heart seizes in my chest, because on one hand, I agree with her. Traveling with a ballet company isn't *really* traveling. It's working, which, as a dancer, means long hours of training and very little time enjoying yourself or the place you're in. On the other hand, this studio has been the first thing to actually make me feel like I'm making progress on finding myself again, and Tonya is a huge part of that.

Losing her, losing this place, is something I'm not sure I can handle right now.

She watches me hawkishly, no doubt seeing every emotion I try desperately to keep hidden from my face.

"You know," she says, leaning back in her chair. It squeaks loudly, but she ignores it. "You could always buy this place."

I stare at her like she's grown another head or suggested a six-year-old purchase her first pair of pointe shoes.

"You can't be serious."

She shrugs again, looking completely unbothered. "That would be the ideal situation. My star pupil, the apple of my eye, the daughter I never had, taking over my business."

"I have no money," I say.

She waves a dismissive hand. "That's not an issue. You could make payments, get a loan, do whatever."

"I have no qualifications."

"You were a professional ballerina. You trained in this studio your entire life. You are a teacher here. How much more qualified do you need to be?"

"I never went to college. I got injured before I even hit my peak as a professional, and I've only been working here for a month."

"Semantics."

I sit up in my chair. "Not semantics. I cannot run this studio. I can't even run my own damn life."

Gray brows lift. "You're crazy if you think anyone can run their life, Elsie. Life happens and we have to adjust to it."

"Well, then, I'm *not* adjusting well."

"No," she says, shaking her head. "You're not, but you're making progress."

I'd thought I was, before last night. Well, before this morning. Before I saw the look of crushing hurt on my husband's face. Before I had to be the one to put it there.

I shake my head. "I can't buy the studio, Tonya."

She holds my gaze for a long moment. I can tell she wants to say more, but thankfully, she lets it go.

"Fine, I won't sell."

I should tell her she can sell if she wants, that she should travel the world and let foreign men buy her expensive alcohol and stand at the top of the Eiffel Tower and see the tulips in Amsterdam in the spring, but I can't make myself. Because although I've grown, it's not enough that I can tell her to leave me, that I'll be fine here without her. Not yet.

And she knows it.

"I'm still mad at you for making him leave again," she says, turning back to the stack of paperwork on her desk.

Me too, I think. I'm growing and I'm healing, but not quickly enough. I'm hurting Beau by asking him to keep his distance and depriving Tonya by not letting her leave. I'm failing everyone, and it feels like the world is closing in on me.

"Excuse me," I say, pushing up from my seat and letting myself out of her office before she notices my expression, heart pounding in my chest.

I'm growing and I'm healing, but I'm *not* okay. Not yet.

FOUR
BEAU
JANUARY

"I SEE YOU'RE WALKING normally," Cooper says. "That means you didn't put in enough effort last night. After a dry spell like yours, you shouldn't be able to stand."

I turn to face him, exhaustion weighing down my shoulders. "Are you sure you've had sex before?"

A wide grin splits his mouth, but I cut him off before he can say something that will make me even more grumpy.

"Never mind. I don't want to hear whatever you were going to say to that."

"Namely, that I have a child," he says, leaning against one of the stall doors in the stables where I came as soon as Elsie asked me to leave. I didn't even bother to head back to my shitty cabin on my parents' property first. I needed to *work*, to drown myself in it so I could forget last night and the look on her face this morning.

Who am I kidding? A lobotomy couldn't make me forget last night.

I look back at my twin, trying to scrub thoughts of Elsie from my head. "I'm still not convinced Ruby is yours. She's way too smart."

He shrugs. "She got that from Willow. She got her good looks from me."

"Her humility too."

"Why the hell would I want my daughter to be humble? She's smart, funny, kind, and beautiful. She should act like it."

He's right, I guess. I'd never want my niece to downplay anything about herself. I want her to be just as confident at sixteen and twenty-six as she is now at six.

I turn to face him. "Maybe she does get some of her brains from you," I concede.

His smile widens. "Do you think you could say that again? I want to record it. Cheyenne will never believe me."

Cheyenne is our younger sister, which means she's seen the worst sides of us our entire lives. When I was a teenager, I used to worry she would grow up to be as crass and combative as Cooper and as stubborn and emotionally reserved as me. I shouldn't have worried. She became all those things but somehow made them charming.

I shove his shoulder. "Leave me alone, Cooper. I need to work."

"Right, those horses won't ride themselves."

I fix him with an annoyed glare. "They literally won't."

"Why are you so grumpy?" he asks, tone losing some of its playfulness. When I chance a look in his direction, concern is in the fine lines of his face. To most, he'd still look carefree and unbothered, but I know him better than that, and he knows me much too well. He knows I'd be acting very differently if things hadn't gone the way they went with Elsie this morning.

I let out a sigh and push my hands through my hair. It's messy from my hands and Elsie's, and I didn't bother trying to fix it before heading for the ranch this morning.

"Elsie told me she wasn't ready for me to come home yet."

Cooper raises his brows, but I see the faint tick of his jaw that gives him away. "So, what, you're just sleeping together now?"

I swallow past the lump in my throat. "No, last night was a mistake."

"And who was the one to say that?" he asks, voice holding a hint of hardness that wasn't there before.

I don't want to tell him because I don't want him to resent Elsie. No one else in our family does. They still love her like she's their own. They've been like that since the day I brought her home when we were sixteen. And the first time I came home without her two months ago, they welcomed me with open arms and said they would do the same with Elsie when she was ready.

Everyone has been patient and understanding. Except Cooper. He loves Elsie like a sister, I know that, but he's also been a little angry that no one seems to be putting me first in this situation. His words, not mine. He thinks someone needs to be looking out for me, and he's taken that job upon himself.

I'm grateful, really, because I've needed the distractions he's been offering, but I won't allow him to speak badly about Elsie, no matter what she does to me.

He thinks he's the only one protecting me, but I *know* I'm the only one protecting her.

"It doesn't matter," I tell him, but, of course, that answers his question.

"How long are you going to let her treat you like this?" he asks.

I understand his anger. Truly, I do. But he doesn't know the full story. He's never lost everything that was important to him. He's never grieved losing his life while simultaneously grieving the one growing inside of him.

He will never understand. I won't either, really. But it's not my job to understand her pain. It's my job to support her through it in whatever way she needs. And if that means staying away, I'll do it every single time.

"You need to learn to ask for what you want, Beau." Cooper sighs, sounding frustrated. "Why is she the only one to get to process this the way she needs?"

His words pierce through me. They're echoes of things I've asked myself when I'm alone and weak in my cramped double bed in the cabin on the ranch.

"Hey, kids," our dad says, walking into the stables. "What're you doing?" He's got a cup of coffee in his hand, the steam from it billowing in the chilly air. It'll be a brew strong enough to put hair on your chest, and yet I choke it down every morning, needing the warmth and caffeine it provides.

Cooper and I catch each other's glance, wordlessly agreeing to drop the conversation about Elsie. I told my parents the basics of what happened when I asked them if I could move into one of the spare cabins on the property usually reserved for ranch hands or travelers looking for a rustic getaway. Neither of them asked questions, and for that, I was grateful. I've shared bits and pieces of the situation with Cooper, but I don't want to talk about my failing marriage with my father.

We won't say anything more about it now, but I know we're not done with this conversation.

Dad looks between us, dark eyes no doubt reading everything on our faces, but he doesn't press. I've always admired that quality about him. Clint Jennings is steady and as immovable as the mountains.

"I'm about to exercise the horses," I say.

Cooper says, "I'm annoying Beau."

Dad loudly sips his coffee. He's drunk out of the same mug every day for as long as I can remember, and he only ever rinses it out with water, hours after the last dregs have dried to the bottom. It's disgusting. One time in high school, Cooper and I washed it as a prank, and he made us shovel horseshit for a week. The ranch hands were happy as clams. We were not.

"Sounds about right," Dad says. He then fixes his gaze on Cooper. "You planning to do any actual work today?"

When Elsie and I moved to Utah, I found a job as a horse trainer, which I loved more than I ever expected to. When we moved back to Larkspur, I took it over at the ranch. Cooper, however, has worked as a ranch hand since he quit his career as a bull rider and moved back home when Ruby was born. None of us ever thought we'd see the day he was working on the ranch, but he's settled into the role easily. He likes the variability of his days as a ranch hand, and neither of us has any desire to take over running the business portion of the ranch. It's just as well, because the honorary member of our family, Morgan Riggs, a local who is a few years older than us and who has worked on the ranch since he was in his teens, is the perfect fit. He didn't have any ranch experience to speak of when he came looking for a job at sixteen, but Dad knew he had a rough home life and decided to take him under his wing. He's been around ever since.

Beside me, Cooper shrugs. "Might get around to it."

Dad laughs into his coffee, the lines surrounding his eyes and mouth deepening. He's spent his entire life in the sun, and he looks like it. Weathered and sun worn.

"Well, we got a heifer ready to give birth, so you might have to get your pretty hands dirty today, son."

"This early?"

Calving season is usually in February and March, and this year, I'm looking forward to the hectic distraction of it. It's one of our busiest times, and I plan to lose myself in it.

Dad nods. "Jade's on the way."

Cooper rolls his eyes, but my heart stops. Jade Dawson is the ranch vet. She's also Cooper's worst nightmare, but Elsie's best friend. I have no doubt Elsie has confided in her about last night, and while I can take questions from my brother, I can't from Jade. She's been a part of our lives since long before Elsie. Our parents have been friends forever, which tends to mean she has no filter with us. No question is too personal.

And I'm not in the mood to discuss my marriage with anyone but my wife.

"You need my help?" I ask Dad, silently begging him to say no.

He shakes his head, and I practically sag with relief.

"Okay, I've got some horses to exercise, then."

I turn on my heel and disappear before either of them can ask any more questions. And damn Cooper, because my thighs are a little sore.

FIVE
ELSIE
FEBRUARY

It's been three weeks since my night with Beau. And my period is late.

I stare inside my medicine cabinet for a long moment, willing a pregnancy test to magically show up on one of the shelves. Or even better, for a period cramp to seize me and blood to gush out of me. What I wouldn't give to ruin a pair of ridiculously expensive panties right now.

Because I absolutely cannot be pregnant right now. Do I want to one day be mentally well enough to try to have a baby with Beau again? Absolutely, yes. Do I think I am anywhere near that right now? Hell no.

No matter how long I stare into the unorganized abyss of my medicine cabinet, a pregnancy test never appears. I feel panic clinging to the edges of my consciousness, fighting to seep into my mind and take over, but I push it down. If there was ever a time to *need* to be calm, this is it.

I take three deep breaths like the useless app I downloaded on my phone tells me to do. It does nothing. So I make my way into the kitchen and fill a glass of water with shaking hands, forcing myself to drink it slowly before pulling my phone out of my back pocket.

I click the second number on my favorites list and listen to the dial tone, letting out a relieved sigh when my best friend's voice fills the line.

"Hey, what's up?"

"I need you to take me to Bozeman to buy pregnancy tests."

She's quiet for a moment, no doubt processing the information. "Okay, why Bozeman?"

"Everyone in this town already hates me for leaving Beau. Can you imagine if they saw me buying pregnancy tests?"

"Right," she says, and I hear a rustling. I imagine her nodding on the other end. "I'm at the ranch right now, checking on a cow. I can be there in twenty."

The mention of the ranch—Lucky Stars Ranch, the *Jenningses'* ranch to be exact—has my heart galloping in my chest.

"Please don't mention this to anyone," I gasp out.

"Of course not." Her voice changes then to something snarkier. "It's just Cooper here, and I wouldn't tell him anything important if my life depended on it."

My pulse ratchets higher and my mind swims. "You're with Cooper?"

"Yes," she tells me, and then I hear a deep voice on the other line. "Mind your own damn business, Cooper. It's my urologist. I have an overactive bladder. Is that what you wanted to know, you intrusive piece of shit?"

Their bickering soothes something inside me, pushes the panic back even farther, and I take my first deep breath since opening my period tracker app this morning and seeing that I was four days late for my period—something that has only ever happened one time before.

"Yeah, I bet you're sorry," Jade says, voice still muffled as she talks to Cooper.

"I'm going to go," I tell her.

She returns to the conversation. "Yeah, I'll be there in just a minute. I need to wash my hands. I just had them up a cow's vagina."

"God, please do."

"How do you feel?" Jade asks me an hour and a half later, staring at me with wide, unblinking eyes.

I swing my head to face her, hands still propped on my bathroom counter. "Pregnant."

"Do you actually feel pregnant, or are you just saying that because there's a positive pregnancy test right in front of you?"

We stare at the *positive* pregnancy test I just took. And when I say positive, I mean *really* positive. I grew up in dance and Jade grew up on a ranch, which means neither of us has ever cared about having any semblance of privacy. She stood in front of the toilet and mocked me for not being able to aim at the stick properly, and then we both watched as two lines started to show up before I even set it on the counter.

"I don't know," I tell her honestly. There have been...signs. Ones I remember from seven months ago, the last time I was pregnant. The nonstop urge to pee. The cramps that feel like my period could show up at any second. The way I've passed out on the couch the last two nights before ever making it to bed.

There were signs that I should have caught, but I didn't. Not when the night with Beau felt like so many other dreams I've woken up from, alone and covered in sweat in our bed. Until looking at those two lines, I was convinced I'd made it up, that he hadn't actually left the fingerprint-sized bruises on my hips or the hickey on my chest.

But now I know that what we did was very, *very* real. And had very, *very* real repercussions.

"Are you okay?" she asks me, and I really don't know how to respond. I meet her green gaze in the mirror. She might have just come from a cattle ranch, but she still looks effortlessly stunning. She has the kind of natural beauty that people pay lots of money to achieve.

"I don't know," I say truthfully.

I'm separated from my husband and pregnant with his child. Just five months after I miscarried our last one.

Oh yeah, and I feel like I'm going to throw up my breakfast.

I let my head fall back, closing my eyes against the bright bathroom lights. "Not good, I don't think."

"So…" She hesitates. "How far along are you? Probably, like, five weeks, right? Unless you guys—"

My eyes connect with hers in the mirror again. "No, we didn't. Again."

Even though I've wanted to. God, I forgot how much I love having him like *that*. I've missed him in so many ways over the last three months. I've missed hearing his laugh and cuddling up to him in the middle of the night when I'm cold and having someone to eat dinner with at night.

But it wasn't until that night three weeks ago that I realized how much I'd missed his hands and mouth and the way he makes me come alive with just one touch. That night felt magical.

And looking down at my flat stomach that will soon start to become rounded with our child, I guess it was.

"Five weeks," I confirm. "If I had to guess."

Jade's voice is softener, less tinged with shock, when she asks, "How do you feel, really?"

I shake my head, so, so many thoughts jumbling around inside it, and turn around to face her in my bathroom. "I'm scared, Jade," I whisper, wishing I could feel the relief of tears.

I've experienced so much hurt, so much *grief* this year, but I've hardly been able to cry. I think I'm broken. No, I know I am.

Jade wraps her arms around me, and I sink into her embrace. She's so much taller than me, and I love the way she always rests her head on top of mine when we hug. It always makes me feel intense comfort, right down to my bones, and this time is no different, even if it doesn't manage to knock all the anxiety away.

"It's going to be okay," she promises, her voice raspy. She has the kind of voice they put in men's deodorant commercials. The ones where ridiculously hot women are talking about how their ridiculously hot partners smell *so* good in this three-dollar deodorant.

"You don't know that," I say into her chest, willing the panic not to take over, not when Jade is here and I can't retreat into myself.

That's all I can think about. How excited I was last time. How finding out I was unexpectedly pregnant was the first bright spot I'd seen in the months following my injury, the first happy thing I'd felt since learning I'd never be able to dance professionally again. It was sunshine after months of rain.

And then I lost the baby.

And the world suddenly felt so dark again.

"I don't know if this baby will make it, Els," she says, and although some people might feel hurt by those words, they feel good to me—validating my fears. "But I do know that whatever happens, you will make it through this. We will. You are so strong."

"I don't feel strong," I choke out around the lump forming in my throat.

She pushes back from me, her hands holding my shoulders tight. Her face is stern as she looks into my eyes. "You are the strongest person I know, do you hear me? You may not feel it, but you are. You danced on blistered feet and twisted ankles for sixteen hours a day, seven days a week."

"I was different then," I say, voicing the fears that have been bouncing around inside my head for the last year. "I knew who I was then. I was a dancer. I don't know who I am anymore, Jade."

My whole life, I'd been chasing one thing. Dancing. Professional ballet. And when I got it, it was ripped away from me.

And I looked at my life and realized I didn't know who I was without it. I realized I wasn't much of anything.

Since then, I've been floundering, trying to figure out who I am and what I want.

And now, I'm bringing another human being into this world when I don't even know where I fit into it.

Jade's face softens, and her hands move from my shoulders down my arms, squeezing along the way. "You're still strong, Els, even if you can't see that."

The other fear I've been harboring comes out before I can rein it in. "I don't know how to tell Beau."

She looks momentarily confused, her perfect, freckled nose wrinkling. "Beau will be ecstatic."

"I know that," I sigh, rubbing my forehead, trying to quell the ache forming there. "But I'm just starting to work on myself, and I'm not ready for him to come home yet. If we lose this one too, it might ruin me, and I'll ruin us. And I can't do that to him, Jade. I can't do it again."

I almost broke us when I collapsed in on myself the last time. I pushed him away and I knew it was killing him, trying to figure out what he'd done wrong, how he could fix it. So I sent him away, told him I needed space and time to figure things out.

I know he thinks I meant us, but I really meant *me*. I needed to figure myself out. Figure out how to be okay in this new reality. Then he could come back and I would be better for him.

But now...

I let go of her and grip the bathroom counter, the stone cutting into my fingers. A welcome, grounding sort of pain. "He's going to want to come home."

Terror grips me as I say it. I'm still too messed up, too confused, too broken. I can't be who he needs me to be, not yet, and I can't let him know that. He's been so patient, but it can only stretch so far.

Jade nods like she expected this. "Yeah, but you don't have to say yes."

My eyes snap to hers, the bubble of anxiety in my stomach popping at the words. "I don't?"

She leans back against the wall, crossing her arms over her chest. "No, Els. You don't have to if you don't want him to yet."

My head starts bobbing, reassuring myself. "Okay, okay. We could..."

"You could date again," she supplies.

I try to focus on what she's saying. Try to make sense of it, of how that would help. I haven't told even Jade why I asked Beau to leave, not the real reason, not that I think I'm too broken for him. I know she would try to tell me all the reasons I'm not, but she doesn't know what it's been like. How *good* Beau has been, and how uneven things have become between us. How I was once a functioning member of society and an equal part of our marriage and how I became a shell of who I once was.

She thinks we were having issues, and that's part of the truth. She doesn't know that they were all caused by me.

"Date?"

"You're married, but that doesn't mean you have to start living like it right away. You could ease into it."

The idea takes shape in my mind, and I latch on to it like a lifeline, an inflatable being thrown out into the raging sea that is my life. Maybe I could date Beau while I try to figure this out. Try to figure myself out. Try to figure out how to bring another person into this world.

I can let Beau in just a little, and I can hide the parts of myself I still don't want him to see. I can have a piece of him and give him a piece of me. Just for now. I have nine months to get my shit together.

Surely that will be enough time. I'll be better then. I can be better for him. For our baby.

I just need time, and then I'll be better.

SIX

BEAU
FEBRUARY
FIVE WEEKS PREGNANT

There's nothing like the bone-deep exhaustion of calving season on a cattle ranch. Between performing prenatal vaccinations, hourly monitoring rotations, and the actual birthing of calves, we're never not busy. My focus is usually horse training, but during calving season, it's all hands on deck.

But I'm grateful for it. When Elsie asked me to leave in November, there wasn't nearly as much to do to keep my mind busy. But after the night we spent together three weeks ago, I've hardly had any time alone. And when I do, it's only to shower and pass out in bed for a couple hours of sleep. It's infinitely better than the days I spent riding through the pastures alone, mending fences and building extra feeders to prepare for calving season.

I'm just stumbling into my cabin to catch a few hours of sleep when a familiar truck pulls into my drive, making fresh tracks in the falling snow. For a minute, I think I'm so exhausted that I'm imagining it. Imagining *her*.

But when she climbs out of the truck and catches sight of me standing on the porch, her feet halting in the snow, eyes wide as she takes me in, I know she's real. For the first time in three months, my wife has come to me.

My heart thunders in my chest when her feet finally begin moving again, closing the distance between us. She waits to speak until she's close, standing at the bottom of the stairs, mere feet from me.

"Hey."

That's all she says, but it's enough to make my heart race, to make my body itch to reach for her. For the millionth time, memories of the night we spent together weeks ago come rushing back to my mind. Things felt different then, different from how they had for long before I left. I don't know when we stopped touching each other like we *had* to, like we needed to in order to survive. Like we couldn't exist one more second without our hands and mouths and skin on each other.

And once again, I wonder if that's part of the reason she sent me away.

"Hey," I breathe, my breath puffing in the cold air. I'm dirty and exhausted, mud caking my boots and staining my hands, sweat beading beneath my beanie, but I'd stay out here for days if it meant I got the chance to talk to her, to *see* her.

She swallows, her eyes never leaving mine, and my skin feels too tight when her tongue darts out to wet her lips. Her hands are pushed into the pockets of her leather jacket, and I can't help but wonder if they are shaking, if she's as nervous as I am. "Can I come in?"

"Yeah, of course." I spin on my heel, trying to fit my key into the lock with trembling hands that I hope she doesn't notice.

The door swings open and I back up, allowing Elsie to go in first. I can't help but observe the cabin through her eyes. It's small, smaller than our house, only one bedroom, and hardly furnished. It came with the essentials, like appliances and furniture, enough to make a short stay comfortable, but I didn't want to buy anything for it. That felt too permanent, and I've always planned on this little cabin being a pit stop only.

Of course, that means it looks like it. Embarrassment creeps up my chest as I watch Elsie's eyes dart around the space. I don't know why I feel it. This is my wife. I don't need to impress her, but I also don't want her to think I'm incapable of taking care of myself.

The place is tiny and hardly furnished, but tidy, and that's really all I need. I've been working myself to the bone since I left, and I really just need a place to lay my head at night before I get up and do it all over again the next day.

"It smells like you," Elsie finally says, and then her lips twitch, cheeks turning pink from something other than the cold. "That's probably a weird thing to say."

I lift my shoulders in a shrug and cross my arms over my chest to keep from reaching for her, wanting to taste that smile. "I've heard weirder."

"At your parents' dinner table," she says, her smile lifting a little. It feels so normal that my chest aches.

"Exactly."

The conversation lapses for a moment, and I watch as the shutters return to Elsie's eyes. "So, I was thinking..." she trails off for a moment, looking everywhere but at me, before her gaze finally snags on mine and holds. Her bottom lip is caught between her teeth like it always is when she's nervous. I hate how awkward this feels. How I can know so much about her and still feel like a stranger.

She hesitates for another moment, the silence hanging heavy between us, and I wonder if she can hear the pounding of my heart in my chest, if she can see it through my shirt.

I watch her swallow, watch the bob of her throat and the way she straightens her shoulders like she used to do before attempting a particularly difficult ballet move. Determination is written in every line of her body.

I'm so focused on it, on her, that I barely hear when she says, "Maybe we could go out." She pauses again. "On a date."

I blink, letting the words settle between us, landing in the grooves of the warped wooden floorboards. My breath catches in my lungs, and I'm sure I haven't heard her right.

"A date?" I ask, then hate myself for it when her expression turns unsure. I don't let her answer me, needing to scrub that look from her face. "Of course I'll go on a date with you, Els."

Her shoulders unknot ever so slightly, like relief is pouring through her. It makes something inside me settle too.

It feels so achingly familiar to when I asked her out for the first time twelve years ago. I'd just gotten my license, and the first thing I wanted to do was see her. So I drove to her house and said those exact words, just like that. I wonder if she remembers, if she asked that way on purpose, but I don't want to say anything, in case she didn't.

I don't know what I expected reuniting with my wife to feel like, but it wasn't this. Hesitant and unsure. Her asking me out on a date when we own a home together and I've still got my wedding ring on and I know what sounds she makes when she falls apart.

It's nothing like I imagined, but I can't say I'm not happy about it. I can't say I'm not willing to take whatever she's giving me.

"Okay," she breathes, and I can't help but wonder how she thought this was going to go. She couldn't have thought I'd say *no*. Not when all I've thought about for close to three months is how to get her back.

"Where do you want to go?" I ask, zeroing in on her lips as she tugs the bottom one between her teeth again.

"Anything is fine with me. Have you had dinner?"

I shake my head. I hadn't planned on eating, or if I did, it would probably have been a ham and cheese sandwich washed down with a beer before passing out on my couch. I would have woken still dressed in my dirty work clothes when dawn started creeping through my windows in the morning.

"How about KC's?" I ask, and something flutters over her eyes, there and gone before I can question it.

Her chin dips in a nod. "That's good with me."

"I'll drive."

She follows me to the door. "You'll just have to drive me back out to the ranch to get my car. KC's isn't far from the house."

I can't help but let my hand settle against her lower back as she passes me, walking onto the porch, and I don't miss the way her breath catches at the contact. "That's fine," I respond, because I want nothing more than for her to ride in my truck with me, just like all the times before. I don't want to follow her off the ranch into town and watch her taillights disappear down the road, heading in the opposite direction as we leave the bar.

Her eyes lift to mine and hold for a moment before she replies, breath puffing out in the chilly air. "Okay, if you're sure."

A knot forms in my throat, and I work to swallow it down. It's taking all of my self-control not to push her right now, to see if she would kiss me back if I pressed my lips to hers. To see if I could make her breath hitch again, if I could hear it against my ear as I lifted her and carried her into my bedroom and laid her on the bed I've hardly slept in the last three months. It always feels too lonely without her in it.

"I'm sure," I say, my voice all gravel.

She nods, eyes drifting from mine. "Let's go."

KC's is packed, but I'm not surprised. There are only a few bars in town, and there's nothing to do but drink during a Montana winter, when the days are short and the air is cold enough to steal the breath from your lungs.

The night doesn't feel that different from the one three weeks ago, when Cooper dragged me here because he said I was spending too much time in my cabin alone. He didn't notice her when we walked in, but I did immediately, my gaze homing in on her like a flashing neon sign.

I'd kept my distance that night, just like all the nights, but something inside me started to fray, watching her sitting alone at the bar, drinking tequila and ignoring the looks the bartender was flashing her way. Four people came up to me to tell me she was here, like it was going to ruin my night, like a glimpse of my wife was going to make me snap.

It wasn't until I saw that tourist slide up next to her, put his hands on her, that I finally did. I'd give her all the time she asked for, but I wasn't going to give up that easily.

Tonight, though, I'm the one here with her. The one with my hand on her back, my chest pressed to her back as she tries to get close enough to speak to me over the loud country music playing on the jukebox.

"There's an empty table over there," she yells, breath fanning my ear, and points to a table in the back corner.

It's as secluded as we could get in a packed bar, and I'm thankful for it. I'm not in the mood to share tonight, and I'm certainly not in the mood to fend off well-meaning townspeople who think it's their duty to protect me from my wife.

"Good with me."

I follow her through the bar, shifting to avoid bumping into people. We make it through the crowd and settle into the rickety, mismatched wooden chairs. The entire bar looks like something out of the Old West, or it probably did when it first opened, but it hasn't been kept up well enough to look like it has any particular decor style. There's a lot of wood, vintage beer posters, red neon signs, a faded pool table and darts in one corner, and a thick layer of dust on everything.

There's also no set menu. Years ago, Elsie and I made nacho fries with extra jalapenos our go-to order, along with whatever beers the bartender wanted to give us.

"The usual?" I ask as we sit. When I look up at Elsie, she's gone white, her normally rosy cheeks bleached of color. Concern lances through me, and I don't stop myself from reaching for her, my hand circling her forearm. Her skin is overly warm beneath my palm. "What's wrong?"

She shakes her head and forces a smile onto her face. "Nothing, that sounds good."

My brow crinkles as I stare at her, trying to figure out what she's not telling me. Briefly, irritation flashes through me, because she's once again hiding something, hiding what she's feeling, unwilling to tell me. But I push it down, try to grab hold of the patience I've been so desperately clinging to like a frayed rope hanging over the edge of a dangerous cliff, and ask, "Are you sure?"

"Yeah, of course," she says, nodding. For a moment, I think about pressing, about asking her point blank what she's keeping hidden behind that brick wall exterior, but I don't.

I need space to calm the roaring in my chest, so I gesture to the bar and say, "I'll go order. Be right back."

My body feels unsteady as I make my way to the bar, and I try desperately to push down the anger that bubbles in my chest. I did so well giving her space, respecting her wishes, until three weeks ago. But that night, something inside me cracked, and I haven't been able to grasp that patience I was holding on to before.

I *hate* that going on a date with my wife feels awkward. I *hate* that there's something going on with her that I don't know about. I *hate* how lost and helpless I feel. I *hate* that I can't fix it and that she won't even let me close enough to try.

I allow myself a look back at her after sidling up to the bar, and something heavy settles in my stomach at how unsure she looks, with her head ducked as she scrolls on her phone, avoiding the gazes anyone from town shoots her way. I want to wipe that look off her face, to make her feel whole again, but I can't, and that feeling threatens to strangle me. I don't know how to love someone who won't let me love them back, and I hate that most of all.

"Hey, Beau," Grant, one of the bartenders, says, wrenching my attention from Elsie. "What can I get you?"

"Two beers and nacho fries with extra jalapenos," I answer.

His brows lift before his eyes dart around the room. He's looking for something, and I know exactly what it is as soon as his gaze settles on the table I just left. On the woman sitting alone beside it.

"You're here with Elsie?" he asks, and I don't miss the tone of concerned reproach in his voice.

Damn small towns. Damn small-town people who think they know what's best for everyone.

A muscle in my jaw ticks, and my hands ball into fists at my sides. Seriously, where the *hell* is my patience? "Can I just get the food, Grant?"

He gives me a long, lingering look, one full of meaning I don't care to parse. "Sure thing, Beau. Give me a minute."

I settle into a bar stool as I wait and allow my eyes to flit back over to where Elsie is seated. Her honey hair is down like it always is when she's not dancing—then it's in a tight bun at the back of her neck—and she's dressed in an oversized turtleneck, her sherpa-lined leather jacket draped over the chair behind her, and jeans that hug her curves so beautifully that I had to force my gaze away from her when we left the cabin so I didn't slip on the ice. That's not what I notice now, though. She looks uncomfortable again, her hand pressed to her stomach beneath the table.

I'm about to head back without waiting for the food when Grant returns. "Nacho fries," he says, sliding a massive plate across the wooden bar top. "And two beers."

I grab it all without looking and shout a *thank you* over my shoulder as I stride back to the table. Elsie glances up as I sit, her eyes blowing wide at the plate of nachos fries, and I stare at her, confused.

"Did you not want these?"

Her attention turns from the nachos to me, and she shakes her head. "No, of course not. This is great. Thank you."

My stomach twists again at how stilted this all feels. Three weeks ago, we didn't have this issue. Of course, there wasn't much talking going on that night. I swallow hard at the thought and shift in my seat before motioning for Elsie to go ahead.

The plate of nachos between us smells amazing, and my mouth waters as I watch steam rising from it. I hadn't realized how starving I was. I was happy to discover that Elsie was eating some when I was at the house last month, but I'm just now realizing I haven't exactly been taking care of myself all that well either. I eat and sleep when I can but mostly work myself to the bone and hope I'll be exhausted enough to pass out without noticing how empty my bed feels without her.

Elsie doesn't look as enticed by it as I am, but she lifts a fry without much substance on it and bites into it. I take a much heftier one and do the same, but I keep my eyes on her. She's chewing slowly, her hand still pressed to her stomach.

"Are you sure you're okay? You look like you're going to be sick."

Her eyes snag on mine and hold. Something passes behind them, and then she pushes her chair back, the legs squealing against the dirty hardwoods. She spares me one more look before darting away. My heart pounds in my throat as I follow her.

She makes it to the bathrooms before me and tries the door to both, but they're locked. I reach her just as she makes a beeline for the front door. She crashes through it a second before me, and by the time the icy air hits me, slicing straight to the bone, she's heaving into the bushes.

I slide my hands beneath her hair without thinking, brushing against her sweating neck. I hold her hair back with one and use the other to rub small circles on her back. The move throws me back in time to every other time I've done this. After drinking too much or during very unfortunate stomach bugs. And then, more recently, months ago, when she would get sick multiple times a day during her pregnancy.

The hand on her back stills as a thought grips me. I'm wrong, I have to be. But the timing adds up. That night flashes behind my eyes again, burned into my memory like nothing before or after it. We weren't careful. In fact, we were anything but. We were *careless* in a way we had only been one other time before.

She finally stops getting sick, standing to her full height beside me. Her body is shaking, and she presses a trembling hand to her mouth before turning to face me. Sky blue eyes lock on mine, and I see the answer there before I even ask, but I have to.

"Els..."

Her shoulders slump, and a tired sigh escapes her. But her eyes still hold mine, a fire behind them that I haven't seen in so long. One that was doused months ago. "I'm pregnant."

SEVEN
BEAU
FEBRUARY

My mind is still whirring when we pull up to our house twenty minutes later. Elsie insisted we head back to the ranch to pick up her truck, and I considered protesting so we could talk sooner, but I think she needed a few minutes alone. And maybe I did too.

I stuff my shaking hands into my pockets so she doesn't see as I step over the threshold. For the second time in three weeks, I'm walking through the front door of my house that I no longer live in, unsure of how I ended up here. I don't know if I expected things to look different, but they look almost exactly the same as they did the last time I was here. It feels strange that our lives are turning upside down, but this house remains untouched, frozen in time.

Elsie stares at me for a long moment, uncertainty written in every line of her face. I want to say something to reassure her, but before I can get a chance, she spins on her heel and disappears into the kitchen. She's all long lines as she presses up onto her toes to pull a glass from the cabinet. I don't miss the way her hands tremble as she fills it with water and walks back to me, liquid sloshing in the glass.

The sight of her, usually so self-assured, looking like she's one second from breaking, has the nerves disappearing from my stomach and determination filling the space they left behind.

Instead of taking the glass she extends, I wrap my hands around hers, steadying them. I can feel her pulse racing beneath my fingertips. Blue eyes catch on mine, wide and unsure.

"Hey," I say, relieved that my voice sounds calm. I sense she needs that. That her mind is a mess of tangled thoughts and that she needs me to be steady. "It's all going to be okay."

Her chest rises and falls as she takes a deep breath. I watch as her walls seem to build back up, strengthening her, but for the first time, it feels like she's allowing me inside them. She's still holding my gaze when she finally nods, and I let go of her hand, taking the glass of water and draining it, needing the feel of it on my parched throat.

She watches me closely, and when I'm done, she asks, "What are you thinking?" She sounds guarded, hesitant.

I stare at her blankly for a long minute, trying to put all my racing thoughts into words. But there's one thought that keeps coming to the forefront of my mind, so I say, "I want to know how you're doing."

Surprise crosses her features before she blinks it away. Bone-deep relief courses through me when she smiles just the tiniest bit, the expression rueful. "Just as sick as last time, if tonight is any indication."

That comment makes the relief sour in my stomach. The reminder that we've been through this before is heavy. We *have* been through this before. Last year, while still recovering from her injury, but finally seeing some marked improvement, she'd started to get sick. *All the time*. We hadn't been tracking things like before, and it took us days to realize why she was sick. I remember standing in our tiny bathroom, watching the second the digital pregnancy test had switched from loading to spell out the word *Pregnant*.

The absence of her morning sickness had been the first clue that something was wrong, although we thought she was finally moving past it. It wasn't until a few days later that we found out it wasn't a good sign, and our relief turned into overwhelming grief.

The fear and anxiety of that same scenario repeating itself feels like a noose tightening around my throat. I swallow hard, mouth dry as cotton.

Elsie must watch the way this all plays out on my face, because I see the way her small smile disappears, her eyes falling to the ground. She pushes her boot against the floor, rubbing at an invisible spot. When she finally speaks, her voice is small.

"I'm scared, Beau."

I don't think before setting my glass down and pulling her into my arms. The knot of anxiety that's been forming inside me loosens when she melts against me. This is going to be all right. *We* are going to be all right.

My hands smooth down her back, her silky smooth hair beneath my fingertips. I know her body better than my own, and the familiarity of having her against me again reassures me even further.

"I know, baby," I whisper into her hair, pressing a kiss to her temple before I can think better of it. I shouldn't have been concerned, though, because all she does is nestle further into my chest, burying her face there like she's done a thousand times before.

I'm not sure how long we stand like that, wrapped together in our kitchen, but when Elsie finally steps back, she's pulled herself together. Her face is blotchy, stained by tears, and her hair is sticking to the wetness there, but the vulnerable look is gone from her eyes, resolution filling them instead. I've seen this look on her face a thousand times, when her feet are blistered or her ankle is twisted and swollen, but she refuses to quit dancing. I've seen it when she's rehearsing a particularly hard or dangerous move, and she's determined to overcome her fear, to push her body to the limit and master it.

I saw it when she asked me to leave that first day and again just a few weeks ago, when she looked ready to break and forced herself to reinforce those steel walls around herself.

My stomach churns seeing it on her face now. And for the first time ever, I feel my own spine straighten at the sight of it. Because tonight, with her eyes hollow from exhaustion and nausea, with my baby in her stomach, I know I can't leave her again, and nothing she says is going to make me.

For the last three months, I've given her the time and space she's asked for, but the clock has run out.

"We obviously have a lot to talk about," she says. "But I'm tired and I haven't had time to process it all, so maybe we can tomorrow...?"

I stare at her for a long moment, wanting to push back, but I bite my tongue when I notice the dark circles beneath her eyes, the exhaustion she's fighting to hide. Nodding slowly, I say, "Yeah, okay." I pause for a moment, square my shoulders. "I'll bring my stuff over after work tomorrow and we can then."

Her expression changes immediately, eyes widening with surprise. "What?"

I cross my arms over my chest, force myself to meet her stare, and stand my ground. "I'm moving back in tomorrow." I hope my tone leaves no room for argument.

I should have known better.

Her head starts shaking before I even finish, blond hair swishing around her shoulders, looking like spun gold in the lamplight. "No, you're not."

"Yes," I reply slowly, voice even, controlled. Unlike how I feel on the inside. "I am. I know how sick you got last time, Elsie. I'm not leaving you alone in this house to take care of yourself. And I'm not going to live at Lucky Stars and be fifteen minutes away if you need me."

My jaw tightens. I don't want to say the last part, but I know I need to.

"I can stay in the guest room if you want, but I'm moving home."

She stares at me, unblinking, for a moment, energy charging in the air between us. We've had arguments like these before, where I've pushed too hard to try to take care of her, something she's never been comfortable with. It's not surprising, considering the kind of house she grew up in, with a former professional dancer who transferred all her dreams onto her daughter and may have nurtured them but never nurtured *her*. My desire to take care of Elsie has always been our biggest friction, and sometimes I've pushed too hard, but in the end,

I've always backed down. This right here—me standing my ground—is uncharted territory for us, and she doesn't look like she knows how to take it.

The moment is fraught with all the things we haven't said, all the time we haven't spent together over the last few months. The air between us feels tangible, crackling with energy. I hold my breath, waiting for her to respond, to tell me to screw myself and get out of her house.

But she surprises me, her shoulders drooping, a tired sigh shaking out of her. "Fine, but you're staying in the guest room."

It's not the answer I wanted, but it feels like the first progress we've had after months of standing still. I feel the relief of it down to my core, making the anxiety knotted inside me loosen just a little.

"Okay," I say, hoping she doesn't hear the way my voice comes out shakier than I'd like. "I'll see you tomorrow."

She doesn't respond as I turn on my heel to head for the door. It feels wrong to leave, but I know tonight will be the last time. I'll make sure of it.

Right before I reach the door, a thought grips me, and I stop dead in my tracks before striding back to her. Surprise lights over her delicate features when I slip my hand beneath her chin and tip it up to me. But something inside me roars with pleasure when she doesn't attempt to pull away.

"I just realized I didn't say it before," I murmur, staring into eyes more familiar than my own, my throat thick with emotion. "But I'm so ridiculously happy that we're having a baby."

EIGHT
BEAU
FEBRUARY
SIX WEEKS PREGNANT

There's nothing I hate more than sleeping in the damn guest bedroom. I thought staying at the cabin was my own personal hell, but I underestimated how much it was going to suck to sleep in the same house as my wife but in an entirely different room.

It would probably be bearable if that distance between us was only physical, but I can't help but feel like every time we're together, Elsie pushes me farther away.

"Okay, what the hell is wrong with you?" Cooper finally asks when I break the ice in the water troughs with just a little too much force, splashing water all over the both of us.

It's not even technically my job to feed and water the horses in the morning, but on this particular morning, I was searching for something extra to do to burn off the anxiety churning in my stomach, loosen the noose-like feeling of helplessness that I haven't been able to shake in a year. The one that's been slowly strangling me.

"Nothing," I mutter with a little too much venom. Cooper sees straight through me.

He hikes his hands on his hips and pins me with a look. "I really thought your sour mood would start improving once you moved back home, but it's somehow gotten worse. What gives?"

I don't want to tell him that I've moved home, but that it hasn't made much of a difference. That every time Elsie and I seem to take a step forward, she takes two steps back. And I sure as hell don't want to tell him about sleeping in the guest room.

But I can tell he's not going to let me bullshit my way out of this.

It's freezing, but I've still managed to work up a sweat, so I wipe my brow and squint at him in the early morning sunshine. "I moved home, but I'm sleeping in the guest room."

His brows reach for the sky. "Oh. Her idea, I'm guessing?"

I nod and palm the back of my neck. "I just thought we'd make more progress, that moving back in would force us to start working through things. But we're basically just roommates."

Frustration claws at me.

When I look at my brother, his jaw is popping and his arms are crossed. "I thought we talked about this. You have to ask for what you want, Beau."

"I did," I practically yell, then sigh and lower my voice. "I did, but there's more going on that you don't know about."

Cooper just stares at me, waiting for me to continue, and I internally debate. I was planning to wait to tell him until after the appointment today, when we had a better idea of how things were going, but the anxiety and the excitement and all the emotions I can't seem to name feel like they're itching to get out of me.

"Elsie's pregnant," I blurt, and watch the words land on Cooper. Shock colors his features, and his arms come uncrossed, hanging down at his sides. "And she still didn't want me to come home, but I told her I was going to anyway, that I wasn't going to let her deal with this on her own."

My brother blinks, processing everything I've just said. "Well, that does complicate things."

I nod, relief coursing through me at having shared this with him. I probably should have asked Elsie first, but she told Jade before she even told me, so I don't think she would mind.

"And I thought things would get better with me home, that the baby would bring us together, but..." I trail off, not sure how much of my soul I really want to bare to him.

Cooper nods like he understands, and for the first time, I realize that while he and Ruby's mom were only ever a one-night stand, they did have to navigate a pregnancy and figure out how to co-parent. My situation is unique, but it's not the first unplanned pregnancy in this family.

And that makes me feel less alone.

He kicks at the dirt at his feet. "I still think you need to be honest with her about what you need and want, but I think figuring this out is going to take time," he says, surprising me.

I look at him, and he must be able to see the emotion written on my face because he laughs.

"I do, occasionally, have brief moments of wisdom," he says, eyes twinkling in the early morning sunlight.

He's doing that thing he always does, downplaying his abilities. I want to tell him he doesn't need to, but an alarm chirps on my phone. I pull it out and press the button to silence it.

When I look up, Cooper is watching me. "I've got to go," I tell him. "We have our first appointment this morning."

"How do you feel?" he asks.

I pause to really think about it, stuffing my hands into the pockets of my work jacket and staring down at the dusty ground, cracked with cold. "I'm nervous," I tell him. "But I'm also so really happy, you know?"

"Yeah," he says, drawing my attention back up to him. He's giving me a soft smile, the one he reserves only for Ruby. "I do."

Elsie is jittery when we climb into my truck an hour later. She's trying to hide it but doing a poor job, her fingers tapping on any available surface, gnawing at her plump bottom lip. I want to reach over and tug it out, tell her she's going to make it bleed, but I know that wouldn't be welcome now the way it used to be.

When I got home and saw the way she was nervously flitting around the house, seeming like she was a million miles away, I forced my anxiety down. I knew today wasn't the day for me to show it, that I needed to be a strong pillar she could lean against.

So I showered off my morning ranch chores and put some gel in my hair in an attempt to tame it, and by the time I came out of the guest room, I felt only excitement. And a concern for Elsie. But I'd sunken so deep into my belief that everything was going to be okay that any other news would have bowled me over.

I found her in the kitchen, hands propped beside the kitchen sink, staring at nothing. But when I said her name, she turned to me, as if noticing I was there for the first time, plastering a fake smile on her face, and asked if I was ready to go.

It made nerves settle in my stomach, but I clung to that optimism and gave her what I hoped looked like a real smile and led her out to the car.

I can see now that it was the right course of action, because Elsie is *not* feeling any of the optimism I am. Her eyes are glazed over as she looks out the window, and she's breathing louder than I think she realizes, her breaths coming in short puffs.

It makes me want to pull the truck over and gather her in my lap, hold her until the fear recedes. Instead, as we stop at a light, I ask, "Can I turn on some music?"

The cab is painfully quiet, only the sounds of the road bumping beneath the tires and Elsie's breathing filling the air. She turns to look at me like she forgot I was there, like she's retreated so far into her head that she doesn't even know how she got here in this truck with me.

It makes worry gnaw at my gut, and I fight to shove it down.

"Yeah," Elsie says, voice cracking with disuse. She clears her throat. "Music is fine."

This truck is so old that the AUX cord is attached to a tape player. I hook it up to my phone and turn on a nineties country playlist before the light turns green. "Strawberry Wine" by Deana Carter starts playing, but Elsie doesn't sing along quietly like she normally would. Instead, she turns back toward the window, lost in her thoughts.

I can feel the tension rolling off her in waves the closer we get to the OB-GYN office, hear the way her breathing becomes more shallow. My heart, the organ I've been trying so hard to protect, shatters in my chest.

"Elsie," I say the second we pull into the parking lot. I turn to face her, and my words fizzle out at the look on her face. She's white as a sheet, staring straight ahead at the office.

"Beau," she whispers, her gaze swinging to mine, eyes wide. "I can't do this."

NINE

ELSIE
FEBRUARY
SIX WEEKS PREGNANT

I HAVE A SECRET, one I've never shared with anyone, not even my best friend or my husband—I have panic attacks.

The first time I had one, I was in elementary school. I told my mom I was scared to try a particular jump in ballet rehearsal, and she told me to not let the fear keep me from doing it. So I pushed myself. And I did it, but not without falling many times. Each time, I felt the noose tightening more painfully around my neck. And the night I finally nailed it, I walked out of the studio and into the bathroom and slid down the wall, clutching my chest, thinking I was dying. I didn't tell my mom about it.

And those panic attacks remained my secret. Even after spending almost half my life with Beau, he still doesn't know about them. He knows certain things make me anxious, but he's never seen the anxiety overwhelm me. I've never let him.

After my injury and the miscarriage, it was too hard to have him around and hide it. So I asked him to leave, and just when I finally felt like I was making progress, I found out I was pregnant and they came back with a vengeance.

The thing is, I'm actually so happy to be pregnant again. I want it to work out so badly. I want to be healthy for this baby, and I want to fix things with Beau and raise our baby together, but I'm so scared of my body failing me again. Of losing this baby. Of falling apart so epically this time that I'll never be able to repair myself enough to let Beau come home.

It's that fear that has me in a chokehold as we pull into the doctor's office. It's the trauma from the last time we were here and the terror that it's going to repeat itself that has me gasping for air, clutching the cracked leather seats in Beau's truck like my life depends on it.

I hear Beau say my name, but he sounds far away. There's a whooshing sound in my ears and my vision is blurry. It feels like the cab is closing in on me, suffocating me. I'm overwhelmed and out of breath, my chest squeezing until breathing is a chore.

Distantly, I think I need to gather myself, to hide this from Beau, to wipe the worried look from his face, but I can't.

I *can't.*

And so instead, I look him in the eye and tell him the truth. "Beau, I can't do this."

He reaches for me, but I wrench open the door, needing *air*. I stumble out of it and round the front of the truck. I can't see where I'm going with tears blurring my vision, so I sink to the ground right there. There's a small part of me that is thankful that I made it to the front of the car before falling apart, that I'm hidden from the view the receptionist has from her window. She may not be allowed to talk about what goes on inside the office, but she wouldn't hesitate to tell the entire town what she saw happening outside.

The dangers of living in a small town.

My breath is heaving when I feel Beau's hand on the back of my neck as he slides down to sit behind me. "Are you about to be sick?"

His voice is so warm and gentle that it gives me the strength to shake my head. He doesn't say anything else, only smooths his hand up and down my back as I gasp for air. It's...comforting. And it keeps me from fully falling apart.

I hate that he's seeing me like this, but the feeling of his hands on me is so good that I can't help but lean into his touch a little more, soak in the warmth he's always radiating. He's the only thing anchoring me right now, and I'm grateful for it, greedy for it in a way that feels as essential as breathing.

I'm not sure how much time passes before my heart rate begins to slow down. When it's happening, I never have any concept of time. Sometimes I sit in my shower, and by the time the water runs cold, I'm still shaking too badly to get out. Sometimes I just need a minute in the janitor's closet at the dance studio. And right now, I have no idea how long I've been sitting on the cold asphalt of the parking lot of the doctor's office, Beau's hand sliding up and down my spine, his fingers brushing the skin of my neck above the collar of my coat before moving back down.

When I finally chance a look at him, he's watching me with those piercing eyes of his. They've always seen more than I want him to. Right now, that divot looks permanently etched between his brows. I think he's going to have wrinkles beside his mouth from frowning so long. He looks ready to fight every single one of my demons.

He doesn't know that they're all just me.

"What happened?" he asks, sounding as wrecked as I feel.

Maybe it's the pregnancy fatigue, or maybe it's the mental exhaustion I always feel after a panic attack, but the truth falls out of me without my permission. "It was a panic attack."

The words hang in the air, heavy and tangible, and my heart races as I wait for him to respond, to ask a thousand questions, to try to help.

But he just nods, and says, "Are you okay now?"

I blink at him in surprise, unsure of how to respond. I *wasn't* okay. I was dreading his response, and fear and regret were clawing up my throat at my accidental confession. But the way he didn't press, the knowledge that I don't have to explain my deepest secret on the cold ground outside of the doctor's office, soothes something inside me.

So when I reply, it's truthful. "Yes, I think so."

He nods again. "Are you ready to go in or do you want to stay out here for a little longer? Or we can reschedule."

I let my eyes drift to the mountains in the distance. I want to run to them and not go inside that office, not experience what I did the last time I was there, when I stared at an ultrasound screen, looking intently for a heartbeat that none of us could find.

But I also realize that running away isn't going to stop anything bad from happening. Squaring my shoulders like I have a thousand times before—when it would be so much easier to let them curl in on themselves—and inhaling deeply, I say, "Let's do this."

Beau holds my gaze for a long time, warm brown eyes assessing. I don't know what he's looking for.

"We can go in," he says finally. "But I just want you to know that we don't *have* to, and rescheduling wouldn't make you any less brave."

His words slice down into the most vulnerable places inside me, stealing my breath, but I refuse to let it show. *This* is why I asked him to leave three months ago. He can see all the pieces of me I've kept hidden for so long, even from him. I've never learned how to show someone everything, but somehow Beau sees it anyway.

I swallow against the lump clogging my throat and will my voice to come out strong. "Thank you, but I'm okay, really."

Instead of answering, he stands and extends a hand to me. I take it, grateful for the warmth of his skin when mine has gotten so cold. Before I realize what he's doing, he's pulled me into a hug, enveloping me in his heat, and I can't help but sink into it.

His lips press to my temple, soft skin and rough mustache. "You're the strongest person I know, Elsie Jennings, even if you don't feel like it all the time."

The words feel like warm honey slipping down my spine, making the cold, dark places inside me feel like they're thawing for the first time in months.

He pulls back before I can push past the lump in my throat to respond. Then he takes my hand and leads me into the doctor's office. All the sour memories of this place come rushing back the moment we walk through the doors, and suddenly, I feel like I'm going to be sick if I have to talk to the receptionist.

But to my surprise, Beau leads me to a seat and leaves to check me in.

I should protest, tell him I'm capable of handling it on my own, but I'm too tired to attempt it. Instead, I sink into the uncomfortable chair and allow my eyes to drift around the place. There are photos of local babies on the sage green walls. I recognize them as some of the kids of people Beau went to high school with. If things had played out differently, maybe our baby would be on that wall right now. It makes an ache stab in my chest.

Beau returns a moment later, sitting in the seat beside me. "All checked in."

"Thanks," I say, and I mean it. My hands are still trembling and my legs feel like gelatin. I'm not sure I would have been able to stand at the desk and accurately answer their questions.

He gives me a small smile. "No problem."

His phone vibrates in his back pocket, and he pulls it out to check it, reading what's on the screen before typing something back. I let my eyes settle on his hands, strong and capable, and I think about reaching for one of them, holding on to it and letting some of his steadiness seep into me. He'd let me hold on to him like he's a pillar in a storm.

But before I work up the courage, a nurse calls my name, standing at the door that leads back to the exam rooms. I recognize her from around town, but I can't think of her name.

My heart is pounding again. I feel it in my throat, in the backs of my knees, in the place between my eyes. We follow her through the doors, and she smiles at us warmly. But despite my best efforts, I can't make myself return it.

"Let's go ahead and get your weight," she says, motioning to a scale up against the wall. Even now, when I'm not dancing, I still avoid looking at the number. It's been years since my body image has been a major struggle for me, but you don't grow up being told by dance teachers that they can see the lunch you ate through your leotard and just learn to accept everything about your body. I'd mostly grown to love mine and all the amazing things it could do before my injury and the miscarriage. Before I'd started to feel like it was betraying me. But in both stages, I avoided looking at the scale. I'd long since determined that that number was none of my business.

The nurse scratches something on her clipboard, and then we head back to the exam room. I sit down in an uncomfortably hard chair and fold my hands in my lap, desperate to hide the shaking. The nurse asks me a hundred questions that I already answered online.

"Is this your first pregnancy?" The question feels like a punch to the gut, and I can't help but let my eyes drift toward Beau's. His grieved expression mirrors what I guess mine looks like. It makes me feel oddly connected to him in this moment, takes the sting out of the answer just the tiniest bit.

"No."

The nurse types something. "Any live births?"

I don't move my gaze from Beau, soaking in his strong, steady presence. "No."

She finishes asking her questions and then finally turns to face me. "There are cups in the restroom for you to pee in and a small door in the wall where you can place the sample. I'm going to head out for a few minutes." She stands and opens a cabinet, pulling out a faded hospital gown. "Go ahead and change into this and get comfortable on the table. I'll be back in a few."

The gown feels scratchy against my hands as I wait for her to disappear. When the door closes behind her, I stand, but the sound of Beau's voice makes me stop in my tracks.

"Hey," he says, and catches my wrist. His hands are calloused, familiar, and make my overly sensitive skin tingle. I meet his eyes. They're sincere, more intense than I've ever seen them. "Whatever happens today, we're going to be okay."

I think he's just now starting to figure out that I didn't ask him to leave because I wanted him gone. That I want him just as badly as I ever have, probably more. That I'm fighting the hardest I ever have to piece myself back together for him.

That I want *us* to be together again.

Emotion clogs my throat, so I can only manage a nod. But his lips curve in the barest of smiles like he understands, and it makes some of the anxiety in my stomach settle.

I can't handle looking at him anymore, so I let myself into the bathroom and lean back against the cool wood, taking deep breaths until my heart rate slows to something bordering on normal.

My hands are still shaking as I pee and change, but I feel calmer, steadier. I let Beau's words sink into me, like I'm a plant that's just been watered after being parched for much too long, its wilted leaves growing full again. They repeat in my mind as I stare at myself in the mirror, gathering my courage. I've done this millions of times over the years, forced my overwhelming emotions into tidy little boxes in my mind. It's harder to do that now than I expected, but I still manage it, letting out one last deep, centering breath before exiting the bathroom.

The nurse has already returned, and she gives me another warm smile. "You ready?"

I nod and climb onto the table, hoping neither of them notice my shaking legs.

She asks me to lift my hips and places a hard pillow beneath them before reaching for the wand. It's already covered in lube that I know from experience will be uncomfortably cold, but I can't even focus on that. My eyes are trained on the TV screen in front of me as she inserts it, waiting to see *something*.

"We probably won't be able to see much today," the nurse says. "Your doctor just wanted to bring you in early to make sure things are progressing as they should."

I knew this. I did my research. But I still can't help hoping there's enough there to calm the beast in my mind, make me feel settled for the first time in a week.

I don't even notice that Beau has sidled up beside me, gripping my hand, until I see the white blob on the screen. It looks a little bigger than our last baby did, because they told us that one had stopped growing sometime between five and six weeks, although it took my body another two and a half to realize it.

"There's your baby," the nurse says.

I stare at the little white blob on the screen in wonder. The anxiety still niggles at the back of my brain, but it's eclipsed by awe and excitement and...love. I don't know how I feel such intense love for a blob on a screen, but I do.

When I look at Beau, his expression mirrors the way I feel. I squeeze his hand, and he squeezes back, three times, the signal he's always given for *I love you*.

"And there's the heartbeat," she says.

I wrench my eyes from my husband to look back at the little flickering she's pointing to on the screen. I know from my research that seeing a heartbeat this early is rare, and I can't help but feel like this little baby is doing it just for us.

I turn to Beau, heart in my throat, and find him already looking at me. I was watching our baby, but he was watching me, and it makes some of the jagged edges inside me heal just a little. I can barely speak over the lump in my throat, but I manage to say, "Beau, that's our baby."

"That's our baby," he says, and then his lips are on mine. It's quick, his kiss, something fierce like he's a man going off to war and this might be his last chance, but it doesn't stop me from feeling it all the way down to my toes.

When he pulls back, he keeps one hand in mine, the other threaded through the hair at the back of my neck. We stare at each other for a long moment, and Beau looks like he's about to say something, but the nurse interrupts.

"There's just one."

I can't help but laugh. "Oh, thank God." I hadn't even considered the possibility of multiples, and I feel that would have been one surprise too many for me in the past few months.

"Heartbeat is 112, so that's good. I'm going to take a few measurements, but you look right on track," she says.

Relief courses through me.

Turning to Beau again, I meet his brown eyes, warm as a Montana summer day. "We're having a baby."

"Yeah, Els," he whispers, pressing a kiss to my forehead. "We are."

TEN

ELSIE
MARCH
SEVEN WEEKS PREGNANT

"When were you planning to tell me you're pregnant?" Tonya asks the minute I walk into her office the Monday after our first appointment.

I stare at her for a moment, slack-jawed. I knew gossip in this town moved quickly, but Beau hasn't even told his family yet, and I sure as hell haven't told mine, so the fact that it's running through town is a cause for concern. I can just imagine Clint Jennings, Beau's dad, at the feed store in town, hearing the news, and it makes my stomach swoop.

I shut the door behind me, even though we're the only ones here. "Who told you that?"

She rolls her eyes. "No one told me. You just look like shit. Even more so than you have the past few months." She motions to her face. "You have this green tinge all the time, like you're one wrong move away from barfing up your breakfast."

Well, she's not wrong.

A heavy sigh puffs out of me, my shoulders slumping against the door. "Thank God."

Tonya leans back in her seat, assessing me. She takes a sip of the green smoothie on her desk, the same one she's had every single day since I've known her. "So when were you planning to tell me?"

I sit in the chair across from her and meet her eyes. Her gray hair is pulled back in a low bun, her deep brown skin just now starting to wrinkle with age. She's as familiar and comforting to me as my own mother should be.

"Today, actually."

She rolls her eyes. "Yeah, perfect timing."

This pulls a smile out of me. "I was. We had our first appointment on Friday."

"And everything was okay?" The way she asks, I know she's clued in to more of my anxiety than I thought I'd let on.

It makes my heart beat a little faster, but I force myself to stay calm.

"Everything looked great," I say, and can't help but smile. They sent us home with two very blurry images of a white blob that doesn't resemble a baby in the slightest, but every time I close my eyes, I see that little flicker of a heartbeat, feel the hope that's taken root and begun growing inside of me.

"Good," she says, and even though it's not much, I know how truly happy she is with just that one word. Just the hint of a smile on her face and the way her shoulders lose the tension they were clinging to. "But you've been sick."

"Ah, yes," I say, leaning back in my chair. "Since I look like shit. When do I not, apparently?"

"When you're happy," she responds, completely serious, and it knocks the breath out of me. "Are you unhappy about this?"

I know she wouldn't judge me no matter what my answer. Still, I tell her the truth. "I'm so happy. But I'm nervous too. Nervous about the pregnancy. Nervous about what it means for me and Beau."

She nods like this all makes sense, and I feel an overwhelming sense of gratefulness toward her. "That's fair. Can you keep teaching?"

We both know I'd have to be on my deathbed not to make it into the studio, but I appreciate her asking anyway. "Yeah, I just step out to puke a lot."

A grin quirks her lips. "Good. Guess this will make you buying the studio a little more difficult."

I let out a breath and roll my eyes. "I'm not buying the studio, Tonya."

She waves me off. "Of course you're not buying it right now. You've got way too much going on."

"I'm not buying it *at all*." I try to emphasize the words, but I can tell she doesn't notice. A bolt of panic slices through me. "You're not going to sell it to that interested buyer, though, right?"

There's way too much change happening in my life right now for me to handle having a new boss, for me to handle not having *Tonya*.

She meets my gaze, her eyes softening. "No, Elsie. I won't sell it to them."

My heart rate slows, and I take a deep breath, exhaling it shakily. "Good."

"But I won't wait on you forever," she says. "Now get out of my office."

I feel a surge of tenderness for her as I leave her office, allowing myself one last look at her before I shut her door. She should get to sell, get to live the life she's worked so hard for, but she's staying, and I know it's for me. I'm not going to be able to buy this place, I know that, but I vow to myself that when I'm better, I'll tell her to sell it. I'll just have to deal with the changes.

The studio is quiet, which is how I like it best. It's usually chaos, filled with screaming, giggling little girls. I love that too, but there's something to be said about the calm before the storm. Maybe it's because I used to spend so much time alone in this studio growing up. Tonya knew I was responsible and just wanted to practice as much as possible, so she gave me a key. I'd be the first one to arrive every morning and the one who would lock up every night. This studio is more familiar to me than my childhood home or the one I live in now. It's where I grew up, and it's where I'm growing into someone new again.

The quiet doesn't last long, as the first of my dancers arrive. It's Maya Delgado, a fourteen-year-old who reminds me so much of myself at her age that I just want to tell her to let go a little, live a little, because as important as dance is, it won't be there forever. But I know she'd never listen, just like I wouldn't have, so I just smile.

"Hey, Maya. How was school?"

She gives me an exasperated look, dropping her bag at her feet. "It's so stupid that I have to go to school when I could be using that time to dance."

My lips roll together to hold back my smile. "I'll let the state of Montana know."

She stares at me for a long moment, brow wrinkled as she tries to puzzle out my statement. "You're being sarcastic."

This does make my smile tug free. "Yes, Maya, I'm being sarcastic."

"I don't have *time* for sarcasm." She says this as she begins to dig through her bag, rooting around until she finds her pointe shoes.

"You're fourteen, Maya. You have nothing but time."

Unlike me, who feels like time is racing. Time I thought I could use to figure things out is now slipping through my fingers. Just the thought of it makes my throat tight and makes the ever-present nausea roil in my stomach.

Maya stares up at me as she begins to bandage her feet, starting with her big toes, which have been causing her issues since I started. "I'm almost *fifteen*, and if I work hard enough, I could go pro as early as sixteen. That's one year to get my act together."

Maybe it's some buried-deep maternal instinct, or maybe I just want to save her from ending up like me, but something drives me to sit next to her. She pauses in her wrapping and meets my eye.

"Maya," I start, searching for the right words. "Dance is...well, it feels like everything. It has a way of making you feel like it's the only thing worth living for. It means testing your body's limits and beating yourself and proving to yourself that you can do things you thought were impossible. It's exhilarating in a way that almost nothing else is."

"Yeah," she breathes, eyes far away.

I feel like I've gotten carried away. So, fixing my gaze on hers, I say, "But it's *not* everything. It can't be. Because no matter how good you are, how hard you work, it can't be forever. So don't make dance your everything, or you'll wake up one day and realize you don't have anything else, okay?" I pause. "I just want you to have everything life has to offer."

She stares at me for a long moment, a ringlet curl falling over her thick, dark brows. It's unfair that a fourteen-year-old is already this pretty when the rest of us had to suffer through awkward years. "Okay, Elsie. I'll try."

A relieved smile hitches up the corners of my mouth. "Good, I've done my good deed for the day. Now wrap those feet and let's get to work."

The grin she gives me is so wide it makes me feel, just for a minute, like everything might be okay. I might not know who I am or what I'm doing, but at least I made a little bit of a difference in one person's life.

It gives me hope that maybe I can get this all figured out. That maybe I'm not too far gone, too broken, to put myself back together. To be the person that Beau and this baby need me to be.

ELEVEN
BEAU
MARCH

THE HORSE IS SCARED. And hesitant. I don't blame her. We rescued her from an abusive home two days ago, so I know I have to be gentle with her. Yesterday, I didn't even attempt to touch her, simply stood near her stall and let her come to me. It was slow going. She flinched and kept her ears pinned back, but I stayed where I was, letting her know I wasn't going anywhere and that I was safe. It took twenty minutes for her to finally come close enough to sniff me, and I considered that a win.

Today, I let myself into the stables and approach her stall slowly, just like I did yesterday. "Hey, Sugar." The American Quarter horse was presumably named for her gray-white coat, but I think it fits her personality too. She's scared now, but I have a feeling she's going to be a sweetheart.

She looks at me, her ears pinning back. "Hey, good girl," I say softly, keeping my voice low. "How'd you sleep? I slept okay." Looking around the stables to make sure I'm the only one here, I turn back to Sugar and say, "I saw my baby yesterday. I can't tell you how relieved I was when I saw that heartbeat."

My quiet words seem to do the trick, soothing her, just as they're doing for me. I didn't want Elsie to know how nervous I was pulling up to that doctor's office, not when I knew how anxious she was. Or I thought I did. Seeing her collapsed on the ground in front of my truck almost did me in. I've never seen her like that before, and I have to wonder if it was the first time that's happened. Something tells me it wasn't, and I don't know what to do about that.

Sugar takes a step forward, and I slowly extend my hand, palm up, in her direction, offering it to her to sniff. She does, her spotted black nose nuzzling against the calloused palm of my hand. I've worked with hundreds of horses over the years, many of them injured or abused or difficult to manage, and I'll never get over the feeling when they willingly come to me, trusting me for the first time.

"I don't know if I have what it takes to be a good dad," I say to Sugar, keeping my voice soft and calm. "My dad is the best dad in the entire world, and I have to think that he taught me something, but I couldn't take care of Elsie the way she needed me to."

Gently, I move my hand to smooth down her nose. When she flinches, I pause, and I wait for some of the tension to leave her body before continuing. Her coat is soft, and I can feel the warmth of her skin beneath my chilled hands.

"I just want to do a good job," I tell her. "For both of them."

I spend a few more minutes smoothing my hand over her nose before moving on to her neck, pausing any time she seems skittish. But the longer I pet her, the more she seems to relax. Horses are like people most of the time. They're slow to trust, especially if they've been hurt in the past. They need to be reassured over and over again that the people in their life are safe. It's hard to do, especially since I mostly work with horses that have been abused or have difficult temperaments. But that only makes it more rewarding when they finally trust you completely. Usually, the ones that take the longest to warm up are the ones I end up having the deepest connection with.

"I've got to go, Sugar," I say. "But I'll be back tomorrow. Maybe then we can try a harness. I bet you'd like some time outside, huh?"

I let my hand trail down her neck one last time before backing up slowly so I don't spook her. She watches me with wary eyes, but she looks less spooked than when I came in a few minutes ago. On the first few days of training a horse that's been abused, I keep our sessions short so they don't get overwhelmed, increasing the time by small increments each day.

It's not until I back out of her line of vision that I see him there—Cooper. He's leaning against the wall a few stalls down, his arms crossed over his broad chest. His deep brown hair is much longer than mine, pushed back from his face below a backward baseball cap that he'll likely switch out for a cowboy hat before heading out on the ranch today. I'm annoyed to see we're wearing the same red flannel shirt.

He arches one dark brow, and I let out a sigh, knowing he heard me talking to Sugar.

Pushing a hand through my hair, I ask, "How much did you hear?"

"So it went well, then? I wouldn't know, since you were ignoring my texts."

I wince and move past him into the tack room, knowing he's following closely on my heels. I hadn't meant to ignore him, but yesterday was overwhelming in so many ways. I needed to decompress after watching Elsie having a panic attack, seeing our baby's heartbeat, and unexpectedly kissing my wife—the wife who still hasn't told me she wants me back.

"I told you everything was fine."

He rolls his eyes. "And then answered none of my follow-up questions."

He sent approximately a thousand, and I just couldn't deal with them. Instead, I lay awake in the guest bed, staring at the ceiling, trying to process all the changes that've taken place over the last few weeks. I finally gave up around four and came to the ranch early.

"We saw the heartbeat," I tell him.

A smile lights up his face. "The best feeling," he says. I could never forget that my brother is a father, but I think I had forgotten that he's been through *this* before.

I rub my palms down my thighs, wiping off the dust clinging to them. I can't help but let a small smile lift my lips too. "Yeah, it really was. I'm going to tell the family at dinner tonight."

His brows lift. "Is Elsie going to come?"

I shrug, but his words pierce me. No part of me wants to tell my family this news without Elsie, but I don't think I can convince her to go. When I mentioned the idea over the weekend, she said she didn't think it was a good idea, but when I asked her why, she changed the subject. I didn't push because right now, conversation with her feels like dealing with Sugar. I have to go slow and steady and not do anything to startle her.

Cooper nods, but I can tell he's not pleased. I want to tell him he doesn't know everything, that *I* don't know everything, that Elsie is perhaps much more fragile than I anticipated, but before I can, he asks, "Are you going to tell Morgan first?"

I palm the back of my neck, thinking. "I probably should."

Morgan is as much a part of our family as any of the rest of us and has become a good friend to Cooper and me. As close as another brother. He's also a single dad to two little boys, so he also knows what I'm going through.

Cooper smirks. "What about Cheyenne?"

"Oh God," I groan. I can only imagine the things Cheyenne will have to say. I think I'd rather rip the Band-Aid off and tell her with the rest of the family, even though she will probably skin me alive for it. "I don't think so."

He laughs, the sound filling the cold air of the stables. "Good idea."

Before I can respond, the big barn door slides open and a familiar voice yells, "*Cooper Jennings*, are you in here? When we have an appointment at seven in the morning, I expect you to be there at seven."

Cooper rolls his eyes and looks down at his watch. "It's seven forty-two, Jade," he calls back.

A minute later, she appears in the doorway to the tack room. "I said I expect you to be there on time. I didn't say anything about me."

"You exhaust me," he responds.

"Just show me which cow I need to shove my hand into before it ends up somewhere else," she says with a pointed look.

"Well, that's my cue," I say, clapping my hands. "Don't kill each other."

"No promises," Jade says, smiling at me with saccharine sweetness.

"Well, spare the animals."

She responds immediately, eyes serious. "Of course."

I look between the two of them, my gaze landing on my brother. "Do whatever you need to with Coop."

"Fuck you," he says.

Jade lifts a brow. "You kiss your mother with that mouth?"

Cooper smirks, one side of his mouth tipping higher than the other and his dimples carving out little divots in his cheeks. When we were small, those dimples were the only way most people could tell us apart—he has them, I don't. "Not her, but I could let you have a turn if you ask nicely."

"You know those statues that people touch over and over for centuries? The ones where the part they touch—a toe or a nose or a hand—rubs off completely?" she asks.

"Mm-hmm," Cooper says.

Jade gives him a charming smile. "I assume that's what's happened to your penis."

His grin broadens. "I'm sure you'd like to find out, wouldn't you?"

"I could throw a rock in any direction in Larkspur and ask the first person it hits, and they'd be able to give me an answer."

Cooper leans in her direction, and I wonder if either of them notices how close they've gotten. "Careful, Jade, you're starting to sound jealous."

"Careful, Cooper, you're starting to sound delusional."

"You guys want to see an ultrasound photo?" I ask, interrupting them, and both heads swivel in my direction, looking like they'd forgotten I was here.

"You have one?" Jade practically squeals, bounding for me.

I nod, pulling the already worn sonogram from my back pocket. I've already stared at it a hundred times, running my thumb over the little speck that is our baby.

The three of us look down at the photos in awe. We never got a sonogram of our first baby, and I hadn't realized how much I wanted one. It makes this photo special for many reasons.

"Can I hold it?" Jade asks, her emerald eyes connecting with mine.

I hand it to her, watching as she examines the photo, tears welling in her eyes. "It's perfect."

There's a lump in my throat, making it hard to speak, so I just nod.

"It looks like you," Cooper says, and it snaps the band of tension.

A laugh rumbles out of me despite my best effort, and I roll my eyes. "Yeah, okay."

"Poor kid," he says.

Jade looks at him over her shoulder. "You two have the same face."

"I'm much better looking than he is," Cooper responds.

"Humble too," I say.

He grins at me. "Yes, that too."

I take the sonogram from Jade and pocket it again, ignoring the urge to stare at it longer. "I really should get back to work. Dad's bound to come looking for us soon, and it won't be good if he finds us."

"Clint wouldn't hurt a fly," Jade says.

"No," Cooper says, "he wouldn't. He would just start yapping and we'd never get anything done."

"True," she replies, and then turns to face me. "Are you and Elsie going to tell everyone at dinner tonight?"

Monday nights are Jennings family dinner nights at the big house and have been happening weekly since long before Cooper and I were born. It's not just Jenningses who are invited, though. There's an open invitation extended to the family we've created over the years—Jade and her mom, who was our vet before her, and her father included. But since the separation, there's been one noticeable absence. Elsie.

I shift on my feet. "I am, but I don't think Elsie is ready to go yet."

"Well," Jade says, wiping her hands on her jeans. "If that's what she wants, then that's what we're going to make happen."

Behind her, Cooper makes a noise under his breath, and Jade and I fix him with hard stares again.

"What's that sound supposed to mean?" she asks before I get a chance.

He doesn't back away from the anger in her eyes. "Why are we always doing what Elsie wants? What about Beau? You think he wants to tell his family he's going to be a dad all alone? They did this together, they should face it together."

"Cooper," I say, voice weary. "It's fine. Leave it."

He holds my gaze for a long moment, and I think he's not going to say anything else, but he does. His words are low and even. "I just think that everyone has been focused on protecting Elsie for a long time, and that's fair. But someone needs to protect you too. And if it makes me the bad guy for doing that, then fine."

I shove my hands into my pockets, unsure of how to respond. Part of me feels grateful. The other part wants to tell him that we're all trying to take care of Elsie because *she's* the one who needs it. More than any of us really know.

But maybe he's right. Maybe I need it too.

TWELVE
ELSIE
MARCH

We haven't talked about the kiss. I think we both know that it happened in the heat of the moment, when emotions were high. But that hasn't stopped me from thinking about it.

I mostly managed to erase it from my mind at work today, but now that I'm back home and *he's* here, it keeps playing on repeat. A scene from a movie that I keep rewinding to watch over and over again.

I've come to the realization that I miss kissing Beau. I miss being with him. After the miscarriage, I could hardly let Beau touch me without feeling like I was going to fall apart. He was so gentle and caring, and it plucked at my frayed and broken heartstrings. At any given moment, I was one kind gesture from falling completely apart. Intimacy—sexual or otherwise—was basically nonexistent. It wasn't until that night at the bar that I realized how starved I was for it. For him.

And I don't know how to handle that desire anymore. It was always so simple before, but now I feel like I'm walking on a tightrope. If I let Beau back into my bed, it means letting him into the bubble I've created around myself, and I'm not sure I'm strong enough for that yet. I need to be better. The parking lot panic attack last week proved that.

So for right now, kissing my husband is off-limits. No matter how badly I might want to.

I look up at Beau from where I'm curled up on the couch. He's dressed for family dinner at the big house, and a small part of me wants to go with him. But a much larger part is worried I won't be welcome, not after the separation. Not after the way I hurt him. The Jenningses have always accepted me as one of their own, but they wouldn't choose me over him, and I wouldn't want them to.

He's wearing Wranglers that hug his ass in the most distracting of ways, a flannel button-down, and a shearling-lined jacket to ward off the cold. Outside, snow falls in fat flakes, coating the ground. If I had to guess, I would say this will be our last big snow of the season. As much as I love it, I'm ready for sunshine and wildflowers. I'm ready to put this winter behind me.

When he checks his reflection in the hallway mirror, he catches me staring and smiles. "See something you like, Elsie baby?"

I've always loved it when he calls me that. It's only ever when we're alone, and it makes my blood heat and goose bumps prickle out along my skin. This time is no different.

Damn the no kissing rule.

"The jacket," I lie. "Can I have it?"

He turns and walks the short distance from the hallway to the living room, his cowboy boots thudding against the hardwoods. "I don't think it's quite your size."

"Well, shit."

"Plus, it's pretty cold out."

I let my eyes drift past him to the huge windows facing the mountains. They're covered in a thick layer of snow, and more falls, faster and faster, as the hours have passed. "Are you sure it's safe to head out to Lucky Stars?"

It's just fifteen minutes down the road, but fifteen minutes down snow-covered country roads is a lot different from driving down a cleared highway.

He walks over to the window, assessing. I appreciate that about him. Cooper would say it was fine without even looking, but Beau has always been more cautious, and he wouldn't leave if he didn't think he could get back safely.

"I think it'll be fine," he says, turning back to me. He holds my gaze for a moment, warm brown eyes searching mine. "You sure you don't want to come?"

My nausea has been surprisingly under control today, probably because I've been sucking on ginger candies since I woke up, but it comes back now. The thought of seeing everyone, of having to watch them hide the disdain and disappointment they're sure to feel for me, makes me sick to my stomach.

I shake my head. "No, I think it will be better if you tell them by yourself." Maybe the news of the baby will soften their feelings toward me.

I expect Beau to leave then, but he surprises me by crossing his arms over his chest, and something flips over in my stomach at the sight of his shearling-lined denim jacket pulling taut over his biceps. "Why do you think that?"

The question pulls me out of my trance, and I meet his eyes. They're harder than I would have expected, a look I don't usually see on him. I can hardly think of a time in the last decade when he's questioned my decisions or the reasoning behind them. He always just rolls with the punches.

"What do you mean?" I ask.

"Why do you think it's going to be better if I tell them alone?"

A thousand thoughts flit through my brain—of his parents' expressions morphing into disdain when they see me, of his siblings accusing me of getting pregnant just to fix things with Beau, of Ruby no longer looking up to me, telling me she wants to be a ballerina just like me when she grows up—but I don't know how to voice any of them without pulling my heart out and pinning it to my sleeve.

"I—" I start, unsure of how to finish my sentence. "They'll take it better from you."

A muscle in his jaw ticks. "How do you think they're going to take it?"

I swallow and lick my lips, watching as his gaze darts down to follow the movement. "I think they'll be happy," I finally say.

"But they wouldn't be if you were there?" he asks. His gaze narrows, like he's trying to piece out this puzzle and he's getting closer with every question. I hate how exposed I feel.

"I don't know," I answer slowly. "And I'm not willing to risk it."

He sighs and pushes a hand through his hair. "Elsie, why would you even think something like that? My entire family loves you. You're as much a part of the family as I am."

I feel myself shrinking into the couch, wanting to hide myself from him, from the emotions that are simmering below the surface of my skin, the ones he seems to have X-ray vision for. Before I can respond, his eyes soften, and the tension in his shoulders loosens. He looks defeated, sad. I wish I could make it better. But if I wounded him with this one confession, letting him see all the dark thoughts in my head would wreck him.

He moves until his knees hit the couch, and he leans down over me, close enough that I can smell the minty scent of his toothpaste. "It's okay if you don't want to go yet, but I need you to know that whenever you're ready, our family will be waiting for you with open arms. They love you and they're going to be so thrilled about this baby." He smiles then, one side of his mouth lifting before the other. "Not as excited as me, of course."

I follow his gaze down to where it's now trained on my stomach, and something inside me turns to mush when he presses his large, calloused hand there and says, "Hey, baby. It's your daddy. I'll be back soon. Take care of your mom for me, and don't make her feel too sick."

Before I can respond, although I don't know how I would over the lump clogging my throat, he presses a kiss to my temple and says, "Be back soon, Elsie baby."

He leaves me sitting on our couch, his words ringing through my head. I'm not sure how long I sit there before there's a knock at the door. I push up off the couch and head for it, swinging it open to find Jade standing on the other side, a huge smile on her face.

"What are you doing here?" I ask, staring at her, confused. She always goes to family dinner at the big house with her parents, who have become close friends with the Jenningses over the years.

She smirks, pushing past me into the living room. "Hello to you too. Get dressed, we're getting dinner. Anywhere that won't make you throw up."

I follow her through the house, watching as she plops down in the exact place on the couch I vacated. "Why aren't you at Lucky Stars?"

She shrugs, like her answer is obvious. "Because I wanted to spend the evening with my best friend."

I give her a grateful smile. I may not have wanted to go to dinner tonight, but I didn't want to spend my evening alone. "Well, I'm glad you came," I say and mean it. "But we can't go out. It's snowing."

She rolls her eyes. "It's just a little snow. If we leave now, we will be back before it gets bad. Now go get dressed."

I look down at my gray sweats. There's a stain on my left boob and a hole in the knee. But they're warm and comfy.

"Can I just wear this?"

She sighs, as if this single question is the last one she has the patience for. "Fine, but we're ordering out and eating in the car, then."

I smile because that's my ideal dinner anyway and she knows it.

She waits for me as I slip a jacket over my shoulders and shove my feet into a pair of boots. The cold is bitter, the wind whipping against any bare skin and instantly chilling me to the bone. Snow falls in thick flakes, piling onto the powder already dusting the ground. Above us, only a few stars penetrate the clouds, lighting our way to her truck.

We climb inside, and she cranks the heat and the radio. "Where to?"

"A burger actually sounds good."

"Really?" she asks, sounding incredulous.

When I laugh, it puffs in the cold air of the cab. "Surprisingly, yes, but if you'd asked me that at lunch, I probably would have thrown up."

"Pregnancy is fascinating."

"It really is."

She turns out of the driveway. The roads are thankfully still pretty clear from the other vehicles that have driven down it. Our house is situated between downtown Larkspur and Lucky Stars, so our road gets a decent amount of traffic. I'm more worried about Beau making it home tonight.

"Beau showed me the sonogram this morning," Jade says.

"Yeah?" I ask. I can't help but feel my frozen heart melt just a little at the thought of a proud Beau pulling out that blurry photo to show her.

She flashes me a smile. "Cutest blob I've ever seen."

A laugh escapes me. "I can't disagree."

"Are you seven weeks now?"

I nod, even though she can't see me in the darkness. "Mm-hmm. Baby is the size of a blueberry."

In the passing headlights of an oncoming car, I see her jaw drop. "She's growing so fast."

"She, huh?" I ask, a smile flirting at the edges of my lips.

"Yes. Jade Jr."

"A perfect name."

She flashes me a grin. "I thought so."

I ask her about calving season the rest of the way to the only burger place in Larkspur, a drive-in that is always packed, regardless of the time or weather. For her, calving season is one of the busiest times. She's employed by Lucky Stars and several other smaller ranches in the area, and they keep her busy.

She tells me about the late nights and early mornings, about a particularly challenging birth that required her, Clint, Morgan, and Cooper to work together to deliver safely. I'm surprised they didn't call Beau, but I'm also glad he didn't have to drive to the ranch in the middle of the night. Clint, Morgan, and Cooper all live on the property, and Jade ends up staying there a lot of nights during calving season when she's too tired to drive home.

The snow is falling harder when we finally make it to Cowpoke Diner, a drive-in, but I'm not surprised to see there's only one stall open. This place is a Larkspur staple.

A crackly voice comes through the static-filled intercom, asking what we want to order. I put in my order for a cheeseburger, fries, and a Diet Coke, and then look out the window as Jade orders. There's a ranch hand I recognize from Lucky Stars in the truck beside us, and he's looking right at me, a disgusted expression on his face.

Shame bites through me, and I look away quickly. Beau might not hold the separation against me, but this town sure does. And I'm not sure they will ever get over it.

"Anything else?" Jade asks, snapping my attention back to her.

I shake my head, and she relays the message to the employee, then rolls up the window.

"God, it's cold," she says, and turns the heat up higher.

When steam gathers on the windows, I'm grateful that no one else will be able to see me in here.

"Hey, Jade?"

She looks at me, green eyes softening at the tone in my voice. "Yeah?"

"Thanks for bailing on dinner."

She bumps my shoulder with her own, her so-dark-it's-almost-black hair falling across her collarbone. "There's nowhere I'd rather be." She pauses, grinning at me in the neon lights pouring into the cab. "Well, except maybe wearing some bull rider's hat in a dingy dive bar hallway. You know what they say. Wear the hat and all."

I roll my eyes and fight back a smile. "Don't let Cooper hear you say that."

She groans and reaches for her phone, pulling up the continuous glucose monitor she uses for her type 1 diabetes to check her blood glucose and adjust her insulin before our food arrives. "Don't talk about Cooper. He's annoying me."

"He's always annoying you," I point out.

"Yes, but he's really annoying me right now," she responds, her focus still on her phone. "This morning he was making all these comments about how someone needs to protect Beau from you."

Her words feel like a slap to my face, and I work hard to keep my expression neutral when Jade drops her phone in her lap, turning her wide-eyed attention back on me. "Shit, I shouldn't have said that."

I wave her off. "No, it's fine. He should. I'm a mess."

The shock drops from her expression, replaced with something hard. "No, you're not."

"No, I am," I say, giving her a look. "I know that. And I haven't been fair to Beau the last few months. I know that, too."

She stares at me for a moment, confusion etched into the lines of her face. "What's that supposed to mean?"

It means that I've been holding myself back from him when he's always given me every part of himself. But I don't know how to do that, how to live like that. I've tried the most with him and with Jade, but even with the people I love the most in this world, I can't make myself let go of the little pieces of myself I've always kept hidden.

Letting out a sigh and rubbing my palms over my thighs, I say, "I just haven't been totally honest with him."

She arches a brow, the neon lights casting her in shades of blue, purple, and red.

"About why I needed time. I've been...struggling," I say, avoiding her eyes. I focus on a spot on the dashboard, a dent she made with the heel of her snakeskin boots one night when I was her designated driver and she was completely wasted after one too many tequila shots at KC's. "I've been struggling, and I haven't wanted him to see me like that. So I asked for time."

It's the most honest I've been with anyone about the separation. Jade asked why when it first happened, but I wouldn't tell her. She probably thought we had problems to work through.

But that was never it. The problem was never us. It was always *me*.

"Els," Jade says with a heavy sigh. "You can't cut out everyone who gets too close."

"I'm not," I reply, even though we both know I'm lying. Finally meeting her gaze, I say, "Or I don't want to. Really, I don't. I just don't know how not to."

The words hang in the air between us, and I watch as my best friend digests them. We've been Jade and Elsie since she took one ballet class at the studio when she was twelve. Ballet didn't stick for her, but we did, and she's stuck with me through thick and thin since. She knows me better than anyone else, except maybe Beau. But she'd say it's a tie.

I'm holding my breath, waiting for her to respond, unsure of what I want her to say. I just said so much, although it really wasn't much at all. But it was enough, and my heart feels raw. I don't think I can handle more tonight, but I owe it to her to try if she wants me to.

"When the food gets here, can I have some of your fries?" she asks. "I got onion rings and I'm already regretting it."

A relieved sigh slips out of my lips and my shoulders drop from where they stationed themselves around my ears. A small smile lifts my mouth. "Yeah, Jade, we can split my fries. As long as you don't let those onion rings in the truck. I think the smell would be my last straw."

She smiles back, although I can still see the words she's holding back hovering on the tip of her tongue. "Deal."

THIRTEEN

BEAU
MARCH

I'M NOT SHOCKED TO find the big house loud and chaotic when I arrive for family dinner. The ranch has been in my family for generations, but my grandparents were only able to have one child—my dad. After they passed, my dad was the only blood relative left of the Jenningses, but he wasn't the only family. Over the years, he and my mom have been collecting people and sewing them into the patchwork quilt that is this family.

The big house is an oversized log cabin, sprawling over three thousand square feet. My parents always said with two boys and a little girl, each one wilder than the two of them combined, they needed space to breathe. They built the new big house when Cooper and I were four or five, and I have distinct memories of Dad letting us nail boards into place and write our names on the walls before they painted over them. This house is as much a part of our family as the people in it.

I make my way into the living room and see Cooper first. He nods in my direction, so I make a beeline for him, wiping my sweating palms on my jeans. Out of the corner of my eye, I see Dad talking to Willow, Ruby's mom, and her husband, Jesse. They look deep in conversation, and I'm thankful for it, because I don't want my dad cornering me. Cheyenne is chasing one of Morgan's boys around, and Morgan is nowhere to be found. Mom is definitely in the kitchen, finishing dinner, and I'd bet my last dollar that Jade's parents are in there too.

I think I'm in the clear. Tonight, I have to tell my family that I got my wife pregnant. Not all that crazy under normal circumstances, but these circumstances are anything but normal. And I'm not ready to face the music just yet.

I remember when Cooper told the family about Ruby. He wasn't nervous at all to tell everyone that he was having a baby with a stranger. He knew that even if they were shocked at first, they'd be thrilled. And internally, I know that too.

But that doesn't make me less nervous, especially since I'll be sharing the news without Elsie here with me. Not having her here feels like I'm missing a vital part of myself, the way people who have lost a limb say that they sometimes still feel phantom pains in the spot it once was.

"You look like you could use this," Cooper says, handing me his beer and pulling me from my thoughts as I reach him. I take it gratefully, the cold, sweating glass bottle a balm against my overheated palms. There's a headache building at the base of my skull and sweat prickling beneath my shirt.

I take a long gulp, welcoming the bitter flavor against my scratchy throat. "That obvious?"

He grins, eyes assessing me, and I swear I see a flicker of concern there. "Not to everyone."

"Just to you?" I ask before taking another sip, practically downing the rest of the bottle.

His smile stretches. "Just to anyone who shares our blood."

To prove his point, Cheyenne sidles up next to me, her blue eyes narrow. Her dark brown hair, the same color as mine and Cooper's, falls in tangles down her back, just like it always does. "What's wrong?"

I let out a sigh and push a hand through my hair, avoiding her gaze. "Nothing."

She steps closer—she's never been one for personal space. I can smell her floral and honey perfume, the same scent she's worn since high school, something she picked out at the mall in Bozeman and still dutifully purchases ten years later. "You're lying. Spill."

Cooper laughs, drawing Cheyenne's stare away from me, allowing me to take a full breath.

"Do *you* know?"

Before he gets a chance to respond, someone asks, "Know what?"

I turn to see Morgan joining our group. He's dressed in worn jeans and one of the plain short-sleeve T-shirts he wears year round, like the cold has no effect on him. The gel I know he haphazardly ran through his dark blond hair is barely holding it in check, the thick waves fighting to break through.

Cooper fixes me with a look, one that I can easily read. He thinks I should go ahead and tell them, and I let out a long breath, knowing he's probably right. I'd planned to pull Morgan aside and tell him before dinner, but Cheyenne will never forgive me if she finds out with the rest of the family.

I look at them each in the eye, taking them in. My twin, who looks the same as me, dark hair and dark eyes, except no mustache and a five o'clock shadow that never seems to grow any longer. My younger sister, tall, wild, carefree. Morgan, a calm, steady presence that I swear he inherited from my father even though he isn't related to us. They've always been there, no matter what, and I know this time will be no different.

"Elsie's pregnant."

Cheyenne's eyes blow comically wide, her mouth falling open, and a ball of chewed-up gum rolls out. "Seriously?"

Cooper snorts and picks up her gum, dropping it into the neck of the bottle I'm only now realizing I've emptied. "No, he's making it up."

She swivels to face him and smacks his arm. "Shut up. This is serious."

Morgan's eyes connect with mine, and I notice a small smile playing on his face. He looks both genuinely happy for me and amused at my siblings' antics. "Congrats, Beau. You're going to be a great dad."

Some of the nerves in my stomach calm at his words. Morgan is a dad as well. He has two rambunctious boys who constantly keep him on his toes. I've leaned on him a lot over the last few months because, although our situations are very different, he's been in a difficult marriage before too. Shortly after the birth of his second child, Ryder, who is now two, he found out his wife had been cheating on him for a year, and he wasn't even sure whether Ryder was his. She left him for the other man, and after confirming his paternity, Morgan was able to get partial custody of both Ryder and Cash.

I give him a grateful smile. "Thanks, Morgan."

Cheyenne turns back to me, eyes alight with a familiar temper that has been getting her in trouble since she could talk. "I better not have been the only one who didn't know."

"No," I say with a shake of my head. "I only told Coop because he was annoying me."

She nods sagely, because we both understand how he can be.

"What are we talking about?" Dad asks, entering the conversation.

I almost jump out of my skin at the intrusion. I can feel my heart in my throat and my face flushing, so I look down at the scarred, knotted wood floor, hoping he doesn't notice.

Before I can think of a way to change the subject, Mom yells out from the dining room.

"Dinner's ready!"

Thank God.

I'm the first to leave the group, hoping to get into the dining room and snag a seat before anyone else asks questions. It's not until I get in there that I notice Jade is absent. I wonder where she is, since she rarely misses dinner at the big house. Across the long dining table, her parents, Wyatt and Tessa, settle into their chairs near Mom and Dad.

I'm about to take my seat when a chubby toddler bounds into my legs, wrapping me in arms that are surprisingly strong for how little they are. A smile creeps up onto my face without trying, and I bend down to pick up Ryder. His blond hair is messy and he has what looks like jam on his face. I imagine it came from Mom. She no doubt slipped him a spoonful in the kitchen while she finished up dinner.

"Hey, Ryder. How you doing, buddy?"

He gives me a broad smile, gaps between his baby teeth. His breath smells like sugar. "Hi, Uncle Beau."

His little voice soothes the last vestiges of nerves inside me. No one in my family could be upset about having another perfect little human like this in the family. It's not even that I thought they would be upset. My only worry stemmed from the conversation I had with Cooper in the stables the other day, when he said he was going to look out for me if no one else would. My family loves Elsie, and nothing could change that, not even her asking me to leave. They may be as in the dark about her reasons as I am, but she's a Jennings too, and nothing could make them stop seeing her that way.

I only wish Elsie knew that. I wish that she was here to see how excited they will be for us. That phantom limb feeling returns, and I look at the empty seat next to me, the one no one has filled for months, awaiting her return.

I tear my gaze from the empty chair, shaking away the grief that's starting to burrow into me, and focus my attention on the little boy in my arms. The one wearing dirty cowboy boots that are sure to leave muddy marks on my favorite jeans. I can't even bring myself to care.

Leaning forward to whisper in Ryder's ear, I ask, "Can you keep a secret?"

His already huge smile grows even larger, and he nods excitedly. He's absentmindedly toying with the collar of my shirt, and every little brush of his fingers makes the warmth inside me grow. "Mm-hmm."

"Auntie Elsie is going to have a baby," I tell him, keeping my voice low. It doesn't feel like a confession. It feels like a promise.

His eyes widen, the same blue-green color as his dad's. "Really?"

I nod and press a kiss to his sticky cheek. "Sure is, bud. You're going to have another cousin."

And then, to my complete horror, Ryder turns away from me and screams to the entire table, "Auntie Elsie is having a baby!"

Eleven sets of eyes settle on me, and to the little boy in my arms, I say, "We need to work on what the concept of a secret is, Ryder."

Everyone takes the news as expected. Mom and Dad are thrilled. Willow tells me that she's still got all of Ruby's baby stuff in her attic and that she will make Jesse get it down for us if we want it. The Dawsons give me warm smiles and congratulations.

When they ask where Elsie is, I tell them she's not feeling her best. It isn't a lie, but it also isn't the whole truth, and I don't miss the look Cooper gives me when I say it. I'm glad he's looking out for me. He's coming from a good place, even if I don't think it's necessary.

I normally love having dinner at the big house. We're all so spread out on the ranch and in town that this is the only time we're all together. But I can't say I'm not grateful when we finish and start heading out. Bitterly cold air smacks into me like a punch, stealing the breath from my lungs, seeping into every inch of exposed skin. I don't notice the way the snow is coming down until we walk out onto the wraparound porch and stare out into the black abyss.

I can't even make out the driveway. In the couple of hours we were inside, talking and laughing and drinking Dad's homemade hot cocoa while Cash, Ryder, and Ruby acted out some play they'd made up, snow piled up on the ground, swallowing up our tires and any tracks we left. The sight of it makes the headache I've been fighting all night pound harder, my mind scrambling.

"Shit," I say, and everyone comes to a stop behind me.

"Well," Wyatt says in that deep voice of his, unfazed as ever.

Jade must have gotten that from him. The only person who has ever been able to rile her up is Cooper. "Looks like we're having a sleepover. Clint, I'm sleeping with you."

Behind him, Dad guffaws, but lead settles in my stomach and a panicky sensation claws up my throat. There's no way

I'm leaving Elsie to wait out a snowstorm alone. I don't think she even knows how to work the generator if the power goes out. Why the *hell* did I never show her how to use it?

Because I never thought there would be a time she'd be there without me. God, was I wrong.

"We can probably make it back to our cabins," Cooper says to Morgan. They live in cabins on the property, ones similar to the cabin but larger than the cabin I moved into when Elsie asked me to leave, though both are bigger. "Ruby, you coming with me, or do you want to stay at the big house with your mom and Jesse?"

My six-year-old niece presses a little finger to her chin, thinking. The sight of it would normally make a smile tug at my lips, but right now, I'm still sorting out how to get home. Because I'm not going to leave my pregnant wife alone for however long it takes for this storm to end and for the roads to clear.

"If I go with you, can we bring some of Papa's hot chocolate?" Ruby asks, looking up at her dad with wide brown eyes.

He smiles down at her, softness in all the lines of his face. "Sure, squirt."

She grins brightly, her light brown hair just as messy as her aunt's. "Okay, I'll go with you."

When I look back at Willow, she's rolling her eyes but smiling, leaning into Jesse for warmth.

Dad claps his hands together, drawing everyone's attention. "Well, let's all head back in and we'll get rooms sorted. Morgan and Cooper, let us know when you make it back safe."

Everyone shuffles back into the house, but I snatch the sleeve of Mom's sweater before she can disappear into the house behind them. Nodding toward the driveway, I say, "I'm going to head home."

Her expression turns hard, and I know she wants to argue with me. My mom is not a soft woman, at least not on the outside. She's deeply caring and fiercely loyal and endlessly strong, but she has a soft spot for the people she loves. I've never seen her cry, never seen her look anxious, never seen her show any emotion she doesn't want to. She's got hair that's turned the color of steel, and I've secretly thought it matches her perfectly.

Right now, she's worried, and it looks like her putting her foot down. Normally, I might try to appease her, just like I do with everyone, but I can't tonight. Not with Elsie just a few miles away, alone.

"Are you sure that's a good idea?" she asks, her gaze never leaving mine.

I nod. "I can't be stuck here while Elsie is sick."

She's studying me now, looking for something. Maybe exhaustion, maybe hesitation. Maybe a reason to tell me to stay.

I can tell she wants to protest, but she only nods, resigned. "Be safe, okay? Let us know when you make it back."

"I will," I respond. I lean down to kiss her cheek, chilled by the wind, before spinning on my heel to head down the stairs that are now slick with ice.

"Beau?" Mom calls.

I turn around to face her, snowflakes dancing in the wind and catching in my hair. The cold cuts through my jacket, and suddenly, all I want is to be home with Elsie, warming up in front of our fireplace. Exhaustion feels heavy in my bones.

My mom is standing on the porch, her arms crossed against the cold, but she still looks like an immovable pillar. Like she's a part of the land that grew up in that exact spot. "I'm really happy for you and Elsie," she says. "Make sure you tell her that."

I give her a smile. Mom may not let others see what she's thinking or feeling, but she never fails to notice it about others. She's observant, diligent, possibly all-knowing. And right now, she sees straight through my excuse that Elsie skipped dinner because she's not feeling well. "I will."

Her hands settle on her hips, despite the rush of cold. "And tell her I want her to come next time."

I push my hands deep into my pockets to ward off the chill. "I want that too, Mom. I'll see what I can do."

FOURTEEN
ELSIE
MARCH

I sit on the front porch for a while after Jade drops me off, wrapped in a heavy flannel blanket, watching her headlights disappear into the snow storm, as she drives away, trying to beat the bad weather.

I've always been a fan of the cold. Maybe it's because the summers in Montana never get overly warm, but I don't think I could handle living in the heat. I come alive in the summer, but I always appreciate the biting cold and windburned cheeks and snowflakes melting on my tongue. The way everything slows down when it snows.

It's not until about an hour or so after Jade leaves that I start to wonder if Beau is going to be able to make it home. If I know the Jenningses at all, they're probably making up beds for everyone right now, not willing to let anyone risk driving in the rapidly falling snow and ice. I left my phone on the kitchen counter, but I'm sure when I go inside there will be a voicemail and a text from Beau telling me he has to stay at the big house. Telling me he hopes he'll be home once they clear the roads tomorrow.

And while I don't want him to risk driving home in this, the house feels empty without him. He's only been home for two weeks, but his presence has always felt larger than life, and I think I've gotten used to having him around again. For the months he was gone, I tried to convince myself I didn't miss him all that much, that I'd made the right decision when I asked him to leave. And when I was shaking on the floor in the middle of an anxiety attack, it felt like a good idea. I didn't have to panic, thinking he could come home at any second and find me huddled in a ball. I didn't have to sneak off to the bathroom when all the thoughts in my head became too much so I could talk myself down, force myself to find things I could see, hear, smell, touch, and taste, just to keep myself from falling off the edge in front of him. This house, with the big blue sky overhead and the mountains in the distance, became my haven. And I started to heal, little by little.

I remember the first day I climbed into bed and realized I hadn't had a panic attack all day. It was late December, two days before Christmas. I stared at the twinkling lights on my tree, the one I'd felt good enough to buy just a few days earlier, and cried, which was something I so rarely allowed myself to do. I cried because it finally felt like I was getting better. I cried because it meant I was one step closer to having Beau again.

Now, here I am, three months later, staring out into the dark, the last snowstorm of the season blocking out even the brightest of stars, wishing he could be here with me. And a very small part of me almost wishes he knew about that day three months ago so he could tell me he's proud of how far I've come. An even smaller part almost wishes he'd been there to hold me while I cried looking at that Christmas tree, so he could have told me he was proud of me then too.

Something in the distance catches my eye, and I blink beneath the porch lights, trying to clear my vision enough to make it out. It's...moving, and for a minute I think it might be a bear, but then the figure stumbles, and I recognize it. *Him.*

Beau.

Walking, in a snowstorm, directly toward our house.

Adrenaline pumps through my veins, and I spin on my heel, running inside to slide my feet out of my slippers and into a pair of heavy boots. I tug my shearling-lined jacket from the hook and pull it over my thick hoodie before heading back outside.

Beau is still there, making his way through snow that is now midway up his calves. I have no idea how it fell this fast. Before dinner, it was hardly coming down, and now, it's almost a whiteout. If I hadn't been searching the darkness for a hint of a headlight, I would have missed him.

I bound down the front porch steps, holding on to the railing for dear life to keep myself from slipping, and into the snow. It's *so much* colder out here in the open than it was on the porch. Up there, I was cold but comfortable in my hoodie, leggings, beanie, and slippers with the flannel blanket around my shoulders. Now, I'm instantly chilled to the bone.

Despite all that, the electricity zinging through me keeps me pushing forward to Beau. I don't know what he's doing outside in the middle of a snowstorm, but a thousand terrifying thoughts run through my head. I don't have time to consider them right now, not when he's stumbling through the snow like a man on a mission, heading right for me.

"Elsie!" he yells when he's close enough to be heard over the roaring wind. "What the hell are you doing out here?"

I stop dead in my tracks for just a moment, stunned. *He's* walking home in a snowstorm and he's going to ask *me* what I'm doing outside?

"You cannot be serious!" I yell back.

We close the remaining feet between us, and Beau's hands land heavily on my shoulders. His eyes look wild and frightened. "Why are you outside right now?" he asks again, no more gently.

"I saw *you* walking through the snow, you idiot. I was coming to help."

He looks ready to snap. "I'm fine. Don't ever do that again. You scared me to death."

I stare at him for a long moment, wanting to say the same thing, to ask him a million questions, but he looks scared, and that triggers a sense of protectiveness in me. I reach up and place my hands on his neck. His skin feels like ice beneath my touch, goose bumps prickling over every exposed inch.

His eyes still look crazed, but his body soothes a little at my touch. I smooth my thumbs down his neck, feeling the tendons there soften beneath my fingertips.

"I'm okay. We're okay," I say softly.

His gaze roves over my face, as if he's searching for signs of injury, and although I want to do the same, I force myself to keep looking at his face. I've never seen him like this before, with fear and panic consuming him. It tugs at my heart, because I know exactly how he feels right now.

Pushing up on my tiptoes in the snow, I press a kiss to his freezing cheek. There's stubble beneath my lips and the smell of his familiar cologne clinging to his neck. "We're okay," I repeat. "Come on, let's go inside."

His warm brown eyes settle on mine, fear still in his voice. "You're okay?"

I nod. "Yeah, I'm okay. But I'm worried about you, so can we please go inside?"

This seems to snap him back into himself, and the calm, reassuring Beau returns. Immediately, his eyes look clearer. When he speaks, he sounds like himself again. "Yeah, of course. Let's get out of the cold."

We trudge back toward the house, my footprints from before already starting to disappear in the rapidly falling snow. I catch myself glancing over at Beau every few steps, trying to assess his mental state. He looks better now that we're heading inside. Stronger, more like his steady, unyielding self, completely unlike the man that was falling apart in front of me just a moment ago.

The door handle is cold to the touch, but the warmth of the inside draws me in, the dying fire cracking in the fireplace calling to me like a beacon. I'm not sure I've ever been this cold, and I can only imagine how Beau must feel.

I step into the almost stifling warmth of the house and turn to Beau. His face is red from the cold, and his hair is wet from melted snow. Snowflakes cling to his lashes, and beneath the mustache that I still haven't gotten used to, his lips look chapped. He looks like he's made from the same stuff as the mountains outside, like he's just as much a part of them as the rocks and trees.

Just the sight of him has relief barreling through me with so much strength that it makes my knees feel weak. I have to grip the edge of the kitchen counter to keep my balance.

"What the actual hell were you doing out there?" I ask, hating the way my voice sounds brittle. I'm so cold I can't think straight.

A smile tugs at the corners of Beau's lips. The fire crackling in the stone hearth casts him in a warm glow, illuminating his tired grin. "Miss me?"

I take a deep breath, some of the adrenaline finally seeping from my body, and shove his shoulder, rolling my eyes. "Seriously, Beau. Where's your truck?"

He sighs and kicks off his boots. Even from here, I can see his socks and the legs of his jeans are soaked through. He has to be freezing. "About a mile down the road in a snowdrift."

My jaw falls open, and I stare at him. Images of him running off the road, his tires stuck in snow that's much too deep, fill my head, making me sick to my stomach. "Why didn't you call me?"

"I did," he says, confusion creasing the lines between his eyes. "How else did you know I was out there?"

"Shit," I breathe, and dive for where I left my phone charging on the kitchen counter. Sure enough, there's a missed call from Beau. And a text explaining what happened. It also says that I shouldn't come after him under any circumstances, but that if he wasn't home in an hour, I should call 911.

I scan the text a second time, incredulity filling up all the places that were filled with concern just a minute ago. Visions of him stranded in the snow race through my mind, making my heartbeat quicken, my throat go tight. The thought that I could have lost him lodges somewhere deep in my stomach, and I feel *sick*.

My eyes snag on his. He's standing here in the middle of the living room, when he so easily could have been *gone*. Because he was reckless and stubborn. A white-hot anger replaces the chill that's seeped into my bones, burning through me until I'm sure I'm going to explode.

"You cannot be serious," I say, waving my phone at him. "You walked *a mile* in a snowstorm and wanted me to just call 911 if you weren't home in an hour?"

"Well, I sure as hell didn't want my pregnant wife to come hiking through the snow to get me."

He says this like it's the most obvious thing in the world, and I have the overwhelming urge to chuck my phone at his stupid, chivalrous head.

"Screw you."

"You're going to have to ask nicer than that," he says, placing his hands on his narrow hips, his voice like a caress in the dark. He doesn't look cold at all. No, he looks warm, inviting, a dangerous smirk lifting the corner of his lips. "You know how I like it when you beg."

I stare at him for a long moment, horrified that I'm too speechless to come up with an appropriate comeback. I finally land on, "I'm going to bed. Don't leave a puddle on my floor."

"That didn't sound like an invitation," he calls out.

I glare at him over my shoulder, brimming with anger but still unable to leave without taking one final look, without making sure he's okay. "It wasn't."

And then I slam the bedroom door closed, hating that I can be so relieved that he's home and feel so safe while also wanting to knock him on his ass. Still, I wait up after climbing in bed until I hear the sound of the shower kicking on. And then I tiptoe back out to the living room and turn the heat up. He might be ridiculous, but he's not going to be cold.

FIFTEEN
ELSIE
MARCH

I WAKE UP TO the sound of a hacking cough in the room across the hall. I lie there for a moment, waiting to see if I imagined it, but when Beau coughs again, I push the covers off and pad across the icy wood floors to the guest room.

The door is closed, and for a moment, I hesitate. I shouldn't feel weird going into his room. We're *married*, after all, but I feel it, nonetheless. I know what he will look like wrapped in flannel sheets, with messy hair and pillow-creased cheeks. I know how he will feel—soft, overheated skin, coated in a sheen of perspiration. I know how he will smell—like musk and leather. I know everything about him except whether he will want me in that room.

My hands shake as I knock on the door, and the coughing inside stops. Time stops, really. I can hear my breathing and the sound of my heartbeat in my ears.

They're so loud, I'm surprised I'm able to make out the rough voice on the other side of the door.

"Elsie?"

It sounds sleepy, husky, and it has that particular quality that Beau has when he's sick. Almost boyish and as close to fragile as he ever sounds. It always makes my heart soften, and this time is no different.

"Can I come in?" I ask, and hold my breath as I wait for his response.

"Yeah, Els, you can come in."

The bedside lamp flicks on as I open the door, illuminating the room in a warm, golden glow. It makes everything feel soft, hazy. Beau is propped against the headboard, his hair in disarray, the blankets twisted around his legs. He's always been a heavy sleeper, barely moving at all, while I'll toss and turn all night. I wonder if he doesn't sleep as well without me either.

"Did my coughing wake you?" he asks, his voice like sandpaper.

My heart squeezes in my chest. Just a few hours ago, he literally walked through a snowstorm to get home to me, and now he's coughing in bed because of it.

I shake my head, and he manages a tired, barely coherent smile.

"Liar."

"Maybe," I say, walking farther into the room, drawn to him like a moth to a flame. When I get close enough to touch him, I reach out slow enough for him to pull away. When he doesn't, his eyes that look almost black in this light never leaving me, I press the back of my hand to his forehead. It's hot, clammy, making me suck in a breath between my teeth.

My eyes lock on his. They're hazy, unfocused. "You've got a fever."

He nods, his movement slow, sluggish, but his gaze remains heavy on me. It makes my skin tingle, sends goose bumps rushing down my spine. "I started feeling sick at dinner."

Swallowing against the feeling, I push down on his shoulder, trying to ignore the firmness of it beneath my palm, the way the muscles bunch and flex, hard as granite. "Lie down. I'm going to get medicine."

"Lying down makes the cough worse," he drawls sleepily, voice rough as sandpaper.

"Mmm," I say, and apply pressure to his shoulder again.

He must really not be feeling well, because he bends beneath it, sliding down onto his pillow. His eyelids flutter, sleep pulling him under. I can't help but run my hand through the thick mass of his dark hair, pushing it off his clammy forehead. Even like this, flushed from fever, he looks beautiful.

Bending down so he can hear me, I say, "I'll be right back."

I swear I feel a phantom touch on my back as I turn, fingertips pressing into the dimples above my waistband, but I don't look back, don't linger. Instead, I slip out of the room, forcing myself to focus on the task at hand. I head into my bathroom and dig through the cabinets, looking for medicine. Back in Utah, I always kept the medicine cabinet fully stocked. A simple cold could ruin a whole week of rehearsals and classes if I didn't tackle it quickly.

I haven't been as good about stocking it since moving, but luckily, I find a box of cold and flu medication that isn't expired. It should get us through the night and into tomorrow. By then, the roads should be clear enough for a trip to the drugstore.

After snatching the box, I pad into the kitchen to make tea. Beau is strictly a coffee man. The habit starts early for ranchers, I guess, due to the early hours. Even back in high school, he drank at least two cups of black coffee every morning before school. I, however, have never been much for coffee. It always makes me jittery, something that isn't especially helpful for a dancer. So instead, I usually have tea or matcha in the mornings, and even when I was at my worst mentally, I was never without tea.

It makes it easy to find some now. I find a bag of peppermint and brew it, then make sure to load it up with honey before heading back into the guest room. Beau is still asleep, his breathing heavy, a wheezing sound pulling from his chest. I almost hate to wake him, but the way his breathing sounds, I know it's only a matter of time before he starts coughing again, and once it starts, it's harder to stop.

I stand at the foot of the bed for a long moment, considering what I should do, hot tea steaming in the cold air around me, the heat of the cup seeping into my chilled skin. Beau and I handle sickness very differently. He's a natural caretaker, and I am...not. But I've never had a problem taking care of him. It comes easily. And it has always frustrated him to no end that I don't let him do much for me when I'm sick. But I don't really enjoy being taken care of. I don't come from a family like Beau's. My needs were always met, sure, but my parents don't show their love the way the Jenningses do.

Still, I don't know if Beau will want me to take care of him now. Not after our fight earlier, not after everything that's happened the last few months. I don't know where we stand, what I'm allowed to do for my husband, and I hate that.

Taking a deep, shaking breath, I decide I'll give him the medicine and make sure he drinks the tea and lots of water before he passes out again. And then I'll head back to my room across the hall. But I won't close the doors behind me, just in case he needs me again.

Slowly, I make my way over to the side of the bed and set the tea and medicine on the bedside table. I let my hand fall to his shoulder, palm smoothing over the slope of it. He's always been muscular. His is not the kind of body honed from hours in the gym, but the kind that speaks to months and years of physical labor. But now, he's bigger, like he's been working more than usual the last few months. I can imagine it easily. While I secluded myself in this house and tried to heal so no one would see how broken I was, Beau drowned his sorrows in hard work. I used to do the same with dance. We're so different in so many ways, but that's something we've always had in common.

A little pang goes through me at the loss of it now. One more way we've changed into people we barely recognize.

Shoving the thought away, I gently nudge his shoulder. "Beau, wake up," I whisper softly. "I'm going to take care of you."

He blinks blearily at me, confusion etched into the lines of his face. "Elsie baby, I can't right now. I don't feel too great."

My lips roll together to keep from laughing. "Your medicine, Beau. I have your cough medicine."

He blinks again, as if he's trying to clear his vision and mind at the same time. "Medicine?"

"You have a fever," I say. "And a cough. You need to take this medicine and drink some tea."

He rolls his face into the pillow, his words muffled. "Don't make me drink the hot dirt water."

This time I do laugh, and at the sound of it, he turns to face me once more, a sloppy smile on his face. "I love your laugh, Elsie. I wish you hadn't stopped laughing."

This sobers me, and sadness settles deep in my stomach. "Me too."

"But you're laughing again. That's good." He pushes himself up onto an elbow, and then half sits, half reclines against the headboard. "You're coming back to me."

I swallow against the lump forming in my throat, wanting to press a hand to the tightness in my chest. "Yeah, Beau, I'm going to come back to you."

He smiles again. "Good."

I pick up the medicine and put two pills in his hand. "You need to take these. They'll make you sleepy, but they'll make you feel better."

His tired eyes settle on me. "I feel better now that you're here."

"Then imagine how much better you'll feel after the medicine."

"Probably good enough to put a baby in you," he drawls, and then looks at me pointedly. "Oops, too late."

A laugh barks out of me, loud in the quiet of the night. "You're delirious."

His grin hitches higher, the same one he wears when he's drunk and handsy. The one that always somehow leads to me with my pants off. "Maybe."

I shake my head at him, fighting a smile. "Take your medicine, Beau, and drink your hot dirt water. I'm going back to bed."

"Wait," he says, his tone more serious, a little desperate. His eyes settle on mine. "Stay with me. Please."

It's the *please* that does it. No, that's a lie. I would have stayed without the *please*. All I needed was an invitation.

"Okay."

His shoulders relax, losing tension I hadn't even noticed had stiffened them, and he pats the spot beside him. I walk around the foot and climb beneath the blankets. The sheets are cool against my legs. Even when it's freezing, I can't sleep in pants. I hate the way they feel twisted against my legs, so I always end up in shorts or just an oversized tee. Tonight, thankfully, I'm in shorts, but I don't miss the way Beau's gaze travels the expanse of my legs as I slide into bed.

It makes my nerve endings catch fire.

I really can't be thinking like this in bed with my sick husband.

I watch as Beau takes his medicine and dutifully drinks his tea, working hard to keep a respectable distance between us. The problem is, I'm used to sleeping in a king-size bed, but this one is a queen, and Beau is a giant. When he bends over to deposit the empty mug on the bedside table and turn off the light, his thigh presses to mine beneath the blankets, and I have to fight to keep from shivering or jumping away.

My skin feels too tight and my nerves feel too sensitive, and I'm acutely aware of how Beau's leg hair feels against my thigh. I'm even more aware of what happened the last time we were in a bed together and exactly how long it's been since then.

I think I might combust.

Before I can wrench myself out of the bed and run across the hall with my tail tucked between my legs, Beau slides down beneath the covers and places his head in my lap. I freeze, but he just says, "Will you scratch my head?"

The heat coiling inside me dissipates, and I slide my hand into his hair, running my nails against his scalp. He hums, the sound muffled by the blankets. I can feel the feverish heat of him through the sheets, hear the wheezing sound he makes when he breathes, although it's a little better since drinking the tea.

"Thank you for taking care of me," Beau whispers, and my heart pinches. His breath is warm against my thighs, his body so familiar against mine.

"I'll always take care of you, Beau."

He rolls his head to look up at me. I can barely make out his features in the moonlight filtering through the windows. "Will you let me take care of you?"

The question hits me in the solar plexus and I have to swallow heavily, weighing my words. "I'm working on it."

He nods and slumps back onto my lap, his hair tickling my exposed skin. "I can live with that."

"Thank you for being patient with me," I say, scratching his scalp lightly. I don't miss the way he makes a little keening noise in the back of his throat, his body sinking deeper into mine, relishing the feel of it.

He's quiet for a long moment, and just when I think he's fallen asleep, he says, "I'll wait as long as you need me to, Els, as long as you promise you will come back to me one day."

Outside, the wind howls, and the clouds block out most of the moonlight, illuminating only a small sliver of the room. It feels like I'm speaking directly into the darkness when I say, "I never wanted to be away from you. I was trying..." I trail off, not knowing how to finish my sentence without revealing too much. I already feel raw from this conversation, and I need to be strong enough to care for him.

"What were you trying?" he asks softly. He's not looking at me now, but that doesn't make this conversion any easier.

I shake my head, even though he can't see me. "Nothing."

For a moment, I think he might push, like he's been doing more and more often of late. I think he might ask again and again until I tell him the truth. But he must be tired, because he just says, "Okay."

The silence stretches between us for a long time after that, but it's not awkward. I keep scratching Beau's head, and his breathing slows until I think he's asleep. I'm tired, too, feeling dragged under by the tempting pull of drifting off in the same bed as Beau, of getting truly restful sleep again. The kind I haven't gotten since the last time he was in my bed.

So I'm surprised when Beau asks, "What happened to the paintings?"

I almost think I dreamed it, but then Beau coughs, and when he shifts his hand up to cover his mouth, I realize he's still awake.

"What paintings?" I ask, even though I have a pretty good idea which ones he's referring to.

"Our paintings."

The ones we made at that drunken paint and sip party. The portraits of each other. The ones that hung over our bed ever since. The ones I took down after he left, unable to look at them anymore.

"They're in the attic."

Beau is quiet for a moment, only the sound of his ragged breathing and the howling wind cutting through the silence. "Why?"

I consider not answering him, or at least not telling him the truth, but I'm so tired, mentally and physically. This is the longest stretch I've gone without vomiting in the last month, and I'm exhausted from growing organs all day.

So the truth slips out, raw and unfiltered. "I couldn't stand to look at them and be reminded of another way I'd failed."

Beau rolls over onto his back, his head still in my lap, but it's too dark for me to make out much besides his shape. Even in the dark, he's so familiar. "What do you mean?" He sounds more alert now.

My heart beats in my chest, and I feel like I'm standing at the edge of a precipice. One that I've been dancing around my whole life, avoiding no matter the cost, and now I'm considering just...falling.

For a moment, I can't breathe. The words are there, pressing against my throat, begging to be spoken. But if I say them, if I let them out, they'll be real.

I exhale, slow and unsteady. Ragged. Then, finally—

"I failed at dance," I say out loud for the first time ever. It's a thought that's been going round and round in my head since my injury, that I *failed* at the one thing I'd been working my entire life for, but this is the first time I've said it aloud. "I failed at dance. And then I failed to keep my baby alive. And then I failed at my marriage. And I would lie awake in bed at night and stare at those damn paintings and be reminded of how I failed at that too." My breath comes out heavy now, jagged. "I just couldn't do it anymore."

"Elsie," Beau says, sitting up.

I cut him off. "No, I don't want to talk about it, okay? I just want to go to sleep. Please." I hate the way my voice breaks on the last word. How brittle and broken I sound.

And Beau, because he knows me better than anyone else, knows it too. He's quiet for two long heartbeats, but he finally says, "Okay, Els. Let's go to sleep."

He lies down then and waits for me to lie beside him before wrapping his arms around me and pulling me close. With his mouth in my hair, he says, "But just so you know, I don't think you failed at any of those things. The dance floor, the canvas, and especially our baby, were lucky just to be touched by you, for however long you had them. Not all endings are failings. Some are just chances for us to start over."

SIXTEEN

BEAU
APRIL
ELEVEN WEEKS PREGNANT

Calving season is officially over, which means I can finally focus on horse training again. Each of my family members has their own job here on the ranch. Mom and Dad handle all the big-picture duties of owning and managing a ranch, although they have a lot more help now that they've officially made Morgan ranch manager. Cooper is a ranch hand and basically floats wherever he's needed day-to-day. It works for him since he's easily bored and needs variety, which can often be hard to come by on a ranch. Cheyenne does horseback riding lessons part time and works part time in town, doing various jobs that she never keeps for long. I spend most of my time training and rehabilitating horses. We have additional ranch hands and a few seasonal workers, but during busy seasons, we all chip in wherever needed.

Now, I stop in front of Sugar's stall, and she eyes me warily. She's warmed up to me a lot over the past few weeks, but every day, without fail, when I walk up to her stall, she looks at me with distrust. I don't know everything that happened to her before she came here, but I want to kill the person who instilled this much distrust in a horse.

"Hey, Sugar, how you doing today?" I ask softly, extending my hand in her direction.

She huffs air through her nose, staring at my hand for a moment before coming close enough to sniff it. When she does, I extend my other hand, holding out an apple chunk, which she hastily nibbles. Sugar, true to her name, loves sugar. I tried rewarding her with carrots at first, but she quite literally turned her nose up at me, so I switched to apples early on. She really loved it when I brought strawberries, but I have to give her those in moderation since they're higher in sugar.

Today, we're going to attempt riding, and if it goes well, Sugar is going to get all the damn strawberries she wants.

"You ready to go for a ride, girl?" I ask her.

She nuzzles my hand again, looking for more treats.

I huff out a quiet laugh. "You'll get more in a bit."

I open the stall slowly to avoid startling her and keep one hand on her neck, moving up and down in slow motions as I hook the lead to her halter. We've practiced this plenty of times now, even on days we don't leave the stall. I wanted her to get used to the sound and the feeling of it before we moved on.

With gentle movements, I lead her out of the stall. We've done this too. We've gone out into a round pen and a pasture, and I've led her on walks so she knows the way.

She's calm as we head for the big barn doors.

"Good girl, Sugar," I say softly, gratification swelling in my chest as she follows my lead. A month ago, she would hardly let me touch her, and now she trusts me enough to follow me out of the barn.

The sun is shining outside, the first somewhat warm day of spring, and I want to soak it in, feel it on my skin. It's a perfect day for riding. I lead Sugar to the tacking area and secure her to a post before taking time to brush her off. I give her another treat before slowly beginning to saddle her up. She's still a little nervous about this part, but she's gotten more comfortable each time we've done it. I smooth a hand down her neck when her ears pin back, and I watch as she slowly settles before I continue. It takes time and patience, but when I'm finished tightening the girth, adjusting the stirrups, and placing the bit in her mouth, I lead her out to an open pasture.

Her mane is long, but no longer tangled, and I let my hand drag down it as I say, "We're going for a ride now, okay, Sugar? Just something slow and steady. Be gentle with me, and I'll be gentle with you."

I fit my boot into the stirrup and lift myself up and onto her back. Pride surges through me when she doesn't even flinch. "Good girl," I say, and have to keep from shouting. I squeeze my calves, urging her forward, and say, "Let's go, Sugar."

I'm riding a high after putting Sugar back in her stall and feeding her a handful of strawberries. My hands are stained red, and I can feel the first slight sunburn of the season pinkening my nose. I feel *good* for the first time in months. Maybe that's why I decide to hop in my truck and head home. It's not until I'm pulling into the driveway that I realize if Elsie says no to my idea, it's going to put a damper on my good mood.

She's sitting on the porch in jeans and a plain white tee, a blanket wrapped around her shoulders, her face turned to the sky, basking in the sunshine like a cat. I want to stop and stare for a moment, soak in the sight of her the way she's soaking in the sunshine, but when she hears me pull up, her eyes open and land squarely on me.

It makes my heartbeat pulse in my throat. My hands grow clammy on the steering wheel, the leather so worn it's gone shiny and slick. When the actual hell did speaking to my own wife make me this nervous?

Her eyes trail me as I climb out of the truck and close the distance between us. I can feel them like a touch, making the fine hairs on my arms stand on end, reminding me of exactly how long it's been since I've had her skin on mine. Confusion is etched into the fine lines of her face as I climb the steps, and I realize I should probably say something, *anything*.

"Hey."

I'm one eloquent motherfucker.

A smile tugs up one corner of Elsie's lips, a lightning bolt straight to my center. In the warm light of the late morning, her eyes look even more blue, reflecting the color of the springtime sky.

"Hey," she repeats. She's still assessing me, although she looks less confused and more...happy. Like the sight of me on a random morning when I should be at the ranch is welcoming.

It makes me climb the last step, narrowing the distance between us. My hand grips the railing, digging into the chipping white paint, as I gather my courage. It shouldn't be this hard. I shouldn't be this nervous.

"Let's go on a picnic," I finally manage to get out.

It's something we used to do all the time in high school, when we were broke. A tradition we tried to keep up after moving to Utah, but it never felt quite the same as lying on a blanket at Lucky Stars under the wide Montana sky.

"A picnic," she says, sounding like she's mulling it over in her head.

I can't help but smirk. "Blanket, preferably red check. Basket of food. Usually ends in sex."

Her mouth falls open, and a laugh rockets out of me. "I was kidding about the sex." I pause, tipping my head from side to side. "Well, I wouldn't be opposed to the sex part."

She rolls her eyes, but something inside me loosens when I see her fighting a smile. "Sure, Beau. Let's go for a picnic."

"Look, you've already got the blanket. Get your shoes and let's go."

"Yes, sir," she replies.

Well, that does something to me.

I force the thought away, watching as she heads into the house, the screen door swinging shut behind her. In the distance, birds chirp, and there's the sound of a plane passing overhead. Wind rustling in the trees and the warmth of the sun beating on my back.

She returns a moment later, dressed in worn black boots and a jacket, a beanie stuffed into the pocket, precariously close to falling out. It may be the first warm day of the season, but that just means we don't need coats to enjoy time lounging outside.

I want to take a long look at her, bask in the sight of her smiling as she heads right for me, but I head back down the stairs, Elsie on my heels, and open the truck door for her.

Her eyes catch on mine for a second before she climbs in, her shoulder brushing against mine. It feels like I'm back in high school again, feeling her for the first time, too unsure to reach out and touch her the way I want.

I have to force myself not to physically react at the contact. It's been weeks since we've touched more than the occasional brush of skin. Not since the night of the snowstorm, when I was sick and she climbed into that godforsaken guest bed to take care of me. It was the first night I didn't hate sleeping in there. But the next morning, when I woke up, she was already gone, the shower in her bathroom running.

I considered bringing up the conversation we'd had in the dark, felt the words on the tip of my tongue, but I knew better than to push her when she was already vulnerable. Elsie is like a frightened horse—I have to be gentle or I risk spooking her. And I knew bringing up what she told me that night in my room would only spook her. It'd halt all the progress we had made, even if it seemed like we'd taken a step forward only to halt again.

Luckily, despite spending a night in a snowdrift, my green '96 Chevy Silverado made it out without a scratch. I close the heavy door behind Elsie without risking another glance at her and run around the front before hopping in on the driver's side. I toss the blanket in the space behind the seat before cranking the engine.

We're quiet, an easy silence filling the cab as I prop my hand on the back of her headrest and reverse out of the driveway. I turn left to head into town in search of food. Beside me, Elsie reaches for the AUX cord and turns on "Rocky Mountain High" by John Denver.

A smile quirks my lips, and I look at her over the space between us. "'Rocky Mountain High' kinda day, huh?"

"Mm-hmm," she hums. "I'm feeling on top of the world today. The sun is shining, and I officially drank an entire cup of coffee without barfing."

"You think the morning sickness might be over?"

She groans and sinks down into the seat. "God, I hope so. Do you know how absolutely vile it is to throw up while brushing your teeth? Every single day?"

My face scrunches, nose wrinkling. "I can't imagine."

"This is all your fault, you know," she says, not sounding malicious in the slightest.

"I take full responsibility," I say, right hand over my heart.

Out of the corner of my eye, I can see her restraining a smile. "Thank you," she responds pointedly.

"I take full responsibility for the four orgasms that led to you getting pregnant," I clarify, and when I feel her staring at me, jaw open, I can't help but laugh. It echoes through the cab, loud and hearty.

When I cast her a quick glance, she crosses her arms over her chest and tries to glare at me. "An orgasm isn't necessary to get pregnant, you know."

I shrug, still unable to wipe the smile from my face. "Maybe not, but you know it's a necessary part of having sex with me."

"You're insufferable."

"You didn't think that when you were taking a ride on my musta—"

"Okay, okay, okay!" she yells.

My laughter fills the cab of the truck once more. This is the most like *us* we've felt in so long, and I want to bask in it the way she was basking in the sunshine earlier, soaking up every second before the clouds return. Right now, it feels like nothing between us could ever be broken again.

We're quiet for the rest of the drive, nothing but old country music playing on the crackly radio, but it doesn't feel heavy. When we get to town, I head straight for Cowpoke Diner, our longtime favorite restaurant in town. When we lived in Salt Lake City, we definitely had more variety of food options to choose from, but we never found a greasy burger joint quite like this one.

There's a dining room, but I pull into one of the drive-in stalls instead and turn to face Elsie. "Is this going to be okay on your stomach?" We've mostly avoided greasy foods since the nacho fry incident.

"Mm-hmm," she says, smiling, eyes alight. She looks so much like herself again that I feel a pang deep in my chest. "I came here with Jade the night of the snowstorm and it was fine, so I'm going to get a cheeseburger and fries."

"Raising our baby right."

I watch as her eyes move down to her stomach, and she presses a hand there. "Most days, other than the debilitating nausea and exhaustion, I don't really feel pregnant." Her gaze moves back to mine. "Is that weird?"

"I've never been pregnant, so I don't think I can be a big help in that area," I say, and she nods. "But I think it's still early, and when you start showing and feeling the baby more, it will feel more real."

I'm silent for a long moment, hesitating before asking what I want to. This outing feels precarious, like one wrong move could set us back again, but I have to know. "Does it..." I hesitate. "...feel like last time. When..."

Her eyes lock on mine, and I know she understands my question. Her head shakes quickly, and relief courses through my veins. "No, not like that. I guess I just feel like I should feel like I'm growing a human."

"What do you feel like?" I ask.

She pushes her honey hair behind her ear, a corner of her mouth lifting. "Mostly like I could nap for days, but I'm finally starting to have more energy again."

"Well, you're growing fingernails and toenails this week."

A look of surprise crosses her features. "How do you know that?"

I shrug and pull my phone out of my back pocket, the worn denim soft against my fingers. "I've got an app."

"You do?" She sounds so genuinely perplexed that I can't help but laugh. I've laughed more today than I have in months, and I don't want to stop.

"Yeah, Els, I want to see what our baby is up to every day." I look at her over the console, her jacket pulled haphazardly over her white tee, blond hair still stuck in the collar. The first freckles of spring popping up on her cheeks. "Do you have one?"

She shakes her head, and her teeth sink into her bottom lip as she looks out the windshield. "No, I...didn't want to get too attached yet." Her gaze turns back to mine slowly. "Is that bad?"

My heart squeezes painfully in my chest, and I resist the urge to place my hand there and try to rub away the ache. Elsie is the strongest person I know, but underneath that tough exterior, she's so tender. She feels everything so deeply, even if she never lets anyone see it. I'm not sure how it's taken me so long to notice that she's not unbreakable.

"No, Els," I say. I reach for her hand, and warmth suffuses the cold places in my chest when she doesn't pull away from it. Her fingers thread through mine, soft against my calloused ones. New and familiar all at once. "I don't think it's bad at all."

"Have you tried to do that too?" she asks, voice softer than I've ever heard it, eyes slowly lifting to mine.

A sheepish smile curls over my lips. "Not even a little. I've been looking at horse auctions online so I can buy the baby a pony and start training it now."

Her laughter fills the car. It sounds like the wind chimes my parents have on the porch at the big house. Like a breeze rippling through them on a perfect summer day. "Of course you have."

"Is that bad?"

Her gaze settles on mine, the exact same shade as the wide Montana sky above. "No, I've always loved that about you."

I lift a brow, heart ratcheting in my chest. "Loved what?"

I expect her to tease me for the way I'm digging, but she doesn't. Instead, her face softens as she says, "The way you love."

My throat feels tight, a lump there that I can't swallow down, but I force words out. "How's that?"

"Like you're not scared," she says simply, without hesitation, like it's something she's thought of over and over again. A worn photograph she's pulled out to examine until she's committed it to memory.

The words hang heavy in the air between us, crackling with an unknown kind of electricity. The moment feels tangible. I think I'll always remember the way her hair looks right now, like spun gold. How her eyes are wide and blue and look like every summer day I've ever experienced in this town. How her bottom lip is red and dented from her teeth, and how I know she must have gone outside in the sun this week because I can see freckles on her nose.

"Are you scared?" I watch the words land. Hear the way her breath hitches ever so slightly. See the way her pulse races in her throat.

But she doesn't shut down or pull away, and it feels like progress, like a step forward when we haven't taken any back. She holds my gaze and says, "All the time."

SEVENTEEN

ELSIE
APRIL
THIRTEEN WEEKS PREGNANT

"I don't think you should go."

Beau stops moving, hands halting where he's applying gel to his hair, and turns to face me. He's shirtless, his skin still glistening from a shower.

I've made a terrible mistake by walking across the hall to the guest bathroom to talk to him.

His hands fall to his sides, and he lifts a brow. "Why's that?"

I avoid his gaze, unsure of how to respond, and end up looking at the broad expanse of his chest, the way the muscles ripple beneath his skin at the slightest movement. It's distracting, and God, I want a distraction from what's coming.

"Elsie," Beau says, forcing me to drag my attention back to him. "Why don't you think I should go?"

The words stick in my throat, and I try to figure out how to tell him what's going on in my brain. Things have been different between us since that picnic a few weeks ago, since I admitted to him how scared I've been. I felt vulnerable and on edge after the admission, but when the dust started to settle, it was nice to know that someone *knew*, that someone was in my corner.

That Beau had me.

I'm not sure if it was that admission or if it was having another successful ultrasound where we were able to see how much the baby had grown and progressed—which made me feel a little less anxious about the risk of another miscarriage—but my panic attacks have been happening more infrequently. There are still times where I hide in the bathroom or pull over onto the side of the road, my heart rioting in my chest, but they're coming fewer and farther between.

I feel more in control than I have in months. But nothing makes me feel more on edge and out of control than seeing my parents. Which is exactly what I'm dreading today.

"Because," I finally say, wiping my sweating palms on my jeans and wincing because I know it's a shitty answer.

Beau's jaw hardens, his eyes going steely, a new determination that is growing more and more familiar. "I'm not letting you tell your parents you're pregnant alone."

My heartbeat quickens, and I wonder if he can see it pulsing in my throat, if I'm half as good at hiding my anxiety as I would like to be. Swallowing, I say, "Might be easier."

He holds my gaze for a long moment, like he's searching for something, and finally, he finds it. "For who?"

The question hits me square in the chest. It would be easier for me, I think. My parents make me feel like nothing I ever do is good enough, and the pressure of always trying to please them is *heavy*. I always leave there feeling exhausted and emotionally spent. It usually takes everything I have to make it back home without falling apart.

And on top of everything else, I don't know if I have it in me today to do that.

Beau steps closer to me, invading my space, and although I know I could move backward, step out into the hall, I don't. I let him surround me. I breathe in his scent. Something in my stomach liquefies when his calloused hands surround my upper arms, a familiar and not unwelcome feeling that's been pushed to the back of my mind the last few months.

He holds my gaze, and I can't help the way my eyes dart to his lips when his tongue reaches out to wet them. "You may not need me there," he says, drawing my attention back to his. "But I want to be there for you. If you decide you need a shoulder to lean on, mine will be right there."

I swallow hard, his words piercing all the tender places inside me, the ones I've ignored for much too long. He's poking holes in all my defenses, but for some strange reason, I can't bring myself to care. For the first time, I want to lean into it, let him shoulder some of the burden that has become so, so heavy.

"They're not going to be happy," I manage to say. My mom is still waiting for me to "get over" my injury and go back to dancing professionally. She says if I'm well enough to teach, I'm well enough to dance in a company. But while I might still be able to dance after tearing my Achilles, I'd never be able to keep up with the demands of dancing professionally again.

His jaw tenses, and my eyes catch on the movement. "I'll never understand them," he says.

I'm shocked by the hardness in his tone, the way his jaw ticks like he's holding himself back from saying more.

Beau has never been the biggest fan of my parents and the expectations they have for me, but he's always been polite, and he's never said an outwardly bad word about them.

"They just want what's best for me," I say, a line I've repeated to myself thousands of times over the years, even though I'm not so sure that's true. I may not be a mother yet, but I can't imagine putting the pressure on my child that my parents put on me.

"No, they want what's best for them, regardless of how it affects you," Beau says, his hands tightening on my arms. Not tight enough to hurt, but enough for me to know he's tense.

"What's that supposed to mean?" I ask softly, genuinely curious.

I'm an only child, and I grew up with only my parents and other dance parents as references. It wasn't until I met the Jenningses that I truly felt like I could be missing something. But just thinking that made me feel like I was betraying my parents, who had only ever given me what I needed to succeed. So they're not overly affectionate, and they usually spend more time pointing out my flaws than my attributes. It's not like I went hungry or without new pointe shoes every week. I was well cared for and given everything I needed.

He shakes his head and stares at the ceiling. My eyes are fixed on his Adam's apple when it bobs as he swallows. He hasn't shaved in a few days, and dark stubble coats his chin. It looks good on him. I want to tell him. I want to change the subject and forget that my parents are waiting for me.

"I just mean that they've always had one idea for you—that you would be a professional ballerina like your mom was," he says, meeting my gaze. It's hard, unyielding, like he's given this a lot of thought. "They never gave you a chance to see if that's what you even wanted. They homeschooled you so you could focus on it and they sent you to camps all over the world and they put all these unrealistic expectations on your shoulders so when you couldn't meet them, you felt like a failure." He stops abruptly, gathering himself. It makes an unknown emotion swoop in my stomach. "And I hate them for it."

I flinch as his words hit me, and he drops my arms, pushing an agitated hand through his hair.

"I'm sorry," he sighs, sounding more like himself. "I shouldn't have said all that."

I stare at him for a long moment, sorting through everything he said. "Is it how you feel?"

His chin dips, eyes catching on mine, sincere. "Yeah, it's how I feel."

"Then you should have said it," I tell him, and I mean it, even if it hurt to hear.

"Do you tell me what you feel?" he asks.

I let my gaze dart away from his, focusing on a point on the wall behind his shoulder. There's a chip in the paint that needs to be fixed from where I accidentally nicked the wall with my hair dryer.

I stare at it, unable to meet his eyes, as I say, "I should probably finish getting ready."

His hand snakes out, wrapping around my arm once more. "Hold on," he says, his voice softer than it was a moment before. "Do you?"

I look up at him, at the familiar brown eyes, the dark hair that's grown a little too long, curling at the edges, the mustache that I've grown to love on him, the stubble covering his jaw, the freckles that are just starting to peek out on his cheeks. He's so different from the boy I met at sixteen, but he's still in there too. Soft, gentle, so very caring. Beau. My Beau, even after everything.

"No, not always."

He nods like he expected this. I shouldn't be surprised. Since he moved back home, it's like he's been finding my puzzle pieces all over the place and putting them together, forming a clearer picture. I don't know how to feel about it. No one has ever seen me all the way, not even him. It's terrifying.

"You can, you know," he says, voice gentle. "You don't have to carry it all yourself."

His words seep into my skin. The thing is, I think I'm starting to realize this. That I can't do it all alone, that I fall apart when I try. But I don't know where to start. How do I tell my husband that I've been hiding huge parts of myself for years? How do I even go about letting him get to know me now?

I try to find a way to respond, but the words are stuck in my throat. I think Beau knows too, because his face softens, and he moves closer.

His breath makes the wispy hairs around my face billow. "Whenever you're ready, Elsie, I'm here." His lips press into my temple, and the warmth of him surrounds me.

I can't help but lean into him, bask in it. A desire that's been dormant the past few weeks flares to life at the feeling of him against me, causing liquid heat to pool somewhere behind my belly button.

It only grows when he doesn't move back, when he keeps holding me, his hand tangling in the hair falling down my back. Awareness sizzles beneath my skin when he gives it a little tug.

I don't know what makes me do it, but I turn my hands out, letting my knuckles drag across his stomach before pressing my palms there. His muscles twitch beneath them, tightening beneath my touch. He's always responded to me like this, like the barest touch from me will bring him to life.

"Elsie," he breathes, more of a groan than anything.

I feel it deep beneath my skin, in the marrow of my bones. The sound of it drags my gaze upward. He's looking down at me, eyes molten, jaw tight. "What are you doing?"

I swallow, my mouth suddenly dry. "I don't know. I just...wanted to touch you."

The noise he makes is strained, but it still manages to make goose bumps prickle along my skin, and I can't help but let my hands drag down his stomach until I reach the waistband of his jeans. My fingers find the belt loops and tug.

His body connects with mine, and we're touching from shoulder to toes. It's the first time in *so long*, and it feels so good that I think my eyes might be rolling back in my head.

I feel Beau's breath rasp against my neck, hear his quick inhale. "Elsie baby."

That nickname. It's like a string connected to the space behind my belly button pulling tight, every single one of my nerve endings catching fire all at once.

"Beau," I say back.

"God, you can't sound like that," he groans.

It makes a small laugh bubble inside me. "Like what?"

His lips brush my neck, the spot that always makes me quiver. Not a kiss, but a tease. A promise of more to come. "Like you want..." he trails off, and my mind fills in all the blanks, just like I imagine his is doing.

The breath in my lungs sucks right out of me like a vacuum on high. "What if I do?"

My knees go weak when Beau licks a stripe up my neck and bites down on my earlobe, tugging it between his teeth. I have to grip his shoulders for balance, hard enough that I imagine I'll leave bruises on the muscle. The thought makes me apply more pressure.

"You always taste so good," he says into my ear, sending a shiver down my spine. "I dream about it sometimes."

"How my neck tastes?" I manage to ask.

His hands slip lower, landing on my ass, tugging me impossibly closer to him.

He shakes his head, the mustache and stubble scraping against my sensitive skin. I hope he'll leave a mark too. "Not your neck, Elsie baby."

I can hear my heartbeat pounding in my ears, feel the want settling lower and lower.

His hands tighten on my ass, gripping me. I can almost feel their roughness beneath my jeans. "Can I touch you? Please." He sounds desperate, like a dehydrated man asking for water. "You don't know how bad I want you."

Warning bells shoot off in my head when I realize how close I am to saying yes, how close I am to *begging*. Because we can't do this. I can't do this. Not yet.

My hands loosen from the tight grip they had on his shoulders, and I step back. My heart catches in my throat at the crestfallen look on his face. He doesn't hide the hurt there, even when he knows I'm looking, and I'm stuck by how damn brave that is. Everyone always talks about my strength, but I'm just now figuring out how much of a coward I've been.

"I can't, Beau. Not yet."

He holds my gaze for so long, no doubt trying to read me, and I wonder if there's anything on my face for him to decipher. I've been hiding my feelings for so long, I don't even know how to show them.

"Okay," he finally says, and some of the stiffness in my shoulders loosens. "But why?"

I feel exposed by his question, because it means he knows there's a reason and that it has nothing to do with me not wanting him.

My hands shake at my sides, and I fight the urge to put them behind my back. Gathering all my courage, I say, "Because I don't want to hurt you when I pull away."

I watch the words land, but surprisingly, he doesn't look hurt by them. He only looks like he's absorbing them for later dissection. "Are you planning on pulling away?"

I shake my head, forcing myself to hold his gaze. "No, but I'm scared I might anyway."

It's perhaps the most truthful thing I've said in a long time. Because I can see now that's what I did when I asked him to leave. I pulled away and retreated into myself to deal with everything on my own. Like I always have. And I thought it would fix it, just like every time before, but I'm starting to wonder whether that's actually true.

I think I've been bandaging my wounds for years instead of treating them. Now they've become infected and I finally have to fix it or risk damaging myself beyond repair.

Beau stares at me for a long moment, and the silence between us feels tangible, but not in a bad way.

"Okay," he finally says, voice softer than I've ever heard it. "Thank you for being honest with me."

I feel the words right in my chest. Like something warm that starts in its center and fans out, making me feel the glow all the way through my body. It gives me the courage to say, "We better go tell my parents we're having a baby."

He holds my gaze for a beat and asks, "You sure?"

No. But I think it will be easier with him there, having his hand to hold and his broad shoulders to lean on. So I say, "Yes."

EIGHTEEN
BEAU
APRIL

My parents aren't poor by any means. They live in a large house and run a profitable ranch in one of the most expensive states in America, but their wealth pales in comparison to Elsie's parents. Growing up, I never knew much about my parents' finances. They're down-to-earth and don't spend their money extravagantly. Elsie's parents, however, live very differently.

I park my truck in front of their oversized house, and the two of us stare at it. I remember the first time I picked Elsie up here. We were sixteen, and I'd just used my entire savings from working at the ranch to buy this truck. I'd followed the GPS on my phone and pulled into a U-shaped driveway, the first driveway I'd ever been on that wasn't dirt or gravel, but inlaid stones. In front of me was this sprawling house unlike any I'd ever seen in my small town. It was modern, with sharp, clean lines and floor-to-ceiling windows overlooking the mountains. Stunning, but out of place in this rugged slice of Montana. It was the kind of home that more and more rich out-of-towners would move here to build on land that they'd bought off struggling ranchers.

I didn't like it then, and I'm not a fan now.

Beside me, Elsie sits with her hands clasped tightly in her lap. I used to think when she did that it was because she was unruffled or poised in the face of a challenge. Now I wonder if she does it to keep her hands from shaking. I'm starting to wonder how many tells she used to give me that I've missed, how many ways I've interpreted her incorrectly.

"You ready?" I ask.

Elsie squares her shoulders and lets out a breath through her nose. Now that I know what to look for, I'm surprised I didn't see these little things for what they are—pushing nerves down, far beneath the surface.

"Yeah, let's do this."

My jaw tightens at the way her voice sounds, like she's steeling herself. It's what makes me blurt out, "Let's make a signal."

She rips her gaze away from the imposing house and finally looks at me, blue eyes confused but clear in the spring sunshine. "A signal?"

I nod, warring with the urge to turn around and drive home. But she's right; we need to do this, even if I don't like it. "For if we want to leave."

"I'll be fine, Beau," she says, her voice unwavering.

I see a glimpse of the Elsie I'm more familiar with then, the one who doesn't need help with anything.

"What if I'm not?" I ask.

She stares at me for a long moment, assessing. I wonder what she's thinking in that brain of hers, and I hate that I can't tell anymore. I hate that I've maybe never been able to tell, that what I thought all these years was actually wrong.

"You've never had a problem with them before," she responds slowly, her eyes narrowed.

That's not entirely true. Her parents have never been the biggest fans of me. They always thought I wasn't good enough for her, that I was going to hold her back from her dreams—or theirs. Even when I left the only job I'd ever planned on having at my family's ranch to follow her to Utah when she entered the dance academy there, they still thought I was going to distract her from her goals. Maybe I did, but I still think dance shouldn't have been the only thing in her life. I think I was the first person to tell her that.

Still, despite their feelings about me, I've never had an issue being around them. I roll with their punches and let the not-so-subtle derogatory remarks they make about me, my family, and my family's ranch slide right off my back, because I know their opinion of me doesn't really matter.

So Elsie knows I'm trying to give her a way out now, and she doesn't like it. I can see her deciphering my intentions and building her walls back up, brick by brick. I'm desperate to keep them down.

"Fine, no signal," I say, "but I'm not making any promises to keep my mouth shut."

Elsie's eyes widen. Years ago, after the first time I watched Elsie perform live, I remember searching for her in the crowd of dancers being congratulated by their families on their performance and finding her with her mom, who was criticizing her for the way her foot turned out during one dance. She was saying it looked sloppy and that she'd never get accepted by a company performing like that. I may have been fine with her mom talking to me like I wasn't worth a damn, but I wasn't going to stand for her talking to Elsie like that.

I walked up to them and made some kind of comment of the sort, but Elsie told me to stop, that it was fine and her mom was right. Later that night, with her flowers sitting in the middle of the bench seat between us in my truck, she told me that she appreciated what I was trying to do, but that it wasn't necessary. That her mom was just helping.

I bit my tongue then, but I'm not feeling particularly like I want to anymore.

"Fine, let's make a signal," Elsie says with a sigh.

I should feel rewarded, but I hate the way this makes her sound tired, like I'm just another task she has to conquer today.

"What did you have in mind?"

The urge to put a smile on her face feels just as necessary as breathing. "I was thinking you could sit on my lap. Bounce around a little to really sell it, you know?"

She rolls her eyes, but I'm gratified when a laugh slips out of her mouth and her hands lose the death grip they have on each other.

"Oh, I know," I say, letting a smile slip into my voice. "You could take your shirt off."

"Come on, Beau," Elsie says, and climbs out of the truck without waiting for me to turn it off.

I follow after her. When we get to the door, she turns to face me, her eyes alight in a way that feels like a punch straight to my gut. She's so stunning it hurts.

"I'll squeeze your hand three times if I want to leave." She holds my gaze as she says it, and I know she's thinking the same thing. That's always been our signal, but it meant something different. Those three squeezes stood for *I love you*, and we did them all the time. Three squeezes to her hips as I'd pass her in the kitchen while she was making stir-fry for dinner. Three squeezes of my hand when we'd attend a wedding and Elsie was feeling sentimental watching the couple exchange their vows. Three squeezes to her thighs when I was between them, showing her how much I loved being there.

I clear my throat, feeling like my heart is stuck in it. "Three squeezes, it is."

Elsie nods once, wiping away the last vestiges of vulnerability from her expression, and squares her shoulders before knocking on the front door.

A moment later, it swings open, and an older version of Elsie stands in the doorway, face sour. "You're late."

"Nice to see you too, Mother," Elsie deadpans.

Diana Huntzberger rolls her eyes in the exact way that Elsie has perfected, her short blond bob tucked neatly behind her ears. "Obviously, it's nice to see you, Elsie." She pauses, then murmurs beneath her breath but purposefully loud enough for us to hear, "It would have just been nicer fifteen minutes ago."

"There were cows in the road," Elsie says, walking into the hall, me on her heels. This is a lie, but it's better than telling her mom she was dry humping my leg while I licked her neck.

Diana's brow wrinkles. "Why must there always be livestock in the roads here?"

"It's Montana, ma'am," I say.

Diana turns to me, looking like she's just noticed me here. Elsie gives me a look, but I don't miss the way her lips roll together to keep from laughing.

"Ranchers should really do a better job of keeping watch over their cattle," Diana says pointedly. "Isn't that why you all are always out mending fences all day?"

"That is one aspect of my job, yes."

"Beau is a horse trainer, Mom," Elsie says with a sigh, pressing two fingers to the space between her brows like a headache is already forming there. "How many times do we have to go over this?"

"Don't worry, I can mend a fence with the best of them."

"Yes, well," Diana says, ignoring both of us, "let's get out of the foyer. Your father is in the living room."

Elsie and I follow her mother through the house, our boots echoing on the marble floors. I always thought white marble floors in rural Montana were stupid, but I guess Diana and Elsie's father, James, aren't spending any time in the dirt. Plus, they're not the ones cleaning the floors. That job belongs to the housekeeper who comes once a week.

We pass the expansive kitchen and end up in the sprawling living room that overlooks the mountains. Even though the house is only on an acre of land, they still have stunning views. I'm sure whatever small ranch home was here before they bought the land and tore it down to build this house was chosen specifically for this view.

"Elsie, you're here!" James pushes up from where he was seated on the couch, setting his iPad in his place. I'm sure that, before we arrived, he was checking stock prices or reading the *Wall Street Journal* or whatever it is an investment banker does in his spare time.

Elsie smiles at her dad, looking a little more relaxed as he closes the distance between them and wraps her in a hug. It makes some of the worry in my stomach settle. I wouldn't say that Elsie's relationship with her parents is bad, but they have a very different dynamic than I do with my family. Diana was a professional ballerina in New York until she retired in her late thirties. She had Elsie two years later and passed her passion for dancing down to her daughter. When they decided they didn't want to raise Elsie in the city and wanted to live in a more "rustic" area, they researched dance studios before even looking at jobs for James. Dance came first, and when they found a surprisingly elite dance studio forty-five minutes outside of Bozeman, James knew he could manage commuting and working remotely.

The three of them put everything into her dance career, hiring tutors to homeschool Elsie so she could focus on ballet during school hours, taking few vacations, even though they could afford them, and making sure Elsie had the most high-end gear. Their family unit was a team dedicated to one thing: Elsie going pro. So when she brought home a seventeen-year-old cowboy her junior year of high school, it didn't go over well.

I'm still not sure exactly where I fit in their unit, but the more I'm learning about Elsie, the more I'm not quite sure she knows exactly where she fits anymore either. Without dance, she's not doing her part, and I think that weighs heavily on her. And now that she's pregnant, there's even less of a chance of her going back to it.

We never told them we were expecting during the last pregnancy, and I'm not sure if she ever told them about the miscarriage. When I asked her after moving home if she told them about our separation, she said no, so I doubt she told them about the miscarriage either.

"How are you doing, honey?" James asks, holding Elsie out at arm's length to examine her.

"She looks tired," Diana says, concern crossing over her features.

He waves her off. "You do look a little fatigued, but your eyes are bright. Teaching keeping you working hard?"

Elsie nods. "Very," she says. "The girls have seemingly never-ending energy."

James laughs, the sound booming through the cavernous home, the lines beside his eyes crinkling. "What I wouldn't give for that."

"You and me both," Elsie responds, smiling softly at her father.

"Enough about work," Diana says, much to no one's surprise. Before Elsie's injury and quitting dance, work was basically our only topic of conversation, but since then, Diana hasn't been interested in talking about it. "Who wants a drink?"

Elsie's eyes flash to mine, looking like a deer in the headlights. "I can make them."

"I've got it," I say, clearing my throat, then head for the bar off the living room. "What does everyone want?"

"Surprise me," Elsie answers quickly, and I know she's hoping I'll cover for the fact that she's not drinking.

"Whiskey, neat," James says.

"My usual," Diana says, meaning a martini with a twist.

I've learned almost nothing of value from these people over the years, but I have learned how to make a good drink. The bar is always stocked, and I usually use it as a chance to experiment, but tonight I want to keep my head clear. I make Diana's and James's drinks before pouring two club sodas for Elsie and me, garnishing them each with a lime wedge.

"So what's been going on the past few months?" Diana asks. "We've hardly seen the two of you. I'm not even sure the last time we saw you, Beau."

"Thanksgiving," I reply, handing everyone their drinks. It was just a few days before Elsie asked me to leave. I'm not sure what excuse she made for me not being at Christmas.

"Right," James says, nodding. "And then the two of you spent Christmas with your family."

"I'm still not sure why you couldn't even manage to come here for dinner," Diana says.

She sounds annoyed, but I ignore it, turning to face Elsie. She's not looking at me, keeping her eyes focused on her parents. My heart twists as I imagine her home alone on Christmas, not wanting to explain to her parents why I wasn't there and feeling like she couldn't come to the ranch.

"We were busy," Elsie responds, not looking at me. "Plus, the two of you went to the New York house the day after Christmas and stayed for all of January."

I clear my throat. "Right, sorry about that."

"Well, I don't think it's fair."

"It's fine," James says, dismissing Diana's comment. "Don't worry about it. We're just glad you're here now, aren't we, Di?"

Elsie's mom purses her lips. "Yes, of course. Anyway, what's new?"

Beside me, Elsie tenses, her hand flexing on her glass.

I know she's not ready to tell them about the pregnancy, so I say, "I'm training a new horse at the ranch. Her name is Sugar."

Diana blinks, completely uninterested, and I have to work to hold back the laugh that bubbles in my throat.

"Is that so?" James asks. "How is it going?" The man has probably never been within twenty feet of a horse, but I appreciate that he always asks about my work and tries to seem interested. The same way I do when he drones on about bonds or whatever the hell he works on all day.

"She's a bit skittish," I say, feeling Elsie's eyes on me. "She's been hurt in the past. It's a fine balance, knowing when to let her do her thing and when to push."

"I'm sure," James responds. "You're a patient man, though. I'm sure, in time, she will trust you fully."

This time, I finally do look at Elsie. Her eyes are narrowed ever so slightly, like she's dissecting my words for hidden meaning and finding it there. "Yeah, I am," I say. "I'm willing to wait on her to trust me."

We're done with dinner and dessert, and Elsie still hasn't told her parents about the pregnancy. I catch her eye from across the table, and she holds it for a long moment before finally sighing, shoulders drooping.

Beneath the table, I tap my foot against hers, trying to silently ask if she wants to do this today or not. I'm this close to leaning across the table and grabbing her hand over the picked-over serving plate of roasted vegetables and squeezing it three times just so she doesn't have to do this. I don't fully understand her hesitation, but I want to wipe it away.

Her parents don't need to know about the pregnancy anyway. They can get a cute selfie of the three of us from the hospital and connect the dots.

But before I can reach for Elsie's hand, she clears her throat, and her parents' eyes swivel to her. They've been deep in conversation about some charity event they have to attend this weekend, and they both look surprised by Elsie's random interruption.

I watch as Elsie tucks her hands beneath the table, and I wonder if it's to hide their shaking. "Beau and I have something we'd like to tell you."

Diana's eyes widen, and she clasps her hands beneath her chin, smiling widely, her bright white teeth on display. "Did you get your spot back at the ballet? I've been making calls for months. Oh, Elsie, I'm so happy."

Elsie's face falls, and I watch the shutters slide over her eyes. I see that response now for what it is—shutting herself off, protecting herself. I don't know how I never noticed it before. "No, Mom, I'm not going back to Utah."

Diana looks between the two of us, confusion written on her features. I ignore her, though, and focus on Elsie. She seems to be caving in on herself, her eyes trained on her lap.

"What, then?"

I keep watching Elsie, and so I see the way she seems to swallow back her indecision. The way her shoulders straighten and her jaw tightens. It's something to behold, really, the way she builds herself up, strengthens her resolve. I used to see her do this when she was rehearsing a particularly difficult move, on nights when I would come to the studio after I got off work, when everyone else had long since gone home and she was practicing alone until she got it right.

"I'm pregnant."

The statement hangs in the air, like the four of us are collectively holding our breath. James breaks it first, his chair sliding against the marble floor as he pushes to standing.

"Congrats, you two," he says, and moves to wrap Elsie in a hug. She sinks into it, and I finally let out the breath I was holding. My gaze turns to Diana, who is still sitting at her end of the table, watching her husband and daughter. Lead sinks in my stomach at the look on her face.

She isn't happy.

And I want to pull her out of this room before she tells Elsie that.

Elsie steps back from her father's embrace and turns to face her mother. I watch the moment she registers her mom's expression, the way her own falls.

"You're not happy for me," she says, staring at Diana.

A muscle in Diana's jaw ticks. "You're never going to go back to ballet now" is all she says.

Elsie sighs, sitting back down in her seat. James stays behind her, hand on the back of her chair. "I was never going to go back, Mom. I can't perform at the same level after my injury. I can't practice like I used to without risking further injury."

"You were at the height of your career," Diana says, voice rising, some mixture of pain and frustration on her face. "You could get back to where you were. We didn't put in this much work for you to quit at twenty-seven."

"Well, I did," Elsie snaps, surprising every single one of us, including her. "I quit, and I started teaching, and I've come to love it. I'm not going back."

"So you're just going to live in this town and teach and have babies? That's what you're going to do with your life?" Diana asks, and none of us can miss the derisive way she says it, the disappointment lacing every word.

"It was good enough for you," Elsie responds, her voice still carrying an edge, and I feel the breath catch in my lungs at the sound of it.

Her mom's jaw tightens. "I danced until I was in my thirties. I lived a full life before I decided to have you. If it makes me the bad person for wanting you to get to have that, too, then fine. I'll be the villain here."

Silence follows her statement, heavy and painful, and I feel the words sinking into each one of us.

"Well, that's not how it worked out for me," Elsie says quietly, the sound of her voice echoing in the vast space. "But that doesn't mean I'm not happy about it."

I wonder if that's true, if she really is happy. She hasn't been for so long, but I want it for her more than anything. I'd do anything to make it happen, and for the first time, I realize maybe that's what her mom has been doing. Maybe she's been working for her daughter's happiness Elsie's whole life, doing it in the best way she knew how. I just don't think she knows what will make her daughter happy, if she's ever taken the time to find out.

"I hope that's true," Diana says, and for the first time, I agree with her.

NINETEEN
ELSIE
MAY
FIFTEEN WEEKS PREGNANT

I STARE AT MYSELF in the mirror, looking at the tiniest bump in the world protruding from my belly. I wasn't sure how I'd feel about my body changing during pregnancy. I've still avoided looking at the scale during my doctor's appointments and I've tried to ignore the way my small boobs have grown too big for all my bras and my once pleasantly round ass has seemed to flatten. I know it's supposed to be magical and women should feel lucky to grow another human, but as someone who grew up in a very toxic, body-shaming environment, I thought I might hate it.

But staring at that little bump in the mirror makes my throat close up, emotion I wasn't expecting clogging it. I didn't know it would feel like *this*. That I would look at that tiny bump and realize I've made it *this far*. I never got to see a bump with my last pregnancy, but right now, my baby is growing enough to show on my body, and I think that's the coolest thing in the entire world.

I smooth my hand over it again, my heart a riot in my chest, and yell for Beau. A moment later, he comes barreling into my bedroom, his face creased with concern, his eyes wandering everywhere, checking me for injury.

"What's wrong?" he asks. He stops when he sees me standing in front of the mirror, my leotard tight over my stomach, my hand pressed to the barely there bump. He's wearing his signature Wranglers, the ones that hug him in all the right places, and he must have just gotten out of the shower, because a lock of damp hair falls over his forehead, making him look even more disheveled.

My heart squeezes at the sight of him.

"I have a bump," I tell him, and watch as his expression morphs from frantic worry to abstract awe. He moves forward as if on instinct, dropping his hand from the doorframe and closing the distance between us, his gaze trained on my stomach.

When he gets close enough, his eyes flick up to mine, unsure. "Can I touch it?"

I swallow hard and nod, just a barely there jerk of my chin, not trusting my voice when he's this close and looking at me like I'm magic. My stomach jumps when his palm covers it, large enough to span from one side to the other. His hand is warm, and I can feel the heat of it through my thin leotard.

"Can you feel it?" I ask, voice the scratch of sandpaper, as he moves his hand over the slight swelling at the bottom of my stomach. I wouldn't be surprised if he couldn't, but I can.

He nods, his fingers lightly tracing the curve, and my skin burns at the feel of it, the path they take. "Mm-hmm."

"I found a stretch mark too," I manage to get out, needing to pull myself out of the trance his touch is lulling me into.

His eyes turn up to mine, warm brown flecked with gold, and I almost want to laugh at the awe I see in them. The reverence. "I want to see it."

I do laugh then, the sound bouncing in the little space between us. "Why?"

He holds my gaze, expression serious, and I can't help the way my eyes drop to his tongue as it darts out to wet his lips. "Because there's a stretch mark on my wife's skin from growing our baby."

My breath hitches in my lungs. I hope he doesn't notice, that he can't somehow feel my heart pounding faster. Swallowing against the thickness in my throat, I say, "Okay."

It's only then that I remember that I'm wearing a leotard.

"I'll need to—" I motion at the leotard straps and watch as Beau's eyes change, the color darkening into something that reminds me of late nights, moonlight pouring through our curtains, our breath the only thing between us.

"Yeah, okay," he responds.

I think his voice is thicker, huskier, that his memories are as relentless as mine. He removes his hands from my stomach, the touch seeming to burn me, and I feel his heavy gaze as I reach for the leotard straps and pull them down my shoulders.

There's not a sexy way to remove a leotard. They're tight and require acrobatics to shimmy into, but Beau doesn't seem to notice. The air in the room seems to thin as his eyes follow the path of my fingers. I slip my arms out and push the rest of the leotard down until it bunches around my waist at the band of my sweatpants. I'm wearing a thin sports bra, but with the way he's looking at me, I feel like I'm standing in front of him naked.

I have a distinct memory of him watching me the exact same way the last time I had my clothes off for him. It's not lost on me that we're just a few feet away from where it happened, that at one point that night, he told me to watch us in the very same mirror we're standing in front of now.

"Where is it?" Beau asks, breaking the silence, snapping me out of my daydream.

I rip my gaze from his, forcing my eyes down to my stomach. Just below my navel, there's the tiniest stretch mark, a strip of skin paler than the rest. I point to it, and Beau moves closer. He reaches out, his thumb smoothing along the strip of skin, and I swear I feel the roughness everywhere—in the backs of my knees and the hollow of my throat and the tips of my fingers.

"It's perfect," he breathes.

My lips tip up in the barest of smiles. "It's a stretch mark."

His eyes lift to mine, and I'm shocked by the sincerity I see there. There's not an ounce of teasing in his expression. "It's *your* stretch mark," he says. "That's what makes it perfect."

My heart rises to my throat, and I try to think of something to say. Last night, when I saw that lighter piece of skin, I got online and ordered stretch mark cream, determined to get ahead of the inevitable. I didn't want my skin to scar, and if it's starting now, when my bump is barely noticeable, then it'll only get worse.

But looking at Beau now, feeling the reverence in his touch as his thumb swipes absentmindedly over my skin, I don't know what I was thinking. I don't know that I'll ever look at the marks on my body and call them tiger stripes or battle scars or any other body positivity term the media tries to rebrand it as, but I do know that if I ever look down at my body and see another stretch mark, I'll remember the look on Beau's face, the sound of his voice calling that little piece of pale skin perfect.

And I don't think I'll be able to hate anything about it then.

I swallow against the lump rising in my throat, for some reason feeling the sting of tears at the backs of my eyes. "I better head to the studio," I say, my voice hoarse.

Beau nods, and to my surprise, his hands move to the straps of my leotard. I have to hold back a shiver as he puts my arms back through them and pulls it slowly back up, calluses scraping against my overheated skin. He's so gentle as he places the straps back in place, and I don't think I imagine the way his hands linger, like he doesn't want to pull them away.

His eyes finally tear away from my shoulders and settle on mine. "Can I come to the studio with you?"

I blink, confused. "Why?"

"I want to spend the day with you," he says with a shrug, without a hint of bashfulness. "I haven't seen you dance in ages."

"I won't be dancing, not really. I'll be...teaching." The words stick in my throat. I've been doing my new job for months now, and I've been surprised by how much I enjoy it, but I can't help the pinch I always feel when I talk about it. The lingering feelings of guilt and shame that were only hammered home after the lunch with my parents a few weeks ago. I wasn't supposed to be a ballet teacher, at least not yet. I was supposed to keep dancing professionally until an appropriate retirement age. This was never the plan, even if I have grown to love it.

A smile tugs up one corner of his mouth and then the other. "Well, I've never seen you teach either, and I'd really like to."

Nervous butterflies take flight in my stomach. No one has watched me teach besides Tonya, and even she is mostly hands off. I'm not even sure if I'm good at it—if I'm too hard on the girls or if I'm not pushing them enough, if my technique is what they need—and I've never allowed people to see me be anything but my best at something. Even Beau, when I would let him watch me at the studio when I was rehearsing. I don't like looking like a failure. I especially don't like feeling like one.

"I don't know…"

One of Beau's brows lifts, and his eyes narrow in that way they've been doing recently, like he's no longer taking anything I say at face value. It's terrifying. "Why not?"

I grasp for an excuse, opening and closing my mouth several times.

The intensity of his stare never wavers. "You'll hardly notice I'm there. Let's go."

And then he walks past me, out of the bedroom, not waiting for me to protest.

The studio is cold, as always, when we walk in. Outside, the sun is shining, and it arcs through the huge windows at the front of the building, illuminating the creamy walls and the high ceilings that are broken up by exposed beams. There's a couch and a desk in the lobby, but just beyond it is the main studio. It's empty, except, of course, for Maya.

She's in her warm-ups, working at the barre. Beside me, Beau shakes his head, and when I look at him, he's grinning.

"So she's a mini you."

I cross my arms over my chest, even though I feel no real agitation. "What's that supposed to mean?"

His smile widens, taking over his face, and it hits me how good he looks like this. I remember how he looked that night at the bar, with that new mustache that had drawn my attention away from the hollows under his eyes and the new wrinkles above his brows, like they'd been furrowed the entire two months we'd been apart.

But now, it's like every day we spend together, every day the sun shines brighter and longer, burning off the last vestiges of our cold, lonely winter, he's seeming to come alive again. I think I am too.

"It's a Saturday morning, and she's here before anyone else," he says, drawing my attention back to our conversation. "How did she even get in?"

I avert my gaze, turning back to face my student. "I gave her a key," I mumble.

Beside me, Beau laughs.

I feel it in my chest, like warmth seeping into me.

"Tonya isn't going to be happy about that."

Tonya hasn't questioned any of my professional decisions, and I doubt she will start with this one. After I moved home, broken and jobless, she showed up at my house and told me I was taking a job at the studio. I was at my darkest point then, just a few weeks after I'd asked Beau to leave, barely making it a day without a panic attack. I didn't think I'd be able to do it—teach the sport that was supposed to be my career. And I told Tonya that, but she ignored me, told me to be at the studio the next morning for class.

I taught my first class the next morning, met Maya and all the other students that were looking at me like I was a goddess, and then locked myself in the bathroom, heaving and gasping for breath, feeling like the world was caving in on me.

I did that every time I taught for the first few weeks, and the first day I didn't, I decided to celebrate by going to the bar in town, the one Beau and I had frequented so many times. I wanted to be close to him in some sort of way, to celebrate my accomplishment in a place where I could feel his presence. I hadn't counted on the way everyone would look at me, like I was gum on the bottom of their shoe, because I had hurt their golden boy. Except when I got there, it didn't feel much like a celebration at all.

And then he showed up, looking angry and raw, and I finally understood their ire. I didn't know how to respond to it—how he looked, how I felt.

I just knew I wanted him so badly that I was willing to let myself have him, even if it was just for one night. For one night, I wasn't going to think about the panic attacks and my failure. For one night, I was going to celebrate my progress, the new life I was carving out for myself.

And now here we were, watching a girl who's following in my footsteps, with our baby growing in my belly and the ghost of his touch still lingering on my skin.

"Tonya gave me a key when I was a student too."

I feel Beau's gaze on the side of my face, but I don't turn to look at him. "She did?"

A smile touches my lips at the memory. "She was tired of me breaking in with a metal coat hanger. Told me I could let myself in and out as often as I wanted, but I had to make a deal with her."

"What was the deal?" he asks, voice soft, his gaze never leaving me. I've never known how to handle the weight of his full attention on me.

Finally, I look up at him, not seeing the man he is now but the boy he was when we met. "That I had to go to the party that Sierra Bennett was having at her house the next night."

His eyes widen, recognition dawning. "The party where we met."

My eyes trace the contours of his face. The strong nose. The full lips that I've always been jealous of. The thick brows that frame searing brown eyes framed by the thickest lashes I've ever seen. The mustache I still can't think about without feeling a hot blush stain my cheeks.

I can still remember that night like it was yesterday. The way our eyes locked from across the room. How I turned away, cheeks burning, and tried to throw myself into conversation with Jade and Sierra, a girl who danced with me at the studio. The feeling of his hand on my elbow when he walked up to me. The sight of that smile that I could feel all the way down to my toes. How he reached his hand out and introduced himself right then and there, and how I knew in that exact moment that I was a goner.

"That's the one."

"So I owe Tonya a thank-you, then," Beau responds, and I think his voice is thicker.

I shrug, guilt surging in my stomach for the way I've handled everything over the last year, how I've drawn away from him, how I've hidden pieces of myself for even longer than that. "I don't know about that."

He moves in front of me, blocking my view of Maya, and when I look up at him, his face is both stern and soft. I don't know how he's managed it.

"I'm going to thank her," he says earnestly. "Because she changed my life that day. She made one small decision that turned my entire world upside down, and I'll get on my knees to thank her for it every day for the rest of my life if I need to. You're the best thing that's ever happened to me, Elsie Jennings," he says, voice dripping with a sincerity I can *feel*. His eyes bore into mine, like he needs me to understand this one truth. "You have to know that."

Before I can respond, before I can think of a way to express to him what his words mean to me, the door to the studio opens, and a horde of giggling teen girls comes crashing in. The cacophony is so familiar that I sometimes hear it in my sleep.

I know I only have a moment before one of them asks if I like their new leotard and another one tells me about the boy she has a crush on at school and another asks if I listened to the Beatles growing up—because they have no concept of how old I am. So before I get sucked into the hurricane that is teenage ballerinas, I lift up on my tiptoes and press a kiss to Beau's stubbled cheek, breathing in the earthy, leathery scent of him. He's always smelled like Montana, even when we lived far away, and it's one of the things I love most about him.

I tell him the only thing I can right now, the only piece of truth I have time for. "You're the best thing that ever happened to me too."

TWENTY

BEAU
MAY
SEVENTEEN WEEKS PREGNANT

When I return Sugar to her stall after a successful thirty-minute ride around the ranch and find my dad leaning against the opposite stall, I know the time for avoiding him has come to an end. Ever since announcing the pregnancy, I've managed to not be alone with either of my parents. I don't want them asking questions I don't have the answers to yet, and I don't want to hear anything negative they may have to say about Elsie. I know they love her like their own daughter, but after the comments Cooper has made, I'm worried they'll also feel protective of me.

"Hey, son," Dad says, and adjusts his hat on his forehead. He might be nearing sixty, but he still has a full head of dark brown hair that's just beginning to streak with gray. His skin is weathered from years spent in the sun, and there are deep creases beside his eyes and around his mouth from a lifetime of easy laughter. He looks like he was formed right out of the mountains and dirt around us, a piece of the land just as unmoving.

I dust my hands off on my jeans and close the stall behind me, stalling for time. It clicks into place, echoing through the barn, and I finally meet my father's eyes. "Hey, Dad."

"I've hardly seen you since you moved back home." He says this without any judgment, just a touch of sadness in his sandpapery voice, and guilt pricks at me for avoiding him. I feel it settle like lead in my stomach.

I glance down at the dirt and drag my boot through it, watching a line form in its wake. "Yeah, things have been crazy."

That's not entirely true. Things at home have been slow moving. Two steps forward, one step back. I feel like things are getting better between Elsie and me, but we're healing at the rate of a deep cut without stitches. It's as frustrating as it is rewarding.

"You're going to be a dad," he says.

I lift my gaze back up to his.

He's still leaning against the opposite stall, one leg bent at the knee and resting on the stall door. There's a small smile tugging at his mouth, lines crinkling the edges of his eyes. "I'm so proud of you."

My lips twitch. "I put in a lot of work for it."

He rolls his eyes at me, fighting back his smile. He's always been so much quicker to laugh than Mom, but I always find it just as rewarding anyway. "I'm sure," he says. "But I meant I'm proud of who you're becoming, and I think you're going to be an amazing father."

His words hit me in places I didn't know were vulnerable, places that have been wounded for possibly longer than I've known. When things went south with Elsie, I blamed myself, even though she told me *she* was the one who needed to figure things out. I thought I wasn't doing enough for her, or I was doing too much. That something about me was wrong. I'd lie awake in that tiny bed in the cabin on the ranch and stare at the ceiling, questioning myself and my choices and what I could have done differently until my eyes burned from the need to sleep and my heart was pounding hard enough in my chest that I could hear it.

It wasn't until I moved back home that I started to realize that even though I definitely needed to work on some things, she wasn't bullshitting me when she said all that. She *does* have things she's working through, things that don't involve me. Still, there's a wound beneath the surface that hasn't quite healed yet, something I think may always linger just a little, a scab that could easily be picked at.

"Thanks, Dad," I say, voice hoarse, and smooth my hands down the legs of my dusty jeans to hide their trembling. The denim scratches against my palms, rough and familiar.

"Let's go for a walk," he says, and turns on his heel, heading for the big barn doors without waiting to see if I'm coming.

I follow after him, dirt kicking up beneath our boots, and we step outside into the blinding sunshine. I have to blink at the change in brightness, but I soak it in, nonetheless.

Summer is officially on its way here. Every day is warmer than the last, and I love the feeling of the sun on my skin and the wind in my hair. I love all the seasons in Montana, but summer is my favorite. I always feel like I'm coming alive—defrosting—when the snow melts and the wildflowers come out and the sun stays out in the sky longer, chasing away the moon.

This year is no exception. I've never looked forward to summer the way I have after this long, hard winter.

Dad leads us out into one of the pastures, and we walk through the tall grasses without saying anything. My dad is like that. I know he wants to talk, to find out what's really been going on in my head the last few months, but he's quiet. He bides his time. He gives people room to breathe, to think.

I'm a lot like him in that way. I've always been the one to give people the space to cool off, to not press when things are getting heated. I'm only just now starting to realize there are times I need to push, people who need pushing. I think he's known that for a long time, because I've seen him do it with my mom and sister when they retreat into themselves. Cooper, of course, has never retreated. He wears his every thought and feeling on his face and sleeve for the entire world to see.

Somehow, Dad has always known just what each of us needs. I hope when my baby gets here, I'll have figured that out too.

In the distance, I hear a meadowlark chirp, and the grasses beneath us swish in the wind. It's calm, the kind of day I always wish for when it's raining. I want to lie down right here and take a nap in the sunshine. Or go get Elsie and bring her right back here for a picnic.

"How's Elsie?" Dad finally asks, breaking the silence. He keeps looking ahead, eyes on the horizon, but I know he's attuned to my every move. That he can read me like a book. It's actually kind of comforting.

I think about his question for a long time. A few months ago, I wouldn't have known how to answer it. I think that's why he didn't ask me then, when I came to him and asked if I could move into one of the cabins on the property that we rent out to people looking for a ranch stay while they're visiting out west. I remember he asked then if Elsie was going to be safe alone, and I knew he meant safe from herself more than from some unforeseen threat. And I knew the answer was yes, that as bad as things might be, Elsie was a fighter first and foremost.

And then he asked if I was going to be safe alone, and I told him that I would be. That seemed to be enough for him.

He never asked how we were doing, if either of us were okay, because I think he knew we weren't, and that neither of us was ready to talk about it. But I am now, and he knows it.

"Better," I answer, stuffing my hands into the pockets of my worn-out jeans. There's a flower in my pocket that Ruby gave me when she saw me in the pasture with Sugar after her riding lesson. I twist the stem between my fingers, feel the dampness against my fingertips.

He looks at me, catching my eye. "Really?" He doesn't sound incredulous or disbelieving, just like he wants to make sure I'm honest, holding nothing back.

I nod, feeling more sure with the movement. "Yeah, she is." Turning back to face the mountains ahead of us, I say, "She's not her old self again, but I don't think she ever will be."

He makes a noise of agreement in the back of his throat, his eyes finding the horizon. "No, I doubt she will be." He pauses for a moment, then asks, "Do you think you can love this new version of her?"

I stop in the grass, and he does too. His eyes are the same dark brown as mine, and right now they're both serious and piercing.

"I never stopped," I tell him, and it's the truth. Even when we were both at our worst, my soul never stopped trying to find its way back to hers.

He holds my gaze for a long moment, as if searching for something in it. "Good."

My shoulders sink, relieved, and we start walking again.

"I don't need to tell you that marriage is hard," Dad says, voice echoing through the pasture, brushing against the grass and lifting in the slight breeze. "Your mom and I have had our fair share of troubles over the years."

I look at him, disbelieving. My parents are opposites in so many ways, but similar in all the ones that count. My mom is fierce and loyal and stubborn as an ox. Dad is easy-going, wise, and steady as the mountains our ranch was built around. They complement each other, like opposite sides of the same coin. I've rarely ever even seen them argue. Sometimes they will have these intense discussions with just their eyes, saying things only the other can decipher, and then a decision will be made and us kids will marvel at the way they made it. I know they have to have had hard times, but I've never *seen* it. They're steady, solid. Unwavering.

"Don't look so surprised," Dad says with a laugh that's raspy from the years he spent smoking when we were kids. It wasn't until his father died of lung cancer when Cooper and I were preteens that he finally quit. I remember the day he threw the cigarettes in the trash can in the kitchen and vowed he would never touch one again. How he made Cooper and me promise we wouldn't either.

"I *am* surprised," I tell him.

He shakes his head, looking at me with the bemused expression he used to wear when I was a teen and thought I had life all figured out. He was right; I did regret those nipple piercings that Cooper somehow talked me into.

"Son, you aren't married for over thirty years without having your problems." He's quiet for a moment, eyes trained on the mountains ahead. "Your mom almost left me when she was pregnant with you and Cooper."

I stop dead in my tracks, and when Dad realizes I'm not following, he does too. He pushes his hands into his pockets and stares at me, like he's gathering his courage. "I wasn't always a good father. Hell, sometimes I'm not now, but back then, I definitely wasn't."

I want to interject, tell him that when I lie awake at night, worried that I'm not going to be a good dad, it's because I'm not sure I can live up to him and the example he's been for me, but before I can say something, he speaks again.

"I was an alcoholic, or I was on my way to being one, at least. The ranch wasn't doing the best at the time, and your mom and I were already arguing a lot about it. She thought we should sell some of the cattle, scale back, and I thought we shouldn't sell the only thing making us money. Then she got pregnant during our worst performing year, and I started drinking more. I would get up earlier than usual and work myself to the bone and then drink myself into a stupor at night. I wasn't kind to her. I didn't take care of her how I should." He sighs at the big Montana sky. "She was carrying twins, for heaven's sake, and I wasn't pulling my weight around the house at all."

I swallow, heart twisting in my chest.

"She fell one day," he says, his eyes taking on a pained look I've never seen on him before.

Not at his father's funeral, although that wasn't that surprising, since they didn't have the best relationship. Not when I asked if I could move home. Never.

"She fell," he continues, voice rougher, more resigned, like he's slipped back into a memory in his head. "And I was at the bar in town until late, and she couldn't get a hold of me. She broke her ankle and had to call an ambulance to get her. I didn't know until I got home and found the note she left me." He scrubs a hand beneath his eyes, and my heart moves up into my throat at the sight of it. "When I finally got to the hospital, she told me I had to quit drinking or she was leaving."

His eyes finally settle on mine, glowing with intensity. "I quit drinking that day, haven't touched a drink since. How could I, when losing the best thing to ever happen to me was on the line?"

His words pierce me, the same ones Elsie and I said to each other just a couple of weeks ago, and I know how he must have felt then, faced with losing my mom. I always knew my dad didn't drink, but growing up, when we asked him why, he just said there were things more important to him than drinking.

I nod, unable to form words against the lump in my throat. It's thick and heavy, and I can feel tears pricking at the backs of my eyes because of it.

"Months later, after you were born," Dad says, his voice husky, "I asked her if she still loved me after everything." He smiles then, even though it's wobbly. "She said she never stopped. I—" he cuts himself off, clearing his throat. "I needed to hear that, even if I didn't deserve to. You make sure Elsie knows that too, okay?"

"I will," I promise and mean it, because I know Elsie feels guilty over making me leave. I know she doesn't regret it, that she still thinks it was for the best, but that she feels remorse over the way it hurt me. And I never want her to doubt that during all of that, I never stopped loving her.

Dad nods and clears his throat again. He wipes his eyes one last time with the back of a hand, his skin wrinkled from long days in the sun. "Good. Good," he repeats. "Our Elsie needs to know she's loved no matter what."

My heart returns to my throat once more at his statement. I love how much he loves her, how much my entire family does, and I wish she knew that too. I wish she didn't think their love, *my* love, was conditional.

I don't think that's what her parents intended for her to learn while she was growing up, and I don't even really think it's true, but I know it's what she's internalized.

And I know what I need to show her moving forward. She asked me to leave once, and I did it because I thought it was what she needed, but I'm not leaving again. This isn't our first rodeo, and one way or another, we're going to find our way back to each other.

TWENTY-ONE

ELSIE
MAY
NINETEEN WEEKS PREGNANT

I CAN FEEL MY heart beating in my throat, a steady thump that accompanies Beau and me the whole way to the doctor's office. Today, we're having our anatomy scan. I felt the baby move for the first time last night, which has helped relieve some of my anxiety, but I'm still nervous about what today could bring as they go over every inch of the baby's body and look for abnormalities.

A warm breeze ruffles my hair as Beau pulls into the OB-GYN office parking lot and picks a spot far away from where I had my meltdown at our first appointment, just as he did at the last two. I can't help but look at it now, remembering the girl I was huddled on the ground, heaving and unable to breathe in the frigid air. The way Beau's hands and voice were the only things to settle me down. It seems so long ago. It seems like yesterday.

Time has felt funny these last few months, like it's somehow both stuck in Jell-O and moving forward at the speed of light. I'm grateful for it, for the way this time we have—just the two of us, while we figure things out—has been trapped in amber. I'm grateful for the time to fix our broken pieces and put ourselves back together so we can be the best versions of ourselves when we bring someone new into our lives.

Beau turns his gaze on me, finding my hand smoothing absentmindedly over my stomach the way it has more and more often of late, his eyes going soft at the gesture. I used to wonder why pregnant people did it so much, if they were trying to emphasize their bump, but now I know it's because you can *feel* it. The baby growing inside you, your organs stretching and moving to make space, the flutter of tiny kicks. It's a certain kind of magic that can't be explained, something I feel so lucky to experience. Something I never could have imagined when I was drinking tequila straight in a bar a few months ago.

"How're you feeling?" Beau asks, his hand landing on the headrest behind me, causing his shirtsleeve to snag on his biceps. I never quit noticing him. It would be impossible to, but lately he's seemed so much more physical, more real. I'm gripped by the need to touch him, but I hold myself back, the way I have time after time, grasping firmly to keep my word, to not push either of us further when I'm not sure I won't pull away.

Instead of answering him immediately, I let myself really think about the question. I feel *good* for the first time in months. For the past few weeks, after Beau leaves for the ranch in the early mornings, I've been slipping outside to walk. It feels good to move my body in a way that isn't productive. I'm walking because I like feeling the sunrise on my skin and the wind in my hair. I like moving my body and working up a sweat. But I'm not working toward anything. At first, I was trying to walk a certain distance each day, but as I've continued doing it each morning, I've stopped paying attention. I'm walking to clear my head, and I like it.

Locking my eyes on Beau's brown ones, I say, "I feel good."

He inclines his head, looking like he's not sure if he believes me, and I don't blame him. I can't count how many times I've told that lie, how much I'd even begun to believe it. But right now I'm telling the truth.

"Really," I say. "I promise."

A smile curls one edge of his lips, pulling my attention from his eyes to his mouth. I've found my attention drifting there more and more of late.

"Any nerves about today?" he asks.

I drag my gaze from his distracting smile and focus on the brown of his eyes. The sun is reflecting on them today, bringing out the flecks of gold that can only be seen in natural light. I shake my head. "Not really." And to both of our surprise, it's the truth. I smooth my hand over my ever-growing bump. I officially look pregnant now, not like I just ate too much at lunch. "I felt the baby moving last night, so I think everything is going to be okay."

Beau's eyes widen. "You did? Why didn't you tell me?"

I can't help but laugh at the betrayal in his tone. "You were asleep. It was the middle of the night."

"You should have woken me up." He sounds incredulous.

"You wouldn't have been able to feel it anyway," I say, still laughing.

He shakes his head, brow furrowed, looking like a hurt puppy. "I don't care. I want to know everything."

My lips curl in a smile. "I guess you'd probably like to know that I can feel them now, then."

His eyes widen comically, and he unbuckles and scoots closer to me on the bench seat, his large hand enveloping my midsection.

"You can't feel it on the outside," I say, laughter bubbling like expensive champagne in my chest. "Only on the inside."

A frown tugs at his mouth, pulling the corners down. "Where can you feel it?"

My hand covers his, so much smaller, shifting it to the spot where I can feel the fluttering in my midsection, the sensation almost like a bubble popping. Last night, I woke up and thought it was indigestion, but when it didn't go away, I pulled out my phone to look it up. When I realized what was happening, I *did* think about running across the hall to wake Beau up, and now I'm regretting staying in bed because I wish he'd gotten to experience this with me the first time.

"Right here," I say when our hands find the spot I can feel the fluttering deep inside.

His gaze fixes on mine, wide and full of awe. "What does it feel like?"

I pause for a moment, trying to think of how to explain it. "Butterfly wings."

At the description, his eyes focus on my stomach. "Hey, little butterfly. It's me, your daddy."

My heart pitches in my chest, like I just jumped off a cliff. I think I can actually feel my ovaries sighing right now.

"Can you move for daddy, please?"

I swear the baby moves at the sound of his voice, and tears prick at my eyes at the feeling of it. "They moved," I breathe.

A smile brighter than the sun breaks across his face. "Really?"

I nod, and I swear I see a sheen behind his eyes, but before I can get a good look, he presses his lips to the spot on my stomach. I can feel the heat of them through the thin fabric of my shirt.

"That's my baby," he says, like he's cheering them on at a baseball game. "You're perfect, just like your mom."

My chest feels full enough to burst when he finally backs up, the feeling of his kiss still lingering on my stomach.

"Come on, let's go see our baby."

An hour and a half later, we're climbing back into the truck with a clean bill of health and an envelope containing the gender of our baby in hand. I'm still in awe after watching our little baby move around on the screen during the ultrasound, knowing they were finally big enough for me to feel just a fraction of the movement.

"Where are we going?" I ask.

When the doctor asked if we wanted to know the baby's gender in the office, take the results home, or stay in the dark altogether, Beau and I agreed that we wanted to know. But he surprised me by saying he wanted to take the results with us because he knew where he wanted to open them.

His smile is wide. "It's a secret."

He backs out of the parking spot and pulls onto the street, heading in the opposite direction of home. When we hit the open road, driving into the mountains, Beau rolls down the windows, letting the summer air in. Nineties country plays on the stereo. The smell of pine and wildflowers dances on the breeze. My little butterfly flutters in my stomach, as if they, too, are enjoying this perfect day as much as I am.

When Beau turns down a nondescript dirt road, I know exactly where he's headed. A place we haven't been to in years. A smile creeps onto my lips as he avoids rough patches in the dirt, narrowly avoiding the dense pine trees on either side. It's a drive he probably could have made blindfolded at one point. It makes me both happy and sad to see that there are no longer any tire tracks in the dirt. Happy because that means that this place is still just ours. Sad because it just goes to show how long it's been since we were here. We've been back in Montana for a year now. This dirt road should show the wear of the visits we've made, but we haven't, and the absence of it feels particularly acute.

Finally, Beau pulls the truck to a stop and backs up so the bed is facing the valley. There's not even a designated spot, just a break in the trees that's perfect to stop and look out at the wide valley below. Beyond, the mountains rise, tall and jagged. Trees surround us on every side and wildflowers that carry the scent of earth crop up beneath our tires.

The place feels like magic. It always has.

"Wait there," Beau says, and hops out, coming to my side to help me down. My heart hammers in my chest at his touch, my throat thick with emotion.

When we round to the back of the truck, Beau releases the hatch, and then his hands find my hips and lift until I'm seated on the edge. Our eyes connect, and for a moment, it's like time stills.

We've been here a thousand times before, and he's always lifted me just like this. The first time we came here as teenagers, when he told me he'd found a place he wanted to show me. Dozens of times after, when we were dying to get away from our parents and the town, when we'd park and barely make it out of the truck before our hands and lips were on each other. The last time we were here, a few months before my injury, on a rare trip home during my off-season.

His hands flex on my hips, fingers digging in, and a part of me wants to pull him close, drag him up until he's laying me down in the bed of this truck, covering me, erasing all the bad memories of the last year.

But I think we're too far past that. I don't think we can go anywhere but forward. And maybe I'm starting to realize I don't *want* to forget it all. I want to remember every aching moment of it, remember how good it feels now, knowing how painful it was then.

Beau backs up before I can move, pulling the envelope the doctor gave me out of his back pocket, and climbs up into the bed next to me. Our feet dangle, knocking together as we stare at the crinkled envelope.

"What do you want it to be?" I ask, my palm finding my bump, pressing the place where the baby is moving.

Beau slides his thumbnail beneath the lip of the envelope, flipping it up and down. "I'd be happy with either," he says, and then his brown eyes lock on mine, the same color as the dirt beneath our feet. "But if I'm being totally honest, I want a girl. One just like you."

My throat feels thick, and I want to cry at the sincerity in his eyes. His hair catches in the wind, blowing over his cheek, and before I can stop myself, I reach up and push it back.

His breath fans across my palm at the touch, his eyes closing, and his body seems to go both pliant and tight, like he's sinking into the feeling, but ready to react to it at the slightest provocation. He's always been like that, and it's always fascinated me. I have visions of him, head tilted back, eyes closed, bottom lip caught between his teeth. I always thought I had him right where I wanted him, and then he'd flip, pin me down and show me I was never in as much control as I thought I was.

I want to tell him that I don't want to have a girl like me. That I don't want my child to be broken like me, to be incapable of being honest with the people they love, to isolate herself when she should let people in.

"I hope they're like you, boy or girl," I say, and it's the truth. The world needs more Beaus.

His eyes open, breath fanning against the wrist I still haven't pulled from his face. I'm entranced by the way his stubble feels against my palm. "Maybe they'll have all the best parts of both of us."

A smile pulls at my lips, and I lift my hand away, dropping it in my lap. "I hope so."

"You want to open it?" he asks.

I shake my head, leaning into his shoulder, sinking into the broad strength of it. "You do it," I tell him.

I can feel the breath let out of him as he slips his thumb beneath the lip of the envelope, opening it slowly. My heart beats wildly in my chest, a steady thump in my ears. Beau pulls out the slip of paper, and I see it the moment before he does.

I see our future spelled out in black and white, and a thousand images flash through my mind. This pregnancy has felt like many things since I watched the test flash *Positive*, but right now it feels *real*, because I can see it. I can see Beau and me and—

"It's a girl," Beau says, turning watery eyes on me. I watch as the future plays out for him the same way it just did for me. It feels bright, much brighter than it has the past year. The first star pricking a moonless sky.

I nod, a smile breaking out over my face. "It's a girl."

His hand finds the back of my head, hauling me in to press a kiss to my forehead before he bends down, eye level with my stomach. With a gentle reverence a man of his size shouldn't be able to possess, he caresses the swell of my stomach with his thumb and places a kiss there too.

"Hey, baby girl. It's me, your daddy."

TWENTY-TWO

BEAU
JUNE
TWENTY WEEKS PREGNANT

When I enter the studio, Elsie is working with one of the teenage girls I recognize. Her name is Maya, the one Elsie talks about a lot at home, the girl who reminds her so much of herself. Looking at the determined expression on the girl's face as she listens to Elsie's instruction and then tries to correct her posture, I can see it too.

When we were in high school, I used to come to the studio on early mornings or late nights with Elsie to watch her practice and try my best to distract her. It rarely worked, but on the few occasions I managed to snag her attention from dance, we made some memories in this studio. But even during the times I didn't manage to distract her, I was fascinated by watching her dance.

After we moved to Utah, I didn't get to watch her rehearse as much, but I tried any chance I got. I loved the way she transformed in the studio, in her pointe shoes, the way she'd become both fluid and controlled. How she could make her body move in these intricate and incredible ways. It was mesmerizing.

She looks different now, her bottom lip caught between her teeth, attention fixed wholly on Maya and the way she works to nail the move. She doesn't notice me standing in the corner, arms crossed, leaning against the wall, but I can't seem to tear my gaze away as her face transforms when Maya perfectly executes the pirouette. She's glowing in a way I've never seen before, eyes bright, cheeks flushed. And when Maya squeals and throws her arms around Elsie's middle, the look on her face transforms into something like awe.

I watch as she hesitates for just a moment, like she doesn't know how to respond, before her body softens and her arms circle around Maya's tiny form, wrapping her in a tight hug. Her lips move, forming words I'm too far away to hear, but I don't miss the way Maya's arms tighten around Elsie's middle, the way Elsie's eyes squeeze shut, like she's trying to hold back tears.

It makes my throat tight and my heart grow too big for my chest.

"She's great, isn't she?" someone says from beside me.

I look down to see Tonya. She's hardly changed in the years I've known her, something I've always appreciated about her. She's steady and unequivocally herself, a pillar of the community and a mentor to so many.

I nod and turn my focus back on Elsie, who is instructing Maya once more. "She really is."

"I wish she'd take me up on my offer."

This catches my attention, and when I look back at Tonya, she's staring directly at me, assessing my reaction. I don't bother pretending I know what she's talking about. This woman has spent the majority of her adult life working with teenage girls; she can sniff a lie from a mile away. "What offer?"

Tonya sighs like she expected this. "I told her I want to sell her the studio."

I quirk a brow, taken aback. "Really?"

She nods and allows her gaze to travel to the two dancers. "I've been getting offers for years from people who want to buy the studio, but I've never really entertained them. But now...I don't know. This town is feeling a little claustrophobia-inducing, and I think I'm ready for a change. I want to get out and travel while I'm still able to enjoy it, you know?"

"I understand," I tell her and mean it. I'm at a point in my life where I'm putting down roots. She's at the place where she wants to rip hers up.

She looks at me again, brown eyes serious. "Despite all that, I wouldn't sell it to anyone but her. That girl is my legacy."

I wish Elsie could hear this, that she could see how plainly her teacher and mentor and boss is proud of her, that she would only trust her business with one single person. I'm not sure if she would believe it, if she's ready to see herself that way yet, but I wish she could know. I wish there was a way to show her, to make her believe in her worth.

"She won't take it, though." Tonya sighs. "Thinks she's not capable."

I don't know how to respond, so I just follow the direction of her stare and watch my wife until she finally notices the two of us standing near the door. When Elsie's gaze finally catches on mine, a startled expression crosses her features for a moment before morphing into a smile that makes my pulse beat wildly.

She turns her attention back to Maya, saying something to her that makes Maya roll her eyes before heading to where her stuff is spread across the floor next to the barre.

"It was good to see you, Beau," Tonya says, patting me on the arm. "Take care of our girl, okay?"

"I will," I promise.

She nods like she believes me before turning on her heel and disappearing into her office and shutting the door behind her.

When I turn back, Elsie is making her way to me, and I can't help but let my eyes drift to the way her rounded stomach pulls tight against her leotard. Elsie has always been beautiful to me, since that very first day, but there's something primal inside me that loves seeing her pregnant with my baby.

"What are you doing here?" she asks, smiling, a little out of breath.

I want to pull her to me, press a kiss to her cheek, but I hold myself back. We've been making progress the last few weeks, and although I want to push us the last little bit, I don't want to spook her.

But damn it, I really want to kiss my wife.

"I wanted to see you," I say with a shrug, and something pinches in my stomach when her smile widens. I want to press my fingertips to the edge of that smile and feel it.

"I wasn't staying late tonight," she responds. "I would have been home in a half hour."

"Too long."

Her smile turns sly, the kind of smile that used to mean things I really, really shouldn't think about right now in a dance studio for children. "That so?"

I force my heart to slow from its wild gallop and say, "I like watching you teach. You're good at it."

A pretty blush stains her cheeks, and she looks down, sliding her ballet flat against the floor. "I like doing it." She's quiet for a moment before her eyes return to mine. There's a shyness in them I've so rarely seen. "I didn't expect to, but I really, really love it."

Before I can respond, Maya slips past us. "Bye, Elsie. See you tomorrow."

Elsie's face transforms into something soft, a wistful smile lifting her lips. "Bye, Maya. You did great today. I'm proud of you."

I tear my gaze from Elsie in time to see Maya's cheeks turn pink. She looks at my wife like she's her hero, like she's everything she wants to be when she grows up. I wonder if Elsie sees it, if she's realized that even though she's not a professional dancer anymore, this teenager still looks at her like there's no one she'd rather be like. My guess is no.

"Thanks, Elsie," Maya says and hurries out of the studio.

Before she can let herself out the door, Elsie calls, "Eat some junk food and watch a movie tonight."

I don't miss the way Maya's eyes roll, but I think she's going to listen anyway.

When Elsie finally returns her attention to me, I say, "You know she wants to be just like you, don't you?"

A shocked look crosses Elsie's face, proving my point. She shakes her head. "She doesn't want to be like me," she says, her gaze returning to the polished floors. "I'm a wash up."

Before I can think better of it, I tip her chin up with the pad of my thumb. Her skin is so damn soft it makes my mind feel fuzzy, and I allow my hand to linger for just a second, reveling in the feel of it. "You don't really think that, do you?"

That exposed look flashes over her features again, and to my surprise, she doesn't try to hide it. Her delicate shoulders lift in a shrug. "I don't regret how things have turned out," she says slowly, deliberately, like she wants me to understand. "But yes, as a ballerina, I'm a wash up."

My brain zeroes in on the first part of the sentence, something that's been tight in my chest finally uncoiling, because I *did* worry that she regretted all of this. I know she's happy about the pregnancy, that she's excited about becoming a mom, but I haven't been able to shake the fear that this entire last year has been cloaked in disappointment—that she regretted moving back here after her injury instead of trying to continue dancing, that she wished she hadn't invited me in that night, that she wished she could take back everything that came after. That if things had been different, she never would have let me come home or begun working on fixing things with me. That she's only doing it because we're having a child together.

But I force myself to store all that away for future examination and focus on the last part of what she said. "Elsie, you're not a wash up." I let out a sigh, wishing she could see herself the way I see her. "You got hurt, but you're so resilient that you picked yourself back up again. You started teaching this sport you love, even though it has to be hard being *here* every day when you'd rather be *there*." My breath heaves out of me, and I push my hand through my hair. I want to mention what Tonya just said to me, but I'm scared to push her too much, to bring up something she's not ready to talk about.

So instead, I say, "And the way that little girl looks at you? You're changing her whole life. *That* is not being all washed up. It's just..." I stare at the ceiling, searching for the words. "Using that passion you have in a different way. Different, but just as meaningful."

When I look back at her, her blue eyes are tipped up to mine, contemplative, like she's never once considered this point of view. She's quiet for so long, the only sounds in the room that of our breathing, that I almost think she's not going to respond.

But she finally says, "Maybe."

A smile touches my lips. "I just gave you an impassioned speech, and all I get is a *maybe*?"

Her lips quirk, eyes dancing in a way that feels old and familiar. "It was a really good speech."

"Thank you."

Her face sobers. "It's just...hard for me to feel that way about myself sometimes."

It's perhaps the most vulnerable thing she's ever said to me. For so long, I looked at her and only saw strength, resilience, unparalleled determination. I knew she had soft spots, but they were for things like lost puppies and elderly people eating alone and *me*. I spent so long loving her and never seeing that she had soft spots that were all hers.

I'm so fucking furious with myself for missing it, for not seeing such big pieces of her, places I should have been protecting, places where she was vulnerable and trying to carry things all on her own.

She's not blameless, of course. She should have told me, showed me hers the way I'd shown her mine, and there's a part of me that's mad at her for that. But I should have *seen* it. I should have noticed the things she kept hidden, the reasons she didn't let me in.

How scared she's been for much too long.

I should have seen it, and I don't know if I'll ever forgive myself that I didn't.

"I wish," I start, voice shaky, "that you could see yourself the way I do."

Her throat bobs as she swallows, and my eyes track the movement, noticing the way her pulse beats erratically beneath her skin. "Me too."

An idea comes to me then, but I hold it back. A secret. A project, really.

"Anyway," she says, straightening her shoulders, the unarmed look on her face morphing into one I recognize. "I better close up."

I nod and follow her through the studio. We begin a well-choreographed dance, one we've performed a thousand times in this very space. First, we adjust the barre, returning it to the correct height before moving it against the wall. Next, I head for the mats left out on the floor and begin stacking them in the corner while she heads down the halls, turning off the lights in the other rooms. Tonya's office is empty, meaning she must have slipped out without either of us noticing.

We meet a few minutes later in the lobby, and as she adjusts the thermostat, I decide to broach the topic I've been meaning to since I got here.

"So, I was thinking…"

Elsie looks over her shoulder at me, one brow lifted.

"I was going to tell my family the news at dinner on Monday."

"That you're an ass man?" she asks, turning to face me.

My eyes slowly trail down her body, lingering on her chest. "We both know that isn't true." My voice is sandpaper, and when I finally look back up at her, I'm pleased to see a flush staining her cheeks.

"What news?" Her voice isn't quite as controlled either, and it drags up memories of us in this very studio many years ago.

Of hands and lips and stolen moments in a dark studio, where neither of our parents knew where we were.

I swallow thickly, the palms of my hands itching. It's been too long since I've touched her, *felt* her. "What?" My mind is buzzing too much to focus on her question, filthy images playing on a loop in my mind.

She smiles then, and it doesn't help the situation. I want to taste that smile. "What news, Beau?"

I shake my head to clear my thoughts, her question finally piercing my brain. *The news.* "Oh, that we're having a girl. Cheyenne will be thrilled."

An indecipherable look crosses over her features, and it makes something in my stomach squeeze. I move forward on instinct, needing to be closer to her, to know what she's thinking.

She smooths her hands down her sweatpants-clad thighs, avoiding my eyes. "Right, of course." Her gaze swings back up to mine, a smile I can see right through pulling at her lips. "I'm sure they'll be happy. Unless they were hoping for a boy, I guess."

I'm finally close enough to touch her, to see in the dim light the way her hands are trembling slightly.

"They'll be happy, Elsie," I say softly but firmly.

Her head tilts up to hold my gaze as I close the last of the distance between us. Her lips press together, her eyes not meeting mine. "Well, good."

"But I was hoping we could tell them together."

I see the way the words pelt her, the way she almost recoils from them.

"I don't think that's a good idea," she responds, voice barely audible, gaze still trained on the floor.

"Why?"

She doesn't respond for a long moment, and I duck to meet her eyes. When they connect with mine, she doesn't look away. I can see the gears moving in her head, the way she's holding back what's really on her mind, debating whether to say it. I get that sickened feeling with myself again, wondering how many times she's done this before and I missed it, thinking she was just choosing her words carefully. That she was *thoughtful*.

"Tell me," I prod, unable to hold myself back. "Tell me, really, why you don't want to see them."

"They have to hate me," she blurts, and I realize it's the first time she's ever done so. It takes me aback, the words and her tone feeling like whiplash.

I reach for her on instinct, my hand lifting to her neck, my thumb settling against the racing pulse in her throat. I feel her swallow against it, and I can't help but drag the pad of my thumb over it.

Her eyes are wide, unblinking. There are so many emotions flitting behind her eyes, but most prevalent is regret.

And I want to erase it. Demolish it.

"They don't hate you, Elsie. They could never."

"The way I treated you..." she trails off, gaze dropping to the hollow of my throat and lingering.

"Doesn't concern them."

She shakes her head. "Doesn't mean they don't have feelings about it."

"They might," I concede. "But they don't see me as some scorned husband, Els. They know there's more to the story, more going on. Things we have to work through. Things they don't need to know and aren't trying to know."

Her eyes lift to mine again, confused. "They haven't asked questions?"

"No."

"None?"

"Well, that's a lie," I say, and her expression falls. "My dad asked how you're doing."

She blinks, and I watch the words wash over her, settling into her bones. When she speaks again, her voice is shaky. "He did?"

I nod, my throat tight.

"Why?"

I shouldn't be surprised by her question, but I am. I'm surprised by how low her self-worth has fallen. That she can't believe that my family would care about how she's doing after losing everything she held most dear in such a short amount of time. That she could think they held the separation against her.

"Because they love you, Elsie." It's so simple, but I can tell it isn't simple to her. That she doesn't believe she deserves their love, that she's shocked as hell that they haven't rescinded it because she fell apart and hurt me in the process.

I watch the thoughts flit through her head again, watch her shut down without saying the darkest of them, but I don't press her. She's been so vulnerable tonight, so brave, and I don't think I've ever felt such a potent mix of pride and love and tenderness at once.

"Will you go with me?" I ask finally, breaking the silence, my heart beating in my ears. "Let's tell our family about our baby girl. Together."

She lets out a shaky breath, and I feel her pulse quicken beneath my touch. Then she nods. "Okay, let's do it together."

TWENTY-THREE
ELSIE
JUNE

MATERNITY CLOTHES ARE ACTUALLY the ugliest things on the planet. Seriously, Jade and I have been shopping for the last hour, trying to find something remotely cute for me to wear to family dinner tomorrow, and there hasn't been a single thing worth spending my money on. I'm tired of living in sweats and leggings. I miss my jeans.

"You're just going to have to get something," Jade says. She's sprawled out on the uncomfortable-looking wooden bench in the dressing room, looking like she's ready to burn this entire store to the ground. I don't even blame her.

"It's all horrible."

Jade rolls her eyes. "You've mentioned that a time or two."

"Maybe Cheyenne's next hobby will be sewing, and she can make me some maternity clothes."

Cheyenne has always had a wide range of interests, which she blames on her ADHD. She hyperfocuses on a hobby for weeks at a time, buying everything she could possibly need for it, only to give it up a few weeks later. It's why her house looks like the inside of a craft store, just much, much less organized.

Jade snorts and moves the pile of clothes from her lap beside her to the bench. "Good luck with that." She pauses for a moment. "Have you talked to Cheyenne...since everything?"

I smooth my hands down the legs of the jeans I've been trying on, avoiding her gaze and looking at my reflection in the mirror. "No. I don't know how everyone feels about me."

Out of the corner of my eye, I see her expression soften, and I don't love it. I don't like feeling pitied, and it immediately makes my hackles rise, but I force myself to push them back down. I'm working on being vulnerable more often.

It sucks.

"Els, the Jenningses could never be mad at you," Jade says, catching my gaze in the mirror.

I swallow, my throat feeling thick, and force myself to hold her gaze. "That's easy for you to say. You've always been a part of their family, and you've never done anything to jeopardize that."

I wish my voice didn't sound so small, that she couldn't decipher how much this has bothered me.

"You haven't done anything to jeopardize that either," she says softly. "You have to know there's nothing that you could do to make them not love you."

All at once, my patience feels frayed. I'm hot, and these pants are both too tight and too loose at the same time. There are so many thoughts in my head, all vying to push to the forefront, and I feel like the room is closing in on me.

And then I realize what's about to happen. That familiar, cloying anxiety clenches at my spine and grips my lungs, making it hard to breathe.

Jade's eyes widen, concern etched in every line of her face. "Elsie, what's wrong?"

I don't remember moving, but suddenly, my back hits the wall, and I slide down it, clutching at my chest that feels too tight. Beside me, Jade drops to the floor, her hands all over me.

"Elsie," she says, sounding panicked enough to clear the fog closing in on me, just a little.

"I'm okay," I manage to get out. "Panic attack."

My breath comes in loud, horrifying gasps, and I force myself to close my eyes, to let the darkness comfort me.

"What can I do?" she asks, voice high with worry.

I shake my head, unable to form any more words, and let the shaking take over. I was so hot a moment ago, but now I'm freezing, my teeth chattering. I force myself to breathe in through my nose and out through my mouth, trying to calm my breathing.

Still, nothing is working.

But then Jade wraps her arms around me, holding me tight. She doesn't say anything, but she rocks us back and forth on the dirty dressing room floor. And something about the tightness of her grip, the gentle swaying of our bodies, cuts through panicked haze. I don't know how long we sit like that, but slowly, my teeth stop chattering, and the uncontrollable shaking of my body eases.

I'm left with that hauntingly familiar hollow feeling in my gut, my head pounding. But I don't feel *alone*. Just like the time Beau was with me, when he sat with me in that doctor's office parking lot, I don't feel the aching loneliness.

Jade eases back from me, her green eyes assessing me. They remind me of the trees outside, the ones that stay green even during the harsh Montana winters. They're steady, constant. Jade is like that, too, and just like I did with Beau, I'm wondering why I hid this from her for so long, why I didn't lean on her when she's like those trees outside, steadfast and unmoving.

"You okay?"

I nod, and the movement makes the pounding in my head intensify.

She watches me closely, and I think she knows my answer was partly bullshit by the way I wince when I nod. "C'mon, let's get out of here."

Jade stands first and helps me up, and to my surprise, she helps me out of the fugly maternity pants and back into my leggings, the only thing that's fit me for the last few weeks. I'm still shaking as she does it, but it's more of a chilled, weak sort of shaking, the kind that always follows my panic attacks.

She gathers our stuff, and I follow her out of the dressing room to where she drops off all the stuff I'm not purchasing and then out of the store. The sunshine immediately warms my chilled skin, and I stop, just wanting to bask in it for a moment, my face lifted to the sky. Jade doesn't ask what we're doing, just stops beside me, her shoulder pressed against mine, her face also lifted like a sunflower arcing toward the sun.

We stand there, side by side, until my breathing finally returns to normal and the sun eases the last of the cold lingering on my skin.

When I finally turn back to Jade, she's watching me, but it doesn't feel as overwhelming as it did in the dressing room. It feels strangely...comforting to know that she just saw me at my worst and isn't acting any differently.

"Ready?" she asks.

I nod, then I follow her to her truck and we hop in. The second she turns it on, Chris Stapleton croons from the speakers, and I settle back into my seat, rolling down my window. I've never felt like this after a panic attack—safe. And that's how I feel now, riding down the road in Larkspur with the windows down and my best friend behind the wheel, the smell of wildflowers and grass and mountain air filling the cab.

She pulls the truck into a parking spot on the main street in town, right in front of the Canteen, a little café in town.

"What are we doing here?" I ask when she turns off the car.

She shrugs and opens the door. "I'm hungry."

I don't really feel like being around people right now, especially people in town, but I can tell Jade isn't in a mood to be argued with, so I suck it up and climb out of the car on still shaky legs. When we walk through the door, a bell chimes, alerting everyone to our presence. I can feel the stares of the other diners, the smiles they give Jade and the barely restrained contempt they reserve for me. I'm shrinking in on myself little by little, but Jade doesn't seem to notice, her eyes fixed on the menu written on the wall above the counter.

"I don't know if I want a burger or a salad," she murmurs, lost in her own head as I try to ignore the stares of the people around us, my skin burning with embarrassment. I want to leave. I want to get takeout and eat it on my couch, away from all these people who loathe me for something I blame myself enough for already.

"What are you getting?" Jade asks, ripping my attention away from where it's fixed on my sneakers.

"What?"

Her expression changes, eyes narrowing, as if she can read the emotions on my face. I hate it. I may have felt safe earlier, but right now, I want to hide. My eyes burn and my throat feels thick. I feel out of control, too bare to anyone who takes a second glance.

"Order me a burger and sweet potato fries. I'm going to the bathroom."

I slip away before she can ask what's going on, feeling everyone's eyes on me as I head down the hall and into the bathroom. The door clicks shut behind me, loud in the silence, and I lean back against it, head pounding. I still feel frail from the panic attack, my body stuck somewhere between fight and flight. No part of me wants to go back out there, to the stares, to Jade's all-knowing gaze.

Deep in my stomach, the baby moves, stronger than she was even a few weeks ago, and I press my hand to try to catch it. There's a little kick, faint, against my palm. So faint, I think I must imagine it, but then it comes again, and my heart stops in my chest.

I lift up my shirt, staring at the now rounded bump, looking for movement, but there's nothing there. It's like she wanted to let me know she's here for just a moment when I need her. It gives me a strength I'm not sure I possess, and I swallow down my fear before turning and heading back out of the bathroom, ignoring the looks shot my way.

Jade is already at a table, a laminated paper number clipped to a table marker. She has her phone in her hand, and I imagine she's adjusting her bolus before the food arrives. Her eyes find me as soon as I exit the restroom, watching me as I walk across the restaurant to where she's sitting.

As soon as I sit down, she asks, "What's going on?"

I let out a little breath that ruffles my long grown-out bangs and meet her stare. "What do you mean?"

Her face flattens and she lifts a brow. "Seriously?"

I can feel eyes on us from around the restaurant, the stares of other patrons making me feel like a bug stuck on a Styrofoam board. I don't want to have this conversation here, but I know she's not going to drop it.

"That was a panic attack," I say, so quietly she has to lean forward to hear me. "I've been having them since I was a kid."

Her brow furrows, confusion clouding her features. "Really?"

I think I notice hurt in her voice, and it makes guilt stab at my chest, because I'd be the same way if she told me she's been suffering with something for years and has never shared it with me.

"Yes," I respond, voice small. I force myself to keep my eyes on her and not on the people around us. "I...I don't really remember life without them, but I was always able to manage them. But after this year—the injury and losing dance and the miscarriage. All of it just kept piling up, and I couldn't take it anymore."

Jade is quiet for a moment, her expression thoughtful. "Does Beau know about them?" She looks like she already knows the answer, like she's piecing the puzzle together in her head.

I shake my head, throat too tight to reply.

She nods, like my answer only confirmed her suspicions. "You didn't want him to know—to see you like that."

I meet her gaze. Her eyes are soft, understanding, without an ounce of judgment in them. Once again, I feel the bitter taste of regret. I should have told her years ago. I should have told Beau. Keeping it from them only hurt us all.

"No," I manage to get out, staring at my lap. "And so I asked him to leave. I was always going to tell him to come back, beg him if I had to." I shake my head, stomach twisting. "It's stupid, I know that now, but I wanted to be better for him. I didn't want to be broken. He doesn't deserve that."

When I finally look back up at her, there's a sheen of tears behind her eyes, and they threaten to loosen the last hold I have on my composure.

"Els," Jade whispers, her hand finding mine across the table. She links our fingers together, holding tight enough to hurt, but I don't let go. "You're an idiot."

A laugh shoots out of me, unexpected. "I know."

Her hand squeezes mine. "But I understand. I wish you hadn't gone through all this alone, that you'd trusted us to help, but I understand."

I hold her gaze. "You do?"

She inclines her head. "I don't agree with it, but I know you, Els. I know the kind of home you grew up in and the kind of person you are. I know how strong and independent you are, and how much you hate asking for help. I'm sure nothing has ever made you feel more vulnerable, and you hate feeling vulnerable."

I let her words sink down into my skin, into the places inside me that feel raw and bruised and battered.

"No," I whisper. "I don't."

"But there's a certain kind of strength in sharing your vulnerabilities, in letting people know where you're soft."

I blink back the tears that threaten to break loose, unwilling to let the other people in the restaurant see me cry. "You think so?"

A smile tugs at the edges of her lips, small and tender. "Has this been easy? Talking about this?"

"No."

"But you did it anyway," she says, letting go of my hand. "You did it, and I think that required a lot of strength."

I assess her words while a server brings our food, rolling them over and over again in my head. She's not wrong. Telling her about my panic attacks, something I've kept to myself for so long, was one of the scariest things I've done—scarier than mastering fouettés, scarier than telling my parents I was getting married weeks before I was supposed to leave for Utah for my first professional ballet job, scarier than the moment I knew I'd injured myself too badly to recover that day in rehearsal.

I want to have the strength to tell Beau the way I just told Jade, to let him know the real reason I asked him to leave, but I'm not sure I'm there yet. But for the first time, I think, one day, I might be.

The minute the waiter leaves, Jade reaches for one of my fries, dipping it in the sauce on my plate before shoving it into her mouth. I'm not even a little surprised; she always does this. "We should throw you a baby shower."

This, however, does surprise me. "No," I say before she can get carried away. This idea needs to be shut down quickly.

Her brows pinch together. "Why not?"

Heat creeps into my cheeks, and I clasp my hands together beneath the table hard enough for my knuckles to hurt. "Because no one would come."

She looks at me like I've grown another head. "What do you mean no one would come? Everyone would come."

I dart my gaze around the room, watching for eyes on us, people overhearing this conversation that makes me want to melt into the ground. I don't know how she hasn't noticed the looks people give me when we're out, the way people have avoided me for months.

"Jade, seriously," I say quietly enough that only she can hear. "Everyone in town hates me for leaving Beau."

She blinks at me. "You cannot be serious."

I stare at her, at a loss for words.

"Elsie, no one hates you."

"Can we just drop this?" I ask, tightening my hands beneath the table, knuckles popping beneath the pressure.

She drops her sandwich onto her plate and wipes her hands on a napkin, her eyes never leaving mine. "No, we can't."

I fight a sigh. "Please, I don't want to talk about it."

"Elsie." She sounds exasperated. "No one is mad at you. Why would you think that?"

My voice drops to a pained, harsh whisper. "Because everyone is always giving me dirty looks, and no one ever talks to me anymore. They cut me off the second I asked him to leave, and I can't even blame them."

She looks at me for so long that I feel the heat creeping back into cheeks and staining my chest with color. "I had three people ask me last week how you're feeling. Last month, Jean Riley ran into me at Bud's and asked if you already had a crib because her baby just grew out of his and she was planning to sell it but wanted to check with you first. My mom asked me yesterday if you had a registry, and I overheard one of your students' moms at the grocery store talking about how much her daughter loves you and how grateful they are that you came back here to teach."

Embarrassment tightens my throat, and my head swims, because *none* of this can be real. I feel like I'm choking on the words when I say, "You don't need to lie to me, Jade."

"I'm not," she promises. She sounds so sincere that I almost believe her. As if she can read my hesitation, she says again, more firmly, "I'm not. I don't know what kind of narrative you've built up in your head about Larkspur, Els, but everyone here loves you just as much as they always have. And they want to support you and Beau. You're just as much a part of this place as he is." She pauses, eyes assessing me. "You belong to this town, and nothing you do could ever change that."

TWENTY-FOUR
ELSIE
JUNE

My stomach is in knots as we pull up to the big house for family dinner on Monday night. I've been sitting on my hands since we got in the truck to keep them from shaking, feeling my heartbeat in my throat.

Beau parks the truck at the end of the long driveway, behind an intimidating line of cars that belong to everyone in his family, then turns to face me. "On a scale of one to ten, how nervous are you?"

"I'm not nervous." The lie slips out before I can even consider speaking the truth, an instinct long ago ingrained in me.

Beau quirks an eyebrow, drawing my attention from the big house, and for a moment, I get lost in him. He looks good tonight. He looks good *every night*. He's wearing jeans that hug him in all the right places and a charcoal tee with a black button-up layered over it, buttons undone. In the evening light, the sunset reflects on his irises, making the greens and golds in them pronounced. His lips are full, tilted in a knowing smile that makes my heart rate quicken.

It's getting harder and harder to resist him, and I don't know why I am anymore. The panic attacks haven't disappeared and I'm not *better*, but I'm getting there, and it's getting easier to share with him what I'm actually feeling. It's like training a new muscle, learning a new dance move. It takes practice, determination. But that, I'm good at.

So it's easier to say, "Seven."

He nods, like this is a fair number. "Why are you nervous?"

He may think they don't hold the separation against me, and maybe they truly don't. It's something that's been running through my head on a loop since my conversation with Jade. I've been going over every interaction I've had with people in town for the last eight months, dissecting each one to see where I misinterpreted things, and I'm starting to wonder if maybe she's right. Maybe the people of Larkspur haven't been holding this against me. But I have been, and I can't stand to look at these people that I love, knowing I hurt their son, their brother, *them*.

My gaze darts away, focusing on the view outside the truck, my hand falling to the swell of my stomach beneath my plain white tee, the hem of which is barely covering my unbuttoned jeans. I still haven't managed to find maternity ones yet, and I'm paying the price for it.

The mountains catch my attention, and I marvel in the way the sun arches through them, coloring the world in shades of gold, and let the view calm me. Settle me.

"They might not be mad at me," I finally say on an exhale. "But I'm still nervous about seeing them after abandoning them for so long."

When I finally glance at Beau, he looks like he wants to protest, but I shake my head, and he stays silent.

"You don't need to correct me. I know..." I pause, searching his face for the right words. "I know that's not what happened, but it's how I feel." My throat feels tight when I swallow. "I'm trying to be honest about how I feel, even when I know my feelings aren't necessarily the truth."

He holds my gaze for so long that I think he might not respond. "Thank you," he says, voice thick. "For what it's worth, I'm proud of you for doing it."

His approval slides beneath my skin, warming me from the inside out. I've always been so susceptible to praise, probably because it was so infrequently given to me growing up. Dancers are most often told what they're doing wrong and how to fix it rather than what they're doing right. It's something I've been trying to do differently as a teacher. When Maya threw herself at me the other day, her thin arms wrapping tight around my middle in a bone-crushing hug, I knew I'd made the right choice.

But from Beau, it feels even more pivotal. All-encompassing. It sinks into my bones, branding itself onto my soul.

"Thank you," I say, and before I can get anything else out, there's a series of loud thuds on my window. I jump, heart racing, and turn to find Cheyenne, grinning like a madwoman.

She rips the door open, squealing at a pitch dogs from miles away would be able to hear.

"You're here!"

She grips my knees and spins me until my feet dangle out the door. Her hands land on my stomach, touching it with awed reverence usually reserved for rare gemstones or the perfect heirloom tomato at the farmers' market. It makes a smile tug at my lips.

Cheyenne's eyes snap up to mine, blinking furiously to hold back tears. I've always admired her ability to feel everything so deeply *and* show it. It must be so freeing. "You're having my baby."

Behind me, Beau laughs. "Mine, actually."

"Ours," Cheyenne corrects, her hands still holding my stomach. "Our communal family baby."

"Pretty sure there was nothing communal or familial about the conception. In fact, it was downright—"

"Please never finish that sentence."

"I'm interested in hearing it," I say.

Beau's eyes glow with mischief. It feels so much like the old *us*, like the new us we're trying to find.

"You're ruining this moment for me," Cheyenne whines.

"Sorry," I say, returning my attention to her and holding back a smile. "We're all having a baby."

Beau grunts and opens his door, climbing out as his sister smooths her hands over my stomach. "Chey, leave my wife alone, please."

Cheyenne rolls her eyes and drops her hands. Her gaze fixes on mine. "I'm going to be an aunt."

She says nothing about the last few months of silence. Nothing about the separation. Nothing about the way I asked Beau to leave and then left them too.

Just genuine, pure delight.

It makes my throat tight. "Yeah, Chey, you are."

She reaches up, wrapping her arms around my shoulders tight enough to hurt, but I don't mind. I hold her back, breathing in her familiar scent. Wildflowers and sunshine.

"I'm so glad you're home."

This time, I can barely speak around the lump in my throat, but I manage to say, "Me too."

"Come on, let's go inside," Beau says, breaking up the moment.

I'm thankful for it, because I need a moment to compose myself so I'm not sobbing as I walk into the big house.

I follow the two of them, barely hearing Cheyenne's chattering over the pounding of my heart, as we head up the wooden porch stairs. My breath catches as I walk over the threshold. The house I grew up in never really felt like home, but this one did from the first moment I stepped inside it.

It's a classic ranch home. Wood everywhere. School portraits and family photos lining the walls. Boots discarded by the door and a hat rack with more than enough hooks. Sunshine bursting through the windows and the smell of earth that never quite leaves. Noise, the kind I never had in my house. Voices talking over each other and laughter and music.

Home. It feels like I'm finally coming home after too much time away.

I don't realize I've stopped in the foyer, but Beau does, and he motions for Cheyenne to keep going and turns back to me. His boots are heavy thuds on the wood floors as he closes the distance between us, matching the heavy falls of my heart.

There are voices coming in our direction, and before I can think about hiding my emotions, putting on a brave face for them, Beau tugs my arm, pulling the two of us into the coat closet and closing us in.

It's dark in here, too dark to make out his expression, but we're close enough for me to feel the pounding of his heart against mine, the heat of his breath on my skin. It smells like leather and shearling and dust in the cramped quarters.

"We're in the closet," I say dumbly.

Beau huffs a laugh, ruffling the hair fringing my face. "Shit, I thought this was a bedroom."

I roll my eyes. "*Why* are we in a closet?"

"You looked like you needed a minute," he says.

My heartbeat slows infinitesimally. He's been seeing more lately, a combination of him looking in the right places and me working hard not to hide as much. At first, it scared me. It still does sometimes. But right now, I'm grateful for it. I'm happy he saw that I was overwhelmed with every single emotion this place drags up in me and gave me a moment to digest it before seeing everyone.

"Thank you," I say and mean it.

His hand snakes around my hip, squeezing it, and the contact feels almost electric in this small, dark space.

Then his thumb slips over the waistband of my jeans, and my breath hitches in my throat.

"Are your pants unbuttoned?" he asks, sounding amused.

"Unzipped too," I say, trying not to focus on how his hands feel on me. How starved I've been for touch the last few months. *His* touch.

A laugh gusts out of him. "Why?"

"They don't fit anymore," I complain.

"We can buy you some new pants," he says.

I can hear the smile in his voice so clearly I can picture it. The way his eyes are crinkling and his lips are curling one edge at a time.

I shake my head, and my hair catches in the stubble on his cheeks. "They're all ugly. I looked."

He laughs again, his thumb still tracing the waistband of my jeans through my shirt in a way that feels all too distracting. "You can't just go walking around with your pants unbuttoned all the time."

"Why?"

"It's distracting," he says.

My breath catches in my throat when his thumb slips beneath the hem of my shirt, touching bare skin.

"How?" I manage to ask, mortified at the way my breath comes out like a pant.

"I won't be able to think about anything else," he answers, his finger tracing the line of my waistband until it gets to where it's folded down just below my belly button. My stomach jumps beneath his touch, and I know he has to notice, but he doesn't remove his hand, just keeps tracing his thumb there. I have to hold in a gasp when he hits the top of my underwear.

"It's not a cute look," I say, my voice embarrassingly breathy. "I'm getting more stretch marks, and I look like a can of biscuits after you crack it open in these jeans."

My breath hitches when his entire hand engulfs my stomach, moving upward, stopping just before he hits anything interesting.

"I like the bump," he says, and it sounds like a scrape of sandpaper.

"Really?"

He shakes his head. "No, that's a lie. I love it." His mouth moves closer, right next to my ear. "I like knowing my baby is growing inside you. I like knowing I did it. It makes me feel oddly...possessive."

"Oh," I gasp.

"Does that bother you?" he asks, again right in my ear, so close I can feel the heat of his breath, the brush of his lips.

"No."

He smiles then, and even though I can't see it, only feel it against the shell of my ear, I know it's wicked. He's so close that I wonder if he can feel my heart race, thumping wildly in my chest.

How the hell did we end up here? In the coat closet at his parents' house, having this conversation?

"Elsie baby," he says, sounding a little desperate and a lot wild.

My heart somehow ratchets up incredibly faster. "Yes?"

"Can I—"

I don't get to hear what he's going to say because the door to the closet is yanked open, and there is Cooper, grinning at us maniacally.

"Hello, brother."

Beau groans against the side of my head, and with a palpable reluctance, slips his hand out from beneath my shirt.

"Elsie, you're looking well," Cooper says, leaning on the doorframe. "Rather flushed."

"Shut up, Cooper," Beau says.

"And you're looking pretty har—"

"How have things been with you, Coop?" I interrupt, trying to will the blush from my face.

"Oh, things have been good," he says, grinning at me. "Not as good as the two of you seem to be, of course."

"Coop, did you find them?" Lottie, Beau and Cooper's mom, yells down the hall.

Cooper holds our gazes for a long moment, drawing out the tension, a smirk playing at his lips. Finally, he answers, "Yeah, they forgot something in the truck. Just walked back in."

I heave out a sigh of relief.

"Come on, you two," Cooper says before spinning on his heel and heading down the hall toward the massive living room.

Beau spares me another look. "Still nervous?"

Yes, but I feel better too. Squaring my shoulders, I say, "I'm good. Let's go."

To my surprise, he wraps his hand around mine and lifts it to his lips, pressing a kiss on the back of it before leading me down the hall. When we finally make it into the living room, the center of all the chaos and noise, I can still feel the echo of his kiss on my skin.

Clint notices us first, his face lighting up when he sees me, and he makes his way across the living room on long legs, eating up the distance between us.

"Elsie," he says, just as he wraps his arms around me in a hug. "I'm glad you're home."

It's an echo of what his daughter said, and it makes my throat and heart squeeze in tandem.

"Me too," I murmur into his chest.

"I'm really glad you're here," he whispers and pulls back. "No more staying away."

I swallow against the lump in my throat. "I won't," I say, and it's true. Now that I'm back here, in this place with these people, I don't think I'd have the strength to distance myself again.

The next few minutes are a swarm of hugs and well wishes, ending with Lottie. She was the one I was most worried about. She's fierce and loyal and protective, and I hurt her baby. But to my surprise, she doesn't seem to hold it against me.

She even hugs me, something I can count on one hand the amount of times it's happened before. And when she does, she whispers "welcome back, Elsie" in my ear in a way that makes me feel the uncharacteristic need to blink back tears.

I don't know who I'm becoming, but I don't think I hate it.

When we finally settle at the table, it's with Cash in my lap, Jade on one side of me, and Beau on the other, his thigh pressed against mine beneath the table. It all feels so, so right in a way I can't comprehend. In some ways, it feels as though I never left. In others, like I've been gone for much too long. Ruby is missing her two front teeth. Cash plays T-ball. Cooper bought a new truck. The Dawsons booked a Caribbean cruise. Ryder has a "girlfriend" at preschool. Cheyenne got a job waiting tables at a new restaurant that just opened in town.

It's overwhelming in the best way possible, and I don't know how I went so long without these people. Without my family.

"Anything new with you guys?" Lottie asks, looking at Beau and me.

I catch his eye, and he nods at me, a small smile playing on his lips. We had a plan of how to tell them—after dinner, when we all sat around the living room with drinks and plates full of summer berry pie.

But the news is bursting inside me, fizzing on the energy of this evening, of being surrounded by the first people to teach me what unconditional love is. And I want them to know *now*. To share in the excitement with us.

"We're having a girl."

"When can we throw you a baby shower?" Cheyenne asks after dinner. Beau finally managed to wrench her hand away from my stomach before disappearing somewhere with Cooper.

I glance at Jade, wondering if she mentioned it to them, but she gives me a small shake of her head before going back to braiding Ruby's hair.

"I, um," I stumble over my words, overwhelmed. "I wasn't expecting one."

Lottie gives me a hard look. "You can't expect to buy everything on your own. You either tell us what you want and let us buy it for you, or you're going to end up with a bunch of stuff you didn't pick out, understand?"

My lips roll together to hold back my smile, and I nod. "Okay."

They dive into plans for a baby shower, all the women present throwing out ideas, and I listen, overwhelmed. Emotion clogs my throat as they volley ideas back and forth—themes, days, times, guest lists—until I finally feel overwhelmed by it, by their forgiveness and acceptance and *love*.

"I'll be right back," I say to the group, who barely spares me a glance as I leave the living room in search of fresh air. I need a minute alone and the sun on my skin, so I head for the back porch, detouring through the mudroom.

I stop in my tracks when I hear voices through the open Dutch door. It's Beau and Cooper, beers in hand, leaning against the porch rail, eyes fixed on the horizon.

"I was wrong about her," Cooper says.

Beau casts him a look before turning back to the mountains, the land that is as much a part of this family as the people in it.

"She's not herself anymore. She's withdrawn." He pauses. "Hurting. I thought she broke you, but she was broken herself."

Beau shakes his head, staring down at his feet. There's a tense set to his shoulders, and I want to smooth it away. I want to reach for him, but my legs stay locked in place, waiting for his response. My throat is thick, my heart beating so loudly I'm surprised they can't hear it. I'm immobile, desperate to hear his reply.

"I should have seen it," Beau says.

My heart cracks in two at how broken he sounds.

"I should have loved her better. I should have seen how broken she was, how much she needed me, but I thought she was…" he trails off. "I don't know what I thought. I thought she didn't need me, that she didn't need anyone. And I was such an idiot to back off and give her space when she needed me to push her to let me in. It's been destroying me, Coop, knowing that I couldn't be there for her the way she needed."

Tears sting my cheeks, falling in fat drops that land on my shirt, and my feet finally start moving, backing away from the door before either of them can see me. I stumble through the house and into the closest bathroom, everything a blur behind my misty eyes.

When I finally manage to lock the door behind me, sobs rack my frame. Guilt, hot and deep, stabs through me.

What have I done?

The thought goes around and around in my head. All this time, I held back, thinking I was protecting him, but I was only hurting him more. *Destroying* him. Breaking him in the way I was broken.

It makes nausea roil in my gut, but I tamp it down. Warm tears streak down my cheeks, and I don't bother to wipe them away. For the first time, I let the years' worth of hurt and guilt and shame wash over me. I allow myself to feel them all, because today is going to be the last day. Today is the last day I hurt others because I'm hurting. I'm done breaking the people I love because I'm broken.

I stay in the bathroom until my tears dry up, until I feel lighter than I have in months. Until I feel stable enough to push up off the toilet seat and splash cold water on my face.

When I catch my reflection in the mirror, I know there's no way to hide that I've been crying. But for once, it doesn't bother me. For once, I don't care who knows that I locked myself in a bathroom and melted down.

I twist the knob and let myself out.

I need to find Beau.

TWENTY-FIVE
BEAU
JUNE

Elsie is quiet on the way home, almost contemplative, but I don't ask her to tell me what's on her mind. I know tonight was overwhelming for her, that she went in expecting, for whatever reason, a much different reaction than the one that she got.

The truth is, I'm feeling a little raw too. I didn't expect to break down during my conversation with Cooper, but the past year came at me like a bag of bricks, knocking the wind out of me. I watched Elsie tonight, seeing her so clearly, wondering how I missed the signs for so long. How I ever brushed off her retreat as resilience. All the times I let her pull away thinking she was strong enough not to need someone to lean on. I failed her, and this last year is as much my fault as it is hers.

The truck bumps over the dirt driveway, the lights slicing over the house. We accidentally left the light on in the front bathroom, and it makes the house glow golden. Looking at it now, I'm overwhelmed that we made it back *here* together. That we're both living in this house again, working toward reconciliation, when we messed things up so royally before.

"Beau," Elsie says, cutting into my thoughts. Her voice is small, quiet, but I hear a determination in it too. Like she's been ruminating on that one word the whole way home. "I heard you with Cooper."

I turn to face her in the darkness of the truck, my heart pounding. The headlights reflecting on the house illuminate her just enough for me to make out her features, the ones so familiar to me I could recite them from memory, trace them in my sleep.

There's a set to her jaw, one I've seen before when she's about to do something hard, like attempt a new jump or get lunch with her mom. But her eyes are soft. The way she's looking at me is so tender I can feel it deep beneath my breastbone.

"What did you hear?" I ask.

"You didn't fail me, Beau."

Her words land like a jackhammer straight to my chest, knocking the wind out of me.

I shake my head. "I should have seen it. I should have." I pause, searching for the words. "I should have known you better."

Her smile is sad, and I swear I see a streak of silver in her eyes. "I didn't let you."

My hands reach out on instinct, pulling her close, and she melts into me like ice cream on a summer day, her head finding the crook of my neck she fits perfectly into, her fingers clasping my shirt right above my heart.

"I'm so sorry," she whispers into my skin.

When I shake my head, my stubble catches in her hair. She smells like vanilla. Like Elsie and every good memory I have in my life. "I'm sorry, Els. I'm so sorry I didn't see you, that I wasn't there for you like you needed me to be."

"I didn't let you," she says again.

"Maybe not," I concede. "But I should have tried harder." I pull back from her then, needing to see her face, needing her eyes on mine when I say this next part. "We both broke us, Elsie. It wasn't just you. But we can put us back together again too."

My heart pounds in my throat as I wait for her reply, half-worried she's going to push me away again.

Her eyes hold mine, as familiar to me as the back of my own hand. I've looked into them so many times. On our wedding day, reciting our vows. The first time I met her, when they caught my attention and I knew I was a goner. All the times I've watched her fall apart, unable to look away. When she told me she was pregnant, the first time with hope in her eyes, the second with fear. I've lost myself in them too many times to count, and right now is no different.

"I want that," she says.

My heart stops pounding. It stops in my chest, just like my breath, waiting for her next words.

She sighs, the breath catching the bangs that have grown out to her chin now. "I want you, Beau."

And then she kisses me, and everything in my body roars back to life, like a live wire sparking and catching flame. I think she intends for it to be something soft, sweet, but it changes tempo in an instant when I drag her across the splitting middle seat and into my lap. It's a tight fit now with the belly, unlike all the times we did this before, but she still fits perfectly against me. She still sighs into my mouth, her hands finding my shoulders and kneading the muscles there like she has a thousand times before.

It feels like a dream, like all the best ones I've had the last year, but better. Because this time it's *real*.

"Inside," she says against my mouth.

I'm nodding, fumbling for the door handle. Warm summer air and the sound of crickets chirping in the moonlight fill the cab a second later. She tries to drop to the ground when I slide out, but I hold her against me, unable to let her go, and I feel her smile against my lips.

"So needy," she mumbles between kisses.

I pull her tighter against me, her hips locking against mine, and she gasps, sending a bolt of lightning down my spine.

"You have no idea."

We stumble through the yard and up the porch steps until her back ends up against one of the columns, my mouth trailing down her neck in a way that's distracting us both. We're so close to the door, twenty steps from our bedroom, our *bed*, but I'm suddenly too impatient for even that distance. Not when she's in my arms, sighing, her nails raking up and down my back in a way I hope leaves marks that sting when I shower in the morning. Not when her legs tighten around my hips, drawing us impossibly closer, the friction making my breath stutter, my heart hammer. Not when she's whispering "don't stop" into my ear as I slide my hand up her thigh and toy with the unbuttoned waistband of her jeans that's been lingering in the back of my mind all night.

I want to devour her right here on our front porch, but there's enough sense left in my mind to make me pull back and shake my head against her neck, the spot that smells like vanilla and tastes like sin. "Not until we're inside, Elsie baby."

The way she whines has the hair on the back of my neck standing at attention, my mind swirling in a million different directions.

I catch her earlobe between my teeth, promise her something filthy that has her sliding down my body until her boots hit the creaky wooden porch boards. "Let's get inside."

My eyes linger on her for a moment longer, unable to look away. Her hair is a mess from my hands, and her shirt has ridden up to expose the unbuttoned waistband of her jeans. Moonlight casts her in silver and the bathroom light from inside bathes her in gold. She looks like something precious. Like *mine*.

She's needy, but I want to take my time with her, show her with my body and my words how much I love her, in a way I haven't been able to in a year.

My boots thud against the porch boards as I close the distance between us, slow and purposeful. My hands find the sides of her neck, thumbs brushing against the delicate skin at the base of her throat. Her lips are swollen, her cheeks mustache-burned.

"I love you, Elsie."

My words calm the hungry, frantic look in her eyes, make them soften. Her palms slide up my chest, leaving a trail of warmth in their wake. It's too dark to make out the shades of blue in her eyes, the white flecks that are only visible up close, but I can see enough to know they're intense, blond lashes framing them, kissing her cheeks as she blinks.

She doesn't look away when she says, "I love you too, Beau. I never stopped."

My lips find hers, slow, tasting, determined to break her down the way she's just done to me. I feel raw, exposed, one spark away from catching flame.

She must open the door, because a moment later, we're walking through it, our hands and mouths never leaving each other. I kick it shut behind me and kick off my boots as she does the same. Then we're making our way down the hall, closing the distance between our bedroom and the front door in meandering, sloppy steps.

And then we're at the bed. My hands tremble with anticipation as she lowers herself onto it, body moving with the grace of a dancer, eyes never abandoning mine. For a moment, I just stand there, chest heaving, looking at her under the moonlight cascading through the windows. It makes her skin look silver, her eyes dark as midnight. Just the sight of her makes my heart ache and the palms of my hands itch with the need to touch her. It's been too long, and I want to make this last. I want to make this good.

I move in slowly, erasing the distance between us, one hand falling to her hip, the other tilting her head up at the angle I want. My lips find her, soft and urgent and filled with all the wanting that's been coursing through me for months. A year. Too long. Too damn long.

Her breath hitches as my hands wander, as they push up the hem of her shirt, my mouth following the same trail. Her skin burns beneath my lips. It's soft, delicate. The feel of it has always driven me nuts. Sometimes I'd wake up from dreams, the palms of my hands tingling, and I could swear I was just touching her, feeling her, loving her, only to realize I was alone.

But not right now. This is real. *She's* real.

"Elsie," I murmur into her skin.

She shivers as my mustache scrapes over a ticklish spot. I can't say anything else. Her name just slips from my lips over and over again like a prayer, an enchantment. Something special, something precious. My entire world in one little word.

She squirms beneath the light touch of my mouth, and I can sense her getting frustrated. It makes a smile pull at my lips, and I press one more kiss to a sensitive spot beneath her belly button before she pulls me up until my mouth is on hers. My weight presses her down into the mattress, and she sighs against my lips, hands tightening on the sheets.

When I palm her hip, knead it, a switch in her flips, and her hands start fumbling at my clothes, exposing skin like she's on a mission, tugging and pulling, knuckles scraping against muscles. She's needy, restless, urgent, but I indulge her for only a moment before stilling her hands, pulling back until all I can see is her face in the moonlight.

"Elsie baby," I pant, chest rising and falling against hers. "Slow down."

Her breath is ragged, and she shakes her head against the white sheets, her hair looking like spun gold against them. "I can't." She sounds desperate, pleading, and it makes my skin prickle, my entire body feel like it could combust.

It almost makes me lose whatever semblance of self-control I'm hanging on to like a lifeline, but I shake my head and I press a kiss to her neck, right below her ear. My breath fans against her skin in a way that makes her shiver beneath me, and I want to memorize the feel of it. "We have time," I tell her. "Let me love you."

Maybe it's my words. Maybe it's the way my hands move in slow, comforting circles against her bare skin, but she seems to settle, melt into the mattress, become pliant and languid.

"Okay," she says with a nod.

My mouth finds her ear again, desperate to say the words that I've been holding in for a year, biting my tongue every time I almost let them slip out.

"I love you."

I don't wait for her to respond. I move down her body, removing clothes as I go, whispering the words over and over again into every inch of exposed skin.

But this time, she says it back. "I love you too, Beau."

TWENTY-SIX
ELSIE
JUNE

"Maya, why are you here?"

She's so wrapped up in her dance that she doesn't even notice me until I say her name. She spins on her heel, turning toward me, a guilty expression on her face.

It's early, hours before the studio is supposed to open, but Beau finally decided he couldn't call out of work another day—after the two we spent in bed; he told his family he was feeling under the weather, when I can say with full authority that he was performing at his peak—and I was lonely in the house that now feels too quiet. I don't know how I lived there for months by myself. Beau's presence is so big, so all-encompassing, that when he's gone, everything seems lifeless.

So I thought I'd come to the studio and get some work done. My first recital as a dance teacher is in six weeks, which means

I'll basically be living at the studio until then. What I *didn't* expect was to find Maya putting her spare key to good use.

"I like coming in this early. It's quiet," she says, her chest rising and falling with her heavy breaths.

My brows lift. "Are you often here this early?"

She looks even more contrite, avoiding my eyes.

"Maya," I sigh, and lean against the barre. "You're always the last one to leave at night. Are you telling me you're dancing for over twelve hours every day?"

"I have to!" she protests, hands finding her hips. "Mom won't let me homeschool, so summer is the only time I actually have to dance like I should."

I know where she's coming from. I've been there, so maybe that's why I feel so strongly about this.

"Maya, you have to have other things outside of dance."

"I went to that party," she says, sounding slightly defensive.

"I'm glad," I say, and I am.

She must be able to tell I'm sincere, because she looks up at me through her lashes. She looks so young like this, in tights that she wears over her leotard, her hair pulled back in a somewhat lopsided bun, her cheeks flushed from exertion.

"But I need more from you."

It's the only way I can think to get through to her—using her desire to please me. It's the same reason I listened to Tonya when I was her age. One day she will realize this was really for her, but right now she's too laser-focused on dance to see that there's more to this world outside of it.

Her eyes narrow with skepticism. "What do you need from me?"

"I need you to love something besides just dance."

Now she rolls her eyes, something that makes her look so painfully like a teenager that I have to roll my lips together to hold back my smile. "I don't understand why this is such a big deal."

I shrug. "No, you wouldn't."

She stares at me for a long moment, expression unsure. "Can I keep dancing, or are you going to make me go home?"

I shake my head, pushing up off the barre. My back is sore from my growing stomach and my feet have begun to swell from the summer heat. There's nothing I'd love more than to sit at my desk for the next few hours, sorting through all the paperwork I've been neglecting and planning out choreography in my head, but there's something more important I need to do right now.

"Come on," I say, and motion toward the door.

Maya moves into action, heading for her pile of belongings on the floor in the corner. "Are you taking me home?"

"No," I answer. "Put some pants on before we leave."

"Where are we going?"

I turn and look back at her. She's on the floor, unwrapping the ribbons tied around her ankles, her hair beginning to fall out of her bun and into her face. "Lucky Stars."

Dust kicks up beneath the truck tires as I turn down the familiar road to Lucky Stars Ranch. It's been so long since I've been anywhere but the big house, but it doesn't make it feel any less like returning home after a long stint away. Lucky Stars was the first place I fell in love with that wasn't the studio, and I'm hoping it has the same effect on Maya.

"Why are we going here?" she asks, her arms crossed over her chest, her voice carrying a hint of a pout. Despite it, her gaze is fixed out the windshield, taking in the beauty that is the ranch. No amount of teenage angst has ever been able to stand up against Lucky Stars. Even when Cooper was in high school and itching to leave Larkspur, the ranch was always his north star, guiding him right back here.

"You need something other than dance."

Beside me, she rolls her eyes again. "So you've said."

My mouth twitches as I fight to hold back a smile. No amount of sassiness is going to deter me. "And this is how we fix that."

"What am I going to do, shovel horseshit?"

I level a flat glare at her, and she looks away, embarrassed, cheeks glowing a pretty shade of pink.

"Sorry," she mutters.

"You're not going to shovel horseshit," I say, and her mouth curves into the barest hint of a smile. "You're going to ride."

Her eyes blow wide. "A horse?"

"No, a unicorn." We pass over a bump in the road that I can feel in my stomach. Something I've noticed about being pregnant is that I am so much more aware of my abdomen, of every movement and jolt. It's not bad, just different.

"I've never ridden a horse," Maya says.

It's practically unheard of for someone who grew up in Montana, but I was the same way. When a person's life is devoted to one thing, it doesn't leave room for much of anything else.

"Luckily, I know the best teacher."

Technically, Beau is a horse trainer, but he taught me to ride. And he taught me to love it. The first day he brought me to the ranch, he took me into the stables and introduced me to the horse I'd later come to think of as my own. Her name is Sienna, and Beau picked her for me because she was calm, which eased my jitters, and nearing the end of her working years, so she wasn't getting as much attention or exercise as she was used to.

That first day, I was too nervous to even go near her. Beau placed his hands on my hips and eased me forward until I finally put my hand through the rails of the stall. I barely contained a squeal when her muzzle tickled my palm. My heart raced in my chest, a fact I tried desperately to hide from Beau, something I was sure he'd see as weakness. Because how was it that I could perform fouettés without a second thought, but I was shaking like a leaf in the presence of a *horse*? But he didn't. He was steady, unmoving, his breath warm on my neck as he inched us forward, his strong body bracing mine. It was the first time I'd ever relied on someone other than one of my dance teachers to hold me steady, to keep me safe, to push me past my limits.

It was the first time outside of dance that I'd ever felt that strange mixture of terror and exhilaration, and I immediately wanted more of it.

And now I hope Maya can find it too.

I pull the truck to a stop in front of the stables, the noise drawing Beau's attention from where he is in the circular pen, his eyes finding mine through the windshield. Even from here, I can see the smile light up his face, brighter than the summer sunshine, and it makes my heart triple its speed in my chest.

As we climb out of the tuck, he hops over the rails, landing in the grass with a puff of dirt beneath his boots. He looks *good* like this. I can't believe I forgot what it's like to see him in his element. He usually cleans up a bit before heading home, washing the dust from his hands and face, and on especially hot days, sticking his head under the sink to cool the sweat that's been gathering beneath his hat. But right now, he's rugged and sun worn, and it does funny things to my insides.

"Hey, Maya," he says, flashing her a smile before his eyes light back on me. "To what do I owe the pleasure?" He leans in, planting a kiss close enough to my ear that I shiver despite the June heat. From his smirk, I know he clocked it.

It's not until he lifts his brows that I remember he asked a question, and my face flames. I press my hand to Maya's back, pulling her from where she's standing slightly behind me until she's next to me.

"I want you to teach Maya to ride."

Beau doesn't miss a beat. He doesn't let Maya know it's not really his job, that he's doing something special for her. "Absolutely," he says, meeting her eyes. "Everyone should learn to ride in their lifetime." A grin crests his lips. "And I know just the horse."

Of course he does. It's a gift he has, pairing horses with people. It's probably because he's spent so much time with them, training them for life on the ranch, but I also think it's something he was born with, something intrinsic. His ability to find someone's soul match in a horse.

We follow him into the stable. Maya, who is normally chatty, keeps quiet, her gaze darting around the stalls, some of which are empty, some full. Beau stops in front of a stall. The nameplate beside it says Freckles. The horse inside is beautiful, its signature spotted Appaloosa coat a stunning deep chocolate and white.

"This is Freckles," Beau says, leaning on the stall door, hand reaching inside to pet her between the eyes. His hands look massive against her muzzle.

"Mmm," Maya says beside me, eyes wide as she takes in the large creature before her.

Beau smiles at her over his shoulder. "Come here."

"I'm good here," she says.

I have to suppress the laugh that bubbles in my chest.

Beau raises an eyebrow. "You're not scared, are you?"

Surprise echoes through me, because it's unlike Beau to push in this way. Despite being a horse trainer, he has given lessons to many people over the years, and when faced with a nervous rider, he handles them much like he did with me, although in a less intimate fashion. He's soft-spoken and reassuring, and he makes them feel like there's nothing to be scared of.

But for some reason, he's taking a different approach with Maya.

And to my shock, it works. Her shoulders stiffen, and I watch as resolve hardens her features. "No, I'm not scared of a horse." It's like when she's learning something in class, challenging herself at something new.

Beau's smile widens. "I didn't think so. So come pet her. She doesn't bite." He waits for Maya to slowly move closer, her hand trembling slightly as she holds it out to the horse. "Usually."

Maya rips her hand back, and Beau laughs, the sound warm and rough as it echoes through the barn. It sounds like sandpaper against wood and feels like a finger sliding down my spine.

"Just kidding," he reassures her, bumping her shoulder with his own. "Here, hold your hand out flat and let her sniff it." He demonstrates the movement for her, and Freckles huffs against his palm before moving to Maya's. She's standing stock-still, determination still in every line of her body.

Watching her, I finally see the differences between us, ones I missed for so long. She may be heading down the same path I was, but she's made of stronger stuff than I am. She's more stubborn, but in a way that will serve her well. If she loses dance, I don't think it will destroy her. I don't think she's *capable* of being destroyed. She's someone who will always land on her feet.

But she still needs this, needs time away from the studio, away from dance. She needs to know what else is out there for her if she ever decides that that world is too small for her. And I don't doubt it will be.

I leave the two of them alone, walking quietly through the stable in search of Sienna. I've missed her in a way that I can't even explain. When we moved to Utah, I hadn't realized how much I'd miss the long rides Beau and I went on through the ranch land. We would sometimes do it when we managed to have a day off at the same time in Utah, but riding one of the horses at the ranch he was working on was never the same as riding Sienna. I used to live for the short visits we'd make back home when we could finally be reunited.

I stop in front of her stall, my heart swelling at the sight of her. She's lying down, asleep, so I just stare at her. She's too old now to ride, but I hate all the time I've missed with her the past year when I was avoiding the ranch, avoiding the people and the memories and the crushing feeling of home that I feel every time my feet hit the soil.

I don't know how long I stand there, admiring her, but eventually, Beau ends up at my side. I look up at him, admiring the way he looks right now, wishing I could drag him away to a secluded spot on the ranch and have my way with him.

"Where's Maya?"

"Bathroom," he says. "I think she and Freckles will be a good match. Freckles is a bit temperamental."

My brows shoot up to my forehead. "You know she's never been on a horse before, right? And you're going to have her start on a temperamental one."

He shrugs. "I guess I should say stubborn."

"You didn't give me a stubborn horse," I say, motioning to Sienna.

He shakes his head, a piece of dark hair falling over his forehead. He ditched the hat when we came inside, hanging it on a hook near the door. His hair is a mess, but it only manages to endear him to me more. "No, you didn't need a challenge. You needed something to come easy to you for the first time in your life."

His words dig into my heart, poking at old wounds there.

"You didn't need to work for affection," he says.

"And Maya does?"

"No, but she needs a challenge or she will get bored and head right back to that studio to do something that *does* challenge her."

Once again, I can't help but marvel at his insight, at the way he can glean so much about someone so easily. Guilt pricks at me, because I know that I had to have built my walls so strongly around myself for him to not have been able to breach them fully. I hate myself a little for it. For not trusting pieces of myself to this man who has only ever proven how well he will love me.

"You're good at this," I tell him.

He turns so his body is facing me, a question in his eyes.

"Your job," I clarify.

A laugh rumbles out of him. "Glad to hear it."

"No," I say, smiling despite myself. "I'm just happy that you found the thing you were made to do."

His eyes search mine. "Do you think you found the thing you were made to do?"

When I first started teaching, I would have said no. I would have said I lost the thing I was made to do and this was the closest I could get to it. But now...

"Yeah," I say, my voice soft. "I think so."

He leans in, pressing a kiss to my temple, his hand landing on my hip and squeezing, sending ricochets of warmth all through my body. "I think so too."

TWENTY-SEVEN
BEAU
JULY
TWENTY-FIVE WEEKS PREGNANT

I PASS BY MAYA in Freckles's stall when I go searching the ranch for Cooper. She's brushing the horse down with a gentleness I wouldn't have expected from either of them. It brings a smile to my face. She's still been at the studio before Elsie in the mornings and has worked harder than any other student while rehearsing for the recital, but I've found her at the ranch most days also, even when I don't have time to spare to give her a riding lesson. It makes something tug in my chest, and I know Elsie is feeling relieved by it. She feels like she's finally made a difference as a teacher.

And I want to celebrate it.

Which is why I'm looking for Cooper. He's nowhere to be found on the ranch grounds, but I have a suspicion he may have slipped inside the big house for lunch. Cheyenne stopped by earlier today and dropped off sandwiches from the café where she started working a couple weeks ago.

Sweat beads across my brow from the summer heat as I make my way up the porch steps to the big house, and I lift my hat off my head to wipe it away before entering. There are hooks by the door for me to hang it, and I kick off my boots. Mom doesn't like us wearing our work boots inside, and I got punished enough as a kid for it to be drilled into my brain now as an adult.

The house smells like it always does. Like wood polish and fresh air, since Mom always keeps the windows open when the weather is nice. She reserves the AC for the hottest of days. There are slightly wilted wildflowers in a vase on the entry table. I can imagine Ruby picking them while she and Cooper walked over for breakfast one morning.

Deep voices filter down the hall from the kitchen, and I recognize them as Dad's and Cooper's. I find them sitting at the breakfast table, one much smaller than the dining table, but still large enough to fit all of us. Cooper has a mostly unfinished deli sandwich on his plate, and Dad's is full of crumbs.

They look up when I walk in, their conversation stilling, and I look between them, feeling like I just walked in on something. I raise my brows, but Dad just smiles. "Hey, son. Cheyenne's sandwiches are good. You here for one?"

I nod at my brother. "I was looking for Cooper," I say. "But I'll take one."

Dad's chair screeches across the floor as he pushes back from the table. "Good, I'll leave you two to it. I need to get back to work." He sends Cooper a meaningful look, something tender and even a little proud. "I like your idea, Coop."

Cooper, to my surprise, flushes the slightest bit, his ears going pink, and he looks down at his hands where they're folded in his lap. "Thanks, Dad."

I look between the two of them as Dad exits the kitchen on socked feet. "What was that about?" I ask Cooper when I hear the front door open and shut.

He waves me off with a flick of his wrist and takes a bite out of his sandwich. "Nothing. What's up?"

I want to press him on it, but his cheeks are still pink and he's avoiding my gaze, so I let it drop and grab a sandwich from the fridge before sitting across from him at the table. "I need your help."

He rolls his eyes. "When don't you need my help?"

Ignoring him, I press on, "Elsie has a big recital coming up in a few weeks. Her first one since becoming a teacher, and she's been working nonstop."

"I'm not going to help you convince her she needs to quit working now that she's in a delicate way, Beau."

"Would you shut up?" I ask..

This makes him smile. "What do you need?"

My gaze drifts to the table, my heart feeling too full for my chest. "I want her to know we all support her on this," I tell him, and lift my eyes back up to his.

He's watching me intently, reading every emotion I'm not bothering to hide.

"It's been hard for her to transition into teaching, and her parents have been no help, but she loves it. And I just want her to know we're proud of her."

He nods in understanding.

"So I was thinking maybe we could all go," I continue. "To the recital. And then I could have a party at the house after, just something small to celebrate."

A small grin tilts his lips. "Let's do it."

It feels like a weight has been lifted off my shoulders. "Thanks, Coop." I unwrap the sandwich in front of me and take a bite. It's extraordinarily good, and I wish Cheyenne sticks it out at this place so we can have more of them, but I don't have high hopes.

"Who do you want to come?"

"Just the family, probably. Can you check with Willow and Jesse? I'll ask Morgan and the Dawsons."

"Can do."

My chest rises and falls with a deep breath. "I'm going to ask Elsie's parents too."

He makes a face of distaste, and I can't help but agree.

"I think it would mean a lot to her if they're there," I tell him. "But I think I need to have a frank conversation with them first."

Cooper's brows lift. I don't blame him. Confrontation has never been my strong suit. I'm still trying to figure out when to push and when to stay. But I know this is a time I need to put my foot down, make a few things clear.

"I don't want them coming if they're not going to be supportive," I say, pleased that my voice sounds steady, that none of the anger that's been bubbling inside me since that disastrous meal with them manages to get out. "They need to know that if they're not going to be positive about this for her, then they shouldn't be there at all."

My brother eyes me, and I think I see respect flit across his features. It settles somewhere deep in my chest. "Good, I agree."

"Elsie would probably kill me if she found out."

He flashes me a grin. "Makes it more fun that way."

My truck never looks more decrepit than when I pull it up in front of the Huntzbergers' house. I didn't call before heading over here. Partly because I didn't want to give them time to speculate about why I was coming, but mostly because I didn't want them to mention it to Elsie. I wasn't kidding when I told Cooper she wouldn't be happy with me for talking to them. She would think it makes her look weak, but I'm tired of them making her *feel* weak, and I'd drive across town any day to tell them that.

Still, my heart races a little as I make my way up to their front door.

Diana answers after one knock, her Botoxed face pulling into its best attempt at surprise. "Beau, we weren't expecting you."

I give her a smile. "I know. I was hoping to talk to you and James about something important."

Alarm fills her eyes. "Is Elsie okay?"

Her concern pricks at me. Despite never learning how her daughter needed to be loved, Diana *does* love her daughter. I wish she could figure out a better way to express it, that she could accept Elsie the way she is and not wish for her to be more, that she could learn that her daughter is more than enough as is.

Some of the tension leaves my shoulders, and I soften my voice. "Yeah, she's great. Better than she has been in a long time."

Diana's mouth pinches shut, any tenderness leaving her expression, and she nods, opening the door wider. "Yes, of course. Come in."

I follow her through the house, glad that I changed out of my work boots and into a pair that aren't crusted with mud and horseshit as we make our way across the white marble, our steps echoing in the silence.

James is seated at the dining room table, a laptop open in front of him, and he looks up when we enter, a smile cresting his face. "Well, this is unexpected," he says, pushing up from his chair and coming to shake my hand.

His is soft in mine, and smaller. The hand of a man who works at a desk and not on a ranch. The differences between us have never been more stark, and not for the first time, I wonder what Elsie saw in me when she was raised in a place like this.

"Good to see you, James," I tell him.

"Likewise. What brings you to this side of town?"

Diana is looking between the two of us, and I meet her gaze. "I wanted to speak to you and Diana about something."

She nods. "So you've said. Can I get you a drink?"

I shake my head. "I'm fine, thanks."

James watches the interaction, and when I turn back to him, his expression is more solemn, the one I imagine he wears at the office. He motions to the table. "Let's sit."

We do, and he closes his laptop, then takes a drink from his steaming white coffee mug. Unlike at the big house, theirs all match, and the set costs more than my parents' entire dining collection.

"So what's on your mind?"

I look at them both in turn. "Elsie has a recital coming up."

Diana's eyes blow wide. "She's dancing again?"

My jaw tightens hard enough that my teeth ache, but I keep my voice steady. "No, a recital for her students. She's been working really hard, and I would love to celebrate it since it's her first recital as a teacher."

Elsie's mom looks like she wants to say something, but bites her tongue. Beside her, James says, "Of course we should celebrate. What did you have in mind?"

I don't meet his eyes, instead continuing to hold Diana's stare. "I've talked to my family, and they're all going to come. And I'm planning a small party at our house after. I'd love for you both to be there."

"We wouldn't miss it," James says.

I can hear the sincerity in his voice, but it's not him I'm worried about.

"I want you to be there," I repeat. "But only if you can be fully supportive."

Diana's eyes narrow. "What is that supposed to mean?"

James shifts in his seat, uncomfortable at her sharp tone.

I look at them both in turn before finally settling my gaze back on Diana. "We both know that you haven't agreed with Elsie's decision to start teaching," I say. When she opens her mouth to interrupt, I continue, "But it is *her* decision. And she loves it. She's good at it." I let out a breath, imagining her in the studio with Maya, the way Tonya looks at her with nothing but pride. "She's better than good at it. And this is what she wants to do. So if you believe you can support her in this, then I'd love for you to come."

When I look at James, there's a tenderness and respect in his eyes that I haven't seen before. I wonder if I'm saying the things to his wife that he wishes he could. That thought urges me on.

"If you can't," I say, meeting Diana's eyes one more time. "Then don't bother."

TWENTY-EIGHT
ELSIE
JULY
TWENTY-EIGHT WEEKS PREGNANT

Today is the day of my first recital as a teacher, and I feel like I could throw up. That could also be the acid reflux that's causing me to pop Tums like they're candy every evening. But tonight, at least some of it is nerves.

Backstage in the Larkspur Performing Arts Center is buzzing, girls in tutus and pointe shoes that are only half-laced running around, finishing getting ready. It's warm and smells of perfume and hairspray. It's a little overwhelming, but also a little comforting. It's the behind-the-scenes magic of ballet.

Still, I excuse myself thirty minutes before the first dance, needing to escape to the bathroom, where it's quiet and cold and I can gather myself.

I've been in this exact same bathroom many times before. I performed dozens of recitals here over the years, and before the first one, I found a secluded bathroom in the basement that I think has been mostly forgotten about. It's small and a little dingy, and the light above the sink has flickered without dying for the last twenty years.

But for the first time, when I step into this bathroom, I don't feel panic seizing my chest. I'm breathing normally—or as normally as I can with my diaphragm compressed by the baby taking up my entire midsection. I haven't broken out in a cold sweat or stored an extra tube of mascara somewhere on my person so I can touch up my makeup so no one knows I was crying.

Tonight, there are nerves fluttering in my stomach, and my skin feels a little clammy. My hands are shaking. But I'm *okay*. And God, it feels so damn good.

My phone vibrates in the pocket of my black silk wrap dress. If I thought finding casual maternity clothes was difficult, I severely underestimated how difficult it would be to find a bump-friendly professional yet elegant dress.

When I glance at the screen, I can feel myself smiling down at it.

Beau: I'd say break a leg, but I feel like pregnancy might make recovery a little difficult.

I'm still grinning as I text him back.

Elsie: Yes, because recovery for a broken leg is usually so easy.

Beau: I could make lying on your back with your feet up for a few weeks worth your time.

A hot blush steals into my cheeks. The last few weeks with Beau have been...busy. We've been making up for lost time.

Beau: Are you nervous about tonight?

I'm proud of myself for not even considering lying or brushing off the truth. I text him back immediately.

Elsie: Terrified.

A knock on the bathroom door comes before his reply, and I stand up straight, quickly examining my reflection in the mirror before opening the door. It's Beau, dressed in dark slacks and a crisp white button-down. He even managed to wrangle his hair back into submission, and he shaved off the stubble that's perpetually covering his cheeks.

He looks good, and I'm stunned to find him here.

"How did you know I was here?" I ask, staring up at him. In the dim light of the basement, his eyes are almost black.

He lifts one solid shoulder in a shrug, causing his shirt to stretch to accommodate it. "Tonya told me I could probably find you here."

I'm not even a little surprised that Tonya knows about my secret spot, and I'm even less surprised that she never intruded on it. It makes my heart swell impossibly larger for her.

I motion at the tiny bathroom behind me. "*This*," I say with a flourish, "is my sanctuary."

A smile tugs up one side of his lips. "I can see why you like the place. It's so rare to find a toilet such a lovely shade of yellow."

I glance back at the toilet that was probably white sometime around Nixon's presidency. "I have good taste."

When I look back at him, his grin is even wider. He points at himself. "I know."

I can't help the smile that curls my lips. He looks so handsome like this, and there's a lightness about him that I didn't realize had darkened in the months we were separated. He looks like Beau again, and there's nothing in this world that makes me happier than Beau.

"So why'd you come looking for me?" I ask, leaning on the doorframe that's covered in a layer of chipping white paint.

His eyes soften, and he lifts a hand to push a stray lock of my hair over my shoulder. The feeling of his skin on mine is like dawn brightening in my chest, warmth filling me up from the inside out.

"I thought you might be nervous."

I hold his stare, meaning the words I say next. "A little less so now."

He brightens a little. "Yeah?"

My chin dips in a nod, and I stare into the eyes that are more familiar to me than my own. I've seen them light up as I walked down the aisle toward him on our wedding day. Seen them fill with tears that I refused to shed when we realized I had miscarried. Seen them burn with fire as his body moved against mine, as he whispered for me to let go. Seen them dim and shutter the day I asked him to leave.

Right now they're impossibly tender, full of a love that never wavered, even when I was hurting him. It's the kind of tenderness I can *feel* deep in my chest, that makes me ache with a matching longing.

"Yeah," I tell him, voice soft. "You make me feel brave."

The recital goes off without a hitch. I've never been prouder of sixty young girls in my entire life. I've never been prouder of myself than when I stand on the stage in front of my town and accept the flowers Tonya offers me.

I've stood on stages all over the country and even a few across the world. I've danced on blistered feet and on one occasion, a dislocated hip. I've broken myself down time and time again for this sport, but tonight, when I stood backstage and hugged a twelve-year-old girl who was on the verge of a breakdown because she was scared she was going to mess up in front of the entire town, I finally felt like I'd accomplished the thing I'd been working toward my entire life. The blisters and the sprained ankles and the fad diets and the hours and years I spent devoting myself to dance felt *worth it*.

And when I heard the wolf whistle that Beau has tried and failed to teach me more times than I can count over the noise of the applause, my throat was too thick to breathe. There, in the front row, were the Jenningses. Each and every one of them.

Now, when I appear from backstage, they're all there, smiles on their faces. Beau is holding a bouquet of wildflowers. And beside him are my parents.

The sight of them hits me straight in the chest.

Dad hugs me first, whispering in my ear. "You did great, kiddo. We're proud of you."

I pull back from him, too stunned for words, needing to feel Beau at my side, his steady, unwavering presence.

But before I can go to him, my mom catches my eye. I can't read the expression on her face. "You put on a wonderful performance, Elsie."

Her praise glows in my chest, because I take it for what it is. I know she still wishes I would go back to dancing professionally, but she's *here*, and she's acknowledging my choice. It's a step in the right direction.

I surprise us both by wrapping my arms around her. She smells like she always does, like expensive perfume and the body oil she lathers herself in after every shower. She smells like my mom, and, strangely enough, I'm comforted by it. "Thank you for coming."

She nods when I pull back. "We will be at the party too."

My eyes lock on Beau's. His expression is locked somewhere between pride and concern. He's no doubt wondering what my parents said in voices too quiet for him to hear over the din of young girls being congratulated by their families.

"Party?" I ask, unsure if I'm talking to my mom or Beau.

He moves closer to me, his hand finding its place on my lower back, a comforting touch that I shamelessly lean into. "Something to celebrate," he says.

I stare up at him, unblinking. "The recital?"

A patient smile coaxes his lips, and he tightens his hold on me. "Yeah, Els. We all want to celebrate your first recital."

The house is lit up from the inside, and I can see the decorations all the way from the driveway. Something swells in my chest at the sight of it, and my throat feels thick with an emotion I can't quite name. Something warm and sticky and tender.

Beau and I drove separately since I had to be at the performing arts center hours before the recital, and he beat me home, along with half of the Jenningses, so when I let myself into the house, I'm followed by a loud burst of applause and congratulations.

I'm clutching Beau's flowers to my chest when he makes his way to me, and all I can think to say is "I can't believe you did all this."

He shrugs like it's no big deal. "I can't believe you did all *that*." He shakes his head, a look of wonder on his face. "You're incredible, you know that?"

The feeling in my chest expands and explodes, effervescent glitter sparkling everywhere.

Behind me, the door opens and Tonya enters, grinning maniacally. "We did it, honey!" she shouts, wrapping me in a hug. I barely saw her after the performance, and when I caught her eye while she was talking to a parent, she shooed me off and told me she'd see me in a bit.

I tighten my arms around her, sinking into her familiar warmth. "We did." I pull back, looking into her dark eyes. "Thank you for everything."

She shakes her head, gray curls bouncing in the warm light. "I didn't do anything. You just needed a soft place to land and someone to tell you that you could do it."

Tears prick at the backs of my eyes, but I push them down and give her one last hug before I truly lose it.

"Let's have cake," Jade shouts from somewhere behind me, pulling a grin out of me and making the tears stay firmly in place.

The night feels magical. I eat enough cake to make my stomach hurt, and I sip on apple bubbly while everyone else drinks champagne. My heart swells enough that my chest hurts, and everyone stops to congratulate me.

Cash and Ryder bring me cards they made. Willow put Ruby in a shirt with a picture of my face on it. Cooper gives me a hug and tells me he's proud of me. Clint kisses my temple and Lottie pats my cheek in that comforting yet practical way of hers. Even my parents raise a glass when Beau makes a toast. And Beau never leaves my side. Any time I turn around, he's there, grinning like he's never been more proud of me, his eyes soft, his body warm beside mine.

"Have you picked out what you're going to wear to the baby shower?" Jade asks as I scrape off another icing flower from my cake and spoon it into my mouth.

"No," I groan. "I was too focused on finding something to wear for this. Maybe I'll just repurpose it."

She makes a face. "Maybe we will just go shopping."

A sigh heaves out of me. "I really don't see why I need to get dressed up."

I finally relented when the might of the women in the family harassed me into having a baby shower. I've been completely out of the planning since I've been devoting every waking minute to the recital, so I don't even know the theme or food or games. But I'm assuming it's going to be low key. They may have convinced me that some of the hostility from the town was all in my head, but they've only managed to make me believe that the people of Larkspur are indifferent to me. They may not toilet paper the house, but they're not going to purchase diaper cream off my baby registry either.

"Because you can no longer get away with unbuttoned jeans," Jade replies.

She's right. They're no longer making it over my hips. I've been relying on Beau's boxer shorts and plain tees that barely cover my growing stomach.

"Fine, we'll go shopping, but I still don't see the point when it's just going to be family there."

She rolls her eyes. "Your pessimism is astounding."

"Your optimism is unrealistic," I tell her.

She only shakes her head. "You'll see, Els. Look around you." She motions at the people gathered around my house, too many to fit on the furniture. "You're as much a part of this town as any of us."

TWENTY-NINE
ELSIE
AUGUST
THIRTY WEEKS PREGNANT

"Aren't you glad I made you go shopping?" Jade asks as I stand in front of the mirror in my bedroom. I'm wearing a flowy floral chiffon dress that we found at a boutique in Bozeman. It's girly and whimsical and makes me feel more put together than I have in months. In short, I love it.

Beside me, Jade is in a pale blue sheath sundress that I would kill to be able to fit into again. She found it in my closet. It's one of the few dresses I reserved for when Beau and I would go on dates or to functions back in Utah. I always liked how it looked on me—blue is one of my colors—but it looks even better against her tan skin and rich brown hair.

"Yes, actually," I tell her.

She grins. Her skin has darkened from all her time in the sun this summer, making her look bronzed and shimmering.

My best friend is gorgeous. I'm struck with how good it is to be able to see her like this again. I missed sharing closets and getting a random coffee together when I was in Utah. My life then feels so distant now, in a way I would have never expected when I was first injured and we decided to move back. Then, it felt like I was cutting away a piece of myself, moving home with my tail tucked between my legs after failing at the one thing I was always destined to do. Now it feels like regaining a piece of magic I didn't realize I was missing so badly.

Jade catches my gaze in the mirror, and I wonder if she can read my expression. The thought doesn't scare me as much as it used to. She finishes up applying her lip gloss and passes me the tube. It's probably a little gross to share, but we've always done it. I coat my lips and can't help but grin at the fact that she's still using the exact same kind we wore to her and Beau's senior prom. Jade is loyal, even to makeup brands.

"You ready?" she asks, giving me a final once-over.

"Let's do this," I say, and slip my feet into a pair of strappy sandals that have started to become too tight with the way my feet and ankles have been swelling the last few weeks. This is probably the last time I'll be able to wear them this summer.

Summer sunshine greets us as we step outside and climb into the truck. The air smells sweet and the sun is pleasantly warm against my skin. In my stomach, the baby moves around, and I wonder if she can feel it too. If she's going to enjoy the sun and summer as much as I do. The thought makes me smile, and I press a hand to my stomach. She kicks it in answer.

Other than the location—Lucky Stars—I know nothing about the baby shower, and I'm glad for it. Life has been hectic enough lately without adding something else on my plate. It's starting to hit me that I'm going to have a baby in just a few short months, that I'm ten weeks away from holding her in my arms, looking at the little perfect mixture of my favorite person and me.

And I think the nesting urge is kicking in, because I drove myself to the hardware store the other day and picked up paint samples for the nursery. After the baby shower today, Beau and I plan to do our final shopping and get started on it. A smile threatens to come loose at the thought of him finally getting to take down the bed in the guest room. Since moving back into our room, he's made his hatred for the piece of furniture known.

"How have things been at the ranches this summer?" I ask Jade over the noise of the wind whooshing through the cracked windows, letting in the warm summer air. She typically works at Lucky Stars and several other smaller ranches in the area, and summers tend to be crazy for her.

"Busy," she says, hands gripping the wheel. "It's breeding season and rodeo season, so I've been swamped with prenatal visits and health checks." She casts a quick glance at me and shrugs. "You know, the usual."

I nod, understanding. Summer at a ranch is never slow, and Beau has been there from sunup to sundown most days, but it's especially busy for a large animal vet like Jade.

"I think Cooper is up to something too," she says, catching my attention.

I raise a brow, watching as her hair catches in the wind and blows around the cab. It's gotten so long in the year since I've been home. "What do you mean?"

"I caught him wandering around a few random places on the ranch. He was carrying a notebook, and I think he even had a spreadsheet," she says, incredulous. "And when I asked him about it, he wouldn't tell me anything."

"I mean," I respond, "him not telling you something isn't exactly new behavior."

Jade and Cooper have been at odds for as long as I've known them. From what Beau has told me, they were like this even as kids. They were always competing for the same things, and Jade would resent when Cooper would win with minimal or no effort. Then, when they were adults, she struggled her way through vet school and made a name for herself in a male-dominated career while he turned down a full scholarship to university to go pro in bull riding. I think she thinks he doesn't care about things and that he hasn't worked for anything he's gotten. And he thinks she's a stick-in-the-mud who judges people too harshly.

I think they both have blinders on when it comes to one another. They're incapable of seeing how great they both are, how *similar* they are. It makes family gatherings loud and combative, but we're all used to it.

"Maybe," she concedes. "But I still think he's hiding something."

"Cooper is an open book."

"Cooper tells people all the things about himself that no one wants to know and keeps all the things he doesn't want people to see very close to his chest," she replies, turning down the road that leads to Lucky Stars.

Her words take me by surprise. Mostly because they make sense, but I've never noticed it before. But she's kind of right. Know your enemy, I guess.

"Enough about Cooper Jennings," she says.

I can't help but laugh. "You brought him up."

She shakes her head. "I've reached my quota of him for the month."

"August *just* started."

She lets out an aggrieved sigh. "And yet, here we are."

Dirt and gravel crunch beneath the tires as we turn down the familiar road to Lucky Stars, passing under the gate with the familiar ranch logo of a lasso forming three stars, one for each of the kids that Beau's great-great-great-grandfather had. The sight of the rusting metal stars always brings a smile to my face, and today is no different. I love the history here, the legacy, and I love that we're celebrating the next generation of Jenningses here today.

The first thing I notice when we pull up in front of the big house is the number of cars parked outside. Dozens. Too many for me to count. Women are climbing out of truck cabs, heading toward the tables that have been set up in the shade of the big house. It looks like a garden party, with pastel tablecloths and flowers lining every surface. Finger sandwiches stacked on a long table off to the side, tiny desserts, and a cake covered in summer berries. A mirror painted with the words "Welcome to the family, little one" in swirling script.

"This can't all be for me," I breathe, the words feeling choked in my throat. My heart is pounding, my stomach tightening reflexively. When I rip my gaze from the party in front of me and look at Jade, she's wearing a soft, patient smile.

"Els, I told you this town would show up for you."

"Not like this." But even as I say it, the words obviously ring false. Because here they are. Women I've barely met at church potlucks and Fourth of July barbeques. Parents of students I teach at the studio. Beau's teachers from high school and his babysitter from childhood. People I've never seen before or only know in passing.

All of them here for me, even after all the hurt I caused. It feels like a balloon filling up in my chest, too much air and close to bursting.

"I don't know what to say," I whisper to Jade, my eyes drifting back to the party. In the distance, I see my mom talking to Cheyenne. Lottie bringing out another doily-lined plate from the big house. Tonya making one of the studio moms laugh.

"Luckily, almost everyone will ask you one single question about how you're feeling and then offer you unsolicited advice about child rearing," she says, shrugging. "At least that's how it was at my cousin's baby shower last year."

My laugh pushes back the tears threatening to spill, and I look at my best friend. Her brown eyes are soft, her smile tender. "Thank you for making me do this," I tell her.

She nudges my shoulder with her own. "Anytime. Now let's go eat some chicken salad. I was here yesterday while Lottie was making it, and she wouldn't let me have any. It's all I've been thinking about since."

"I bet she let Cooper have some," I say, climbing out of the truck, careful not to let my dress get stuck.

Jade glares in my direction. "Don't even start."

THIRTY

BEAU
AUGUST
THIRTY-THREE WEEKS PREGNANT

"You should really just let me do this and you watch," I try to tell Elsie for the fifth time this morning, but from the stubborn tilt of her chin, I know she isn't going to listen.

"I can paint, Beau."

"There's a lot more to do than just paint." The guest room, the room I slept in for far too many months, is going to be the nursery. I moved all my stuff back into our room a couple of weeks ago, but the furniture is still in there. It needs to be taken apart and moved out before we can paint and begin to set up the nursery furniture and decor. It took three trips to bring home all the stuff gifted to us at the baby shower, and it's all been sitting in random corners of the house, waiting for us to get started assembling and organizing it. And as often as I've tried to convince Elsie that I can handle the heavy lifting, she refuses.

"I can move a mattress," she says this with an eye roll, but I don't miss the way she absentmindedly massages her lower back. She's been trying to hide the pain from me for the last few weeks. Like I don't know that she has a growing human sitting on her nerves and compressing her organs.

"Not according to your obstetrician."

Elsie waves a hand dismissively, avoiding my gaze. "What does she know?"

I heave out a sigh and open the bedroom door. It's been weeks since either of us has been in here, and it's already developed a closed-off, musty smell that will soon disappear when I prop open the windows to let the summer breeze in.

It takes me a moment to realize Elsie has stopped in the doorway. I crane my neck over my shoulder to look at her as I push up the window. She's staring at the wall above the bed.

"The paintings," she breathes.

Only now do I remember them there. I can still feel the cold air of the attic as I climbed into it late one evening while she was still at the studio. The cobwebs that clung to my clothes. The dust that had gathered on their surfaces. I remember the tight feeling in my chest as I looked at them, unsure of whether we'd ever get back to the people who had painted them, drunk on cheap wine and handsy, laughing as we made love after returning home and hanging them on the wall.

We didn't make our way back to those people, but I'm not sure I would want to. I like who we are now so much more.

I finish pushing the window open and turn to face her, feeling the breeze rush in, catching the curtains and wrapping them around my thighs. "I got them out of the attic," I say, stuffing my hands in my jeans pockets. They're worn, soft against my skin.

Her eyes peel from the paintings and settle on mine, bright blue in the light peering through the window. "Why? When?"

My shoulders lift in a shrug. Maybe I should be embarrassed that I wanted them back, that I wanted to fall asleep beneath them, but I'm not. "A few days after you told me you put them up there. I…" I trail off. "I missed them."

Her eyes settle on the paintings once more, her expression softening. She looks beautiful like this, her hair catching in the breeze, her skin golden from the sun, her entire body relaxing like she's at peace, something neither of us was sure she'd ever be capable of feeling again. "Yeah, I think I did too."

I move to stand beside her, the bare skin of her arm brushing beneath the sleeve of my shirt as I reach for her hand. She entwines it with mine, and I can feel her pulse against my palm, beating in rhythm with mine. We stare at the paintings for a long moment, and I wonder if she still looks at hers and thinks it's ugly, or if she sees what I do. If she remembers the way our teeth clinked together when we laughed in our bedroom after hanging them, too drunk to unbutton her jeans. If she remembers ending up with my painted fingerprints staining her ribs because the edges weren't completely dry. If she remembers us touching up the paint on the wall in our apartment when we moved out for the same reason. If she remembers what it felt like to make something together, to be the people we once were. If she likes who we've become even more.

"We should put them back in our room," she says.

My heart skips a beat, my chest filling up with something that feels like bubbly champagne, popping and exploding.

I try to steady my voice when I ask, "Yeah?"

She smiles up at me, so bright in this dark room, the one that always felt so lonely. The one that will never feel like that again. "Yeah. And maybe after the baby is born, we can have a date night and paint some terrible pictures of her to hang in here to embarrass her with until the end of time."

A grin splits my mouth and the warm bubbly spreads from my chest, invading every part of my body until it feels like sunshine in my veins. "That sounds perfect."

We take the bed apart, and I manage to move the mattress on one of Elsie's frequent bathroom breaks. She acts like she's annoyed, but I know she isn't, not when every time I look at her, she's holding back a smile. I know she thought we wouldn't get here. Us, but mostly the baby. That this pregnancy would end the same as the last. That she held herself back from being excited, but that she's finally allowing herself to now.

It pours out of her, filling the room with its warmth.

We chose a muted blue color for the walls, one that matches the summer sky outside. It was Elsie's choice, and I couldn't have been happier with it. This room felt so dark when I lived in it. The walls were a medium gray color that we had never gotten around to changing after we moved in. The furniture and decor were mismatched pieces we'd acquired over the years. Nothing about it felt intentional or personal. It felt lifeless.

And I couldn't be more excited to bring new life into it.

Elsie paints, and we both pretend I don't notice the way she stops every few rolls to place a hand on her lower back. I have to suppress a smile each time, knowing that she won't stop, no matter what I say.

I cover three walls in the amount of time it takes her to do one, but we don't acknowledge that either.

We talk as we paint. I ask her about the lunch she had with her mom last week, the one Diana initiated. It surprised us both, and I offered to go with her, but she went alone. It went better than either of us expected. There's still tension between them. Diana still thinks she knows best, but she's trying, and that's more than she did before.

We discuss baby name options. We haven't found anything that sticks out to either of us, and I think we both thought we would by now. Elsie says she feels like time is closing in, but I tell her I think we will know when we meet her, so we leave it at that.

She asks if Cooper has been acting weird and tells me about her conversation with Jade. I tell her about the comment Dad made, the way Cooper brushed it off. We both agree something is going on, but that Cooper will tell us when he's ready.

Time moves at an easy pace, and before we know it, we've finished all the walls, the color making the entire room feel like summer. We settle on the carpet that will need a good cleaning before we begin to move in furniture and admire our handiwork. It already looks better in here, and the sight of it soothes that part of me that was broken for so long.

Elsie leans her head on my shoulder, sleep tugging at her eyes. She hasn't been sleeping well the past few weeks, and she's gotten progressively more uncomfortable as her hands and feet have been swelling, but she refuses to slow down.

"Let's take a picture," she says. Mumbles, rather. She mentioned something about a headache earlier, and I wonder if it's lingering despite the pain reliever she took.

I pull out my phone from my back pocket. "Of what?"

Her head moves on my shoulder, her gaze catching mine. There's a slight tilt to her lips, a tired smile. "Of us. We don't have any pictures during the pregnancy."

I smile back and lift the phone to snap a photo of us. She looks so exhausted, but she's beaming too, the sun slanting through the window and making her skin look golden.

She takes the phone from my hand, examining the picture, expression wistful. "I wish we had taken more. I've taken a few bump pictures, but I...wasted so much time during this pregnancy. I didn't document it because I was too stuck in my head." Her voice is small, regretful, and it makes my chest feel tight.

My hand covers hers, retrieving the phone to click on an album before returning it to her. "I've been documenting it." I watch her as she scrolls through the album. There's a look on her face I can't quite decipher and silver lining her eyes. A fat drop crests her eyelid, rolling slowly down her cheek.

The album is full of photos and videos, candid ones I've been taking of her for months. Memories for us, sure, but also living proof for our daughter that even when things were rocky between us, that even if we had never figured things out, *she* was always loved.

Elsie stops scrolling and clicks on the first video in the album. My voice fills the empty room. "Hey, baby, it's me, your dad. I wanted to introduce myself now because you'll never know me when I'm not a dad. And you'll never know your mom when she's not your mom. She's going to be the best mom in the entire world. I just know it, baby. But I want you to see her now, too, when she's just the best woman in the world."

The camera flips, and then Elsie is on the screen, humming as she cooks dinner. She's so inside her head that she doesn't hear my whisper. "Isn't she beautiful? I can't believe she's growing you *right now*."

The video ends and Elsie clicks on another. This one was taken at her studio. In the video, she's demonstrating something to Maya, and the girl watches her with rapt attention, soaking in her every instruction.

"Hey, baby, it's me, Dad," my voice says. "But enough of me. Look at your mom. She's dancing. I wish you could have seen her dancing on the stage, but I think she's even better here. She's the best dancer in the entire world. I know she probably wishes you could have seen her dancing in a company, but I'm glad you'll get to see her like this, the way she lights up as she teaches these kids about the thing she loves most."

She scrolls through more photos and videos, dozens, her tears falling freely now. When she speaks, her voice is thick. "I can't believe you were doing this the whole time."

I wrap my arm around her, pulling her body into mine. She fits so perfectly here. It makes me wonder how we went so long without it, how we ever felt whole when we were apart.

"I was...terrible to you," she says, voice tinged with something like regret. "And you were making videos, talking about how perfect I am."

"Elsie," I breathe, and turn my body so I'm facing her fully. Her cheeks are tearstained, her eyes red. She looks heartbroken. "You were never terrible to me."

"I was," she says, nodding vigorously. "I asked you to leave and then I let you come back, but I still didn't let you in. I held you at arm's length for so damn long and you *still* loved me. I don't—" She sighs, wipes hard beneath her eyes. They're bloodshot, the skin around them red. "I don't deserve you."

"Elsie," I say more firmly, needing her to understand. "You were hurting, and grieving, and *broken*."

She just shakes her head again, pushing to her feet and pacing the room that smells like paint. "That's not an excuse."

"No, it's not," I agree, propping my forearms on my bent knees as I watch her. Her hair is falling down her back in messy waves from the clip she was wearing. Her feet are bare and her

T-shirt doesn't fully cover her protruding bump. "But it's the truth. You were hurt and you hurt me."

She stops pacing, her eyes connecting with mine, hard and so unforgiving toward herself. There's a crack in her voice when she says, "I was broken and I broke us."

I stand and move closer to her, but she backs away until she has nowhere else to go, her body just a hairbreadth from the wet walls. I have no such qualms. I place my hand beside her head, blue paint staining my palm, and lean in until we're nose to nose.

"You were healing and you put us back together."

"It doesn't erase what I did," she whispers, voice cracking again.

"Maybe not," I say. "But we're past it now. I've forgiven you. Now you have to forgive yourself."

Her eyes meet mine, blue as the skies outside the window. "I don't know if I can."

I drop my hand from the wall to land on her lower back, pulling her closer to me, erasing the last little bit of distance between us. "You want to know what I thought when I saw those paintings today?" I wait for her nod, then continue. "I was thinking about how, when I hung them up in here, I was praying we could get back to those people, to the ones who made those paintings."

"Me too," she says, and it sounds raw, like it was scraped out of her.

I shake my head, her nose brushing against mine with the movement. "But then I realized I don't want to be them again. I *love* who we are now, who we've become through all of this. It hurt, but we're better for it, Els. You have to see that. We may have broken, but when we put ourselves back together, we made something more beautiful than what we were before."

She blinks up at me, looking wrecked, but I see a sliver of hope behind her eyes, how desperate she is to believe what I'm saying. "Do you really believe that?"

My lips find hers, pressing against them in the barest touch, letting her feel my words as I say them. "I do, Els. I really do."

She nods, mouth brushing mine. "Okay."

I pull back enough to see her eyes, enough for her to be able to read the sincerity in mine. "You'll be able to forgive yourself. It might take time, but we have endless amounts of it."

THIRTY-ONE

ELSIE
SEPTEMBER
THIRTY-SIX WEEKS PREGNANT

"Beau, I'm going to be fine, I promise. It's not that big of a deal," I say, turning the truck down the street toward my doctor's office.

He lets out a frustrated sigh, and I can imagine him pushing a hand through his hair. "Yes, it is. I haven't missed any appointments."

Beau and Cooper left early this morning to pick up a rescue horse from a town two hours away. He would have had plenty of time to be back for the appointment if the trailer hadn't gotten a flat tire on the way there or if they hadn't run into trouble loading the horse up when they arrived. Apparently, he was even more skittish than they had anticipated, and they had to take things much more slowly, meaning Beau is just now on his way back to Larkspur.

"I promise it's fine. They're just going to check my vitals and do a group B strep test. I'll be in and out in no time," I tell him. "Please don't beat yourself up over this."

The line is quiet for a long minute, and I know he's trying to think of a way to argue with me, but I've used his own line against him. For the past few weeks, since I had the meltdown in the nursery, any time I start thinking about the last year, about everything we've been through, he tells me I can't keep beating myself up over the past, that we have to move forward to our new future or something along those lines.

"Fine," he huffs. "But can you please at least write everything down so I know what I missed?"

My lips roll together to hold back my smile. "Yes, of course."

"And I wrote down some questions I wanted to ask her. I'll send you a photo."

"Everything will be fine," I promise one last time as I pull into the doctor's office.

"You're right. Everything's fine," he repeats, and I can tell it's more to himself. "I'll be home as soon as I can, okay?"

"See you soon. Love you," I tell him, and end the call before pulling into a parking spot. I pull down the sun visor to check my reflection in the mirror before heading in. My face has started to swell in the last two weeks, along with my hands and feet, even more so than they were before. The straps of my sandals—the only shoes I could fit into this morning—are digging painfully into my feet. The summer sunshine beats down through the window, baking me in the cab of the truck and making sweat glisten on my brow. Not exactly the pregnancy glow I was promised. I look as uncomfortable as I feel, and I'm not sure how I'm supposed to make it through another four weeks of this.

But on the plus side, I'm too uncomfortable to be nervous. For the first time in this pregnancy, I don't feel the rush of nerves that I usually do when I sit in this parking lot, preparing myself to go inside.

Cool air hits me as I walk into the doctor's office, and I bask in it. My truck is too old for the AC to get as cold as I'd like it, and I've spent the hottest weeks of summer dreading riding around in it. To my surprise, the woman at the desk smiles at me as I approach. I wonder if she's been doing this all along, if I was just projecting the looks of indifference. I allow myself to fully look at her instead of avoiding her eyes like usual, and shock ripples through me as I realize she was at my baby shower. She must be a friend of the Jenningses.

"Good afternoon, Elsie. How are you feeling?"

I blink, taken aback, and then feel myself relax and smile back at her. "Good," I say, and then laugh a little. "Actually, I'm exhausted and hot."

A chuckle rumbles out of her. "I'm sure. I had my youngest in August, and I was miserable all summer." She gives me another warm smile. "I'll let the doctor know you're here."

My name is called a few minutes later, and I prop a hand on my back and waddle through the door the nurse has open for me, my feet screaming as the sandals cut into my skin. I thought my days of sore muscles and blisters and foot pain were over, but I underestimated pregnancy and the toll it would take on my body.

We go through the routine of taking my weight—which I still avoid looking at—and head back into a room. I take a seat in the chair next to her small desk against the wall, thankful to be off my feet once more.

"How are you feeling?" the nurse asks. I've had her before, and she's always been kind. She's younger than me, fresh-faced and always wearing a smile.

"Swollen and tired," I tell her. "And I've been getting these terrible headaches for the past couple of weeks. They were originally getting better with medicine, but now even that's not touching it."

A look of alarm passes over her face, but it's gone so quickly I almost think I've imagined it. She types something into the laptop and reaches for the blood pressure cuff. "I'm sorry. That sounds miserable. Let's go ahead and get your blood pressure."

She hesitates when she goes to wrap it around my arm, her eyes fixed on my hand. Last week Beau had to massage my hand with lotion to get my wedding ring off, and I haven't put it back on since. My hand feels bare.

"Swollen hands?" she asks, glancing up at me. I nod, and she looks back down, this time at my feet. "Feet, too, it looks like."

"Very," I say. "These are the only shoes that still fit."

She nods absentmindedly and slips the blood pressure cuff onto my arm before pressing her stethoscope to my elbow. The band tightens around my arm, the sound of her squeezing the ball the only sound in the room. I can feel the blood rushing in my arm and even more clearly, the feeling of the baby kicking me right in the rib. It brings a little smile to my face.

Until I see the nurse's expression change. "163/111."

My heart stops, and I look at the pressure gauge. "That can't be right." My blood pressure has always been a little elevated, most likely due to my anxiety, but never enough to require medication. Over the last few appointments, it's been slightly higher, but my doctor said it wasn't high enough to be concerned.

But this number is critical.

"I'll go get the doctor," the nurse says, pushing up from her chair and flashes me a smile. "No need to worry."

She leaves me alone, and all the anxiety that has been slowly diminishing over the course of the pregnancy comes back with a vengeance, threatening to cut off my oxygen. I need Beau, and of course, it's the one time he isn't here.

I can feel my heart pounding in my chest, my lungs burning, and the walls seem to be closing in. My palm lands on my stomach, a protective instinct I don't quite understand. In the quiet of the room, my breath comes in loud gasps.

But for some reason, the panic doesn't fully take over. Not like before. It stays thrumming in my chest, present enough for me to feel it, but distant enough for me to use every ounce of mental strength I have to push against it.

"It's going to be okay," I whisper to myself over and over again, but I don't hear it in my own voice. I hear it as if Beau is next to me, whispering it in my hair, his hand making soothing circles on my back.

I look down at my stomach, watching as a little foot or hand pushes against it. "It's going to be okay, baby. I promise."

The door opens, wrenching my attention away from my stomach. The doctor gives me a reassuring smile, but I can see the look of concern lingering beneath it.

"So your blood pressure has shot up," she says, sitting in the chair the nurse vacated and opening her laptop. "I think you know that was a seriously high number."

I nod, my throat tight.

Her eyes soften as she looks at me, and she drops her hands from her keyboard, settling them in her lap. "The good news is this isn't anything we haven't seen before. We're going to run a test to check for protein in your urine. If it's present, it would be an indicator of preeclampsia, which is a severe condition that can lead to complications for both you and baby."

My heart rate quickens, and I can feel it everywhere in my body.

"Luckily, if that's the case, you're in the best place. While we wait on the results of your urine test, we will do a Doppler to check on baby and hear her heartbeat. I want to make sure she's doing okay, and I think that will ease some of your fears too. Sound good?"

An uneven breath whooshes out of me, and all I can manage is a nod.

She finally looks around the office. "Where is Beau today?"

"Two hours away, picking up a rescue horse."

The doctor smiles then. "Of course he is." She's a few years older than Beau and Cooper, closer to Morgan's age, but she has known the Jenningses for most of her life. "Well, I'll escort you to the restroom, and when you're finished, you can come back here and we will hear the heartbeat."

I follow her out of the room and use the bathroom before returning. We've listened to her heartbeat on the Doppler at every appointment in the second and third trimesters, but hearing the *whoosh-whoosh* of it never gets old, especially today. It eases some of the pounding in my chest, the thoughts running on a loop in my mind.

And then she leaves me alone. I stare at the phone in my hand, wondering if I should tell Beau yet, but I decide to wait. He's two hours away, and he will only worry. Until I have concrete news, he doesn't need to know just yet.

The room is quiet, and I listen to the clock ticking on the wall, my hand pressed against my stomach, feeling my baby move around inside it. It's crazy how clearly I can feel her movements now, when just a few months ago, they were barely there flutters, butterfly wings brushing against my insides. Now, I can see the outline of her foot even through the fabric of my T-shirt.

Beside me, the door opens once more, and the doctor returns. I can't read her expression, but my heart skips a beat in my chest regardless.

"There was protein in your urine sample. We're going to go ahead and send you over to labor and delivery to be induced. Congratulations, Elsie. You're having a baby."

THIRTY-TWO
BEAU
SEPTEMBER

"WE'RE GOING TO WRECK, and then you're really not going to make it," Cooper says from the passenger seat. I've been driving back to Larkspur as fast as humanly possible with a quadruped-filled trailer attached to my truck since I got the call from Elsie almost two hours ago. Cooper insisted we pull over for lunch, so I was in a fast-food parking lot when she called and told me they were taking her to labor and delivery. Cooper has kept up a steady stream of conversation since, probably in an attempt to keep me calm, but I think this is the first thing that's actually registered.

He's right. I need to get back home, but I also need to do it safely. I lift my foot off the gas ever so slightly. I have a skittish horse in the trailer, and driving recklessly is only going to make him harder to deal with when we get back to the ranch.

I heave out a breath, and some of the tension in my shoulders relaxes just a bit. "I'm freaked out," I admit into the quiet of the cab. "I missed one single appointment, and *this* happened." I risk a glance at my brother.

He's watching me calmly, a look of understanding on his face. "I was terrified when Willow went into labor," he says.

Surprise ripples through me. I wasn't aware that my brother was scared of anything.

A laugh rumbles out of him at the look of shock I must be wearing. "Any man who says they're not terrified when their partner goes into labor is lying."

"I just need to be there with her," I tell him.

"You'll get there." He's quiet for a minute. "And when you do, you'll be scared as hell but also relieved and also feel like you're going to throw up just a little bit."

This pulls a smile from me.

"But birth is so cool. And Elsie is strong. She and the baby are going to pull through like champs, okay?"

I squeeze the wheel a little harder, my knuckles turning white. "What if she doesn't?" I ask the question into the void, refusing to look at him. The fear has been nagging me since she called, since I heard the waver in her voice. Since I pulled up the web browser on my phone and looked up what we're dealing with. Preeclampsia. It terrified me. Most cases turn out fine, but the risks, the complications put a fear in me like I've never felt before.

"I just got her back," I tell him, my voice cracking. "I just got her back. I can't lose her, Coop."

"You're not going to lose her." He sounds calm but firm. Steady. He sounds like a father. He sounds like *our* father, and it soothes some of the jagged edges of fear inside me. "At this time tomorrow, you're going to have a healthy wife and baby." He pauses. "Well, hopefully."

I cut a sharp look at him, and he laughs.

"What? Labor can take forever."

I slump against the steering wheel. "God, Cooper. Choose your words a little more carefully next time."

He chuckles again. "They're going to be okay, Beau. And you're going to be a dad."

"I'm going to be a dad," I whisper.

Elsie is uncomfortable by the time I finally make it to her hospital room. To my surprise, everyone in my family except my father—who was waiting for us at Lucky Stars to assist Cooper with the horse so I could head to the hospital—is already in the labor and delivery waiting room. I brush by them, telling them I'll report back as soon as I see Elsie. Then I run up to her room, my heart thumping in my chest.

Jade is there with her, helping to adjust the pillow Elsie is leaning on. Elsie's face is scrunched in pain, but when she sees me, everything in her body softens with relief. "You're here."

"I'm here," I say, and move to the side Jade isn't on, grabbing her hand and pressing a kiss to it. "I'm sorry it took so long."

She shakes her head. "It's okay. I'm just glad you're here now."

"I told her I could deliver the baby if you didn't get here," Jade offers. "How much harder can it be than a calf or foal?"

"Beau isn't delivering the baby," Elsie tells her in a tone that makes me think this isn't the first time she's said it.

Jade shrugs. "Offer still stands."

"Thanks for being here with her," I tell Jade.

She smiles. "Of course."

I look back at Elsie, relieved at how much more relaxed she looks now than she was when I walked through the door. I can't believe my presence did *that*, and it makes me want to strangle myself even more for not being here before.

"My entire family is in the waiting room," I say.

Elsie's eyes widen. "Why?"

A smile cracks my lips. "Because they have no sense of boundaries."

She shakes her head, managing a smile of her own. "They should go home. I'm only a centimeter dilated. This is going to take a while."

"I'll try my best."

Jade pushes to standing, reaching for Elsie's hand to give it a squeeze. "I'll handle them. You guys handle the having a baby part."

"Thank you for being here."

Jade's expression softens. "Of course, Els. Always." She looks at both of us in turn then. "Keep me posted, okay?"

Elsie nods. "I'll send selfies the whole time."

"Make sure to get one while pushing."

"Definitely," Elsie says with a smile.

Jade gives her hand one last squeeze before leaving.

As soon as she's gone, Elsie's face pinches in discomfort. She lets out a breath through her nose. "Contraction."

Her hand tightens on mine, and I grip hers back, breathing with her, trying to funnel my strength into her as best as I can. A minute later, it's over, and the tension releases from her body.

"I'm not a fan of those."

"Have they given you the epidural yet?" We talked through her birth plan together and with her doctor over the last few appointments. She told the doctor she planned to get an epidural, but that she wanted to wait until her contractions were really uncomfortable.

Elsie shakes her head. "Not yet. I want to hold out a little longer."

"Okay." I look around the room. It's larger than I expected and less clinical. There is, of course, all the medical equipment—the hospital bed and the monitors Elsie is hooked up to—but there's also a couch and a chair that can convert into beds, a sink, and cabinets that I would guess hold extra linens. "What can I do?"

When I look back at Elsie, she's smiling softly. "Nothing yet. You being here is nice enough."

Guilt pricks through me again. "I'm sorry, Els. I hate that I wasn't here."

She grabs for my hand again, holding it tight as she looks into my eyes. "Don't beat yourself up, remember? I'm just glad you're here to do this with me now." She pauses, her eyes going a little misty. "We're having a baby, Beau. It's really happening."

All the stress and anxiety from the last few months evaporates because she's right. We're *here*, doing it. In a day or two, we're going to be holding our baby in our arms, looking at this perfect thing we created.

"Yeah, Els, we are."

The next hours pass in a blur. Elsie insists I eat even though she's not allowed to since she's getting magnesium through an IV to prevent seizures from preeclampsia. It makes her uncomfortable and nauseous, and although the epidural she gets eventually helps with her pain, it doesn't help with those symptoms. It makes the time pass slowly, and I hate seeing her become more and more miserable.

I text updates to my family and hers. I assure Jade that everything is progressing and let her know how far along she is after cervical checks. I ask the nurses for refills on ice chips the second Elsie finishes her cup of them and sneak bites of protein bars when she isn't looking, even though she's the one who texted my mom to bring them to me.

Night falls and Elsie manages to sleep. I do too, I think, but I mostly sit in the chair and stare at her, check her monitors to make sure her blood pressure doesn't get too high and her vitals look good. I take a photo of her in the early morning light and add it to the album I've been compiling for the baby. I want her to see how strong her mom is right now, when she's doing the hardest thing she will ever do.

Throughout the morning, Elsie's labor intensifies. The sun slants through the windows, indicating the passing of time, as we hunker down. My hand is sore from Elsie's hold on it, but I'd let her break every bone in my hand if it brought her relief.

I don't know what time it is when things change, when a nurse tells us Elsie is in transition. Time is moving differently, and my focus is entirely on Elsie. I don't feel the fatigue hanging heavy on my shoulders, don't feel the grumbling in my stomach indicating it's been too long since I last ate a protein bar. I don't notice anything except the sweat on Elsie's brow, the monitor that beeps when her blood pressure goes a little higher, the way she grits her teeth at the feeling of pressure as another contraction hits.

At some point, the nurse returns, smiling, and tells us it's time for Elsie to start pushing. It simultaneously feels like I just got here and like we've been in this room for weeks, waiting on this moment. Now time narrows to the seconds of pushing during contractions, the windows of time between them. I'm whispering words to Elsie, unsure fully of what I'm even saying. I tell her she's strong. That she's doing great. That it's just going to take one more push until we see her.

I don't know how long I tell her these things, only that, eventually, the doctor and a NICU team arrive, in case the baby needs immediate intervention when she gets here. Then there are bright lights that heat up the room, people that fill it up until there's not much space. I tighten my grip on Elsie's thigh, my other hand in hers. I tell her it's happening, it's time.

She nods, that determined look I've seen on her face a thousand times filling her expression. She's done so many hard things. She's danced on blistered feet and sprained ankles. She's woken up at the crack of dawn and stayed at a studio until well after dark, her muscles quivering and lungs burning. She's watched all her hard work come crumbling down after a devastating injury and picked herself back up again. She's lost a baby and held herself together through the fear of losing another. She's found her way back to herself and to me. She's done so many hard things, and I know she can do this.

I tell her that too.

Time slips, a ripple in the universe, a shooting star that you make a wish on, there and gone in an instant. And then I hear it, a cry. I look from Elsie to the baby the doctor is holding. My baby, *our* baby. And when I turn back to Elsie, she's already watching me, awe written in the exhausted lines of her face.

I lean down, my lips finding hers. "You did it," I whisper against them. "You did it, Elsie."

Her tears are salty, mingling with the taste of mine, as she says, "We did it, Beau."

THIRTY-THREE
ELSIE
SEPTEMBER
ONE DAY POSTPARTUM

"Beatrice—one who brings joy."

I shake my head and adjust the baby in my arms. "Mmm, I don't like it."

"Me neither, actually," Beau says.

He's been throwing out baby names for the last hour, and we're no closer to picking one. Our theory that we'd know a name when we met her was wrong. The only thing I knew was how much I loved her, immediately. I'd never felt anything like it before.

I snuggle her a little closer, and she sighs contentedly, continuing to nurse. She caught on like a champ, latching within minutes of the doctor putting her on my chest. She was healthy and crying, so the NICU was able to leave, unneeded. The rest of the nurses and doctor soon filed out too, and then it was just the three of us alone, Beau counting her fingers and toes as I fed her for the first time. It felt like magic, like something too good to be true. A dream I couldn't have perfected if I'd tried.

"Did you know Beau means beautiful?" Beau asks, grinning at me. "So does Bella. We should name her Bella so we can both be called beautiful every day."

I roll my eyes, suppressing a laugh. "No Bella, too *Twilight*."

"*Twilight* was our make-out movie in high school."

"I know, so we can't name our child after the main character."

Beau sighs and stretches, his shirt lifting to reveal a slice of tanned skin. "We had some good times during those movies."

Heat licks at my cheeks. "Pick a name, Beau."

He flashes me another grin, and I can't help but notice the dark circles beneath his eyes. I don't think he's slept in days. "What about Rose?"

"What does that mean?"

"Rose," he replies.

A laugh slips out of me, jostling the baby back awake from where she'd drifted off.

"I should have guessed."

"Felicity means happiness."

I tilt my head from side to side. "I like it but don't love it."

"Chloe. Eveline. Celeste."

My eyes find his, and I let out a sigh. "None of them feel right."

His chin dips in a nod of agreement. "I know, I don't think so either."

"Shouldn't it just come to us? Your mom said she looked at you and Cooper and just knew your names."

"Have you met Cooper? His personality was formed directly out of the womb."

"She's just sweet," I tell him, holding her a little closer to me. She's drifted off again, and I pull her away from my chest, clipping my gown back in place before returning her to my body. She snuggles against me, and I swear my heart sighs. When I look at Beau, his expression matches the way I feel inside. Like mush that's in love.

"She is sweet," he says, and pushes up out of his chair, coming to stand beside us. When he lifts her off my chest and holds her against his own, I think I could cry just from looking at them. I can't believe this almost didn't happen. That if I hadn't stepped into a bar eight months ago, he never would have taken me home. I never would have kissed him, and he never would have peeled my clothes off. I never would have stared at that positive pregnancy test and known my life had just flipped upside down. Again. We never would have found our way back to each other.

If it weren't for that perfect little baby in his arms, we never would have had our second chance. We never would have made something new out of the rubble.

I pull out my phone and snap a photo, knowing I'm going to frame the image of Beau holding our daughter, haloed in the golden morning light, and put it on my nightstand so I can look at it for the rest of time.

He's humming to her now, rocking back and forth. He's a natural at this. Last night when she cried, I fed her and he sang to her until she fell asleep on his still bare chest. I can still hear the sound of it, his deep voice singing softly in her ear. I thought my heart might explode just watching them.

Ripping my gaze from them, I pull up the web browser on my phone and type "baby names that mean new" into the search bar. Name meanings have never seemed that important to me before, and I still think if I found a name that we both loved that meant something like *desert dirt*, I'd probably still choose it. But right now, we're at a loss, and I'm ready to chase down any lead. I'm tired of not knowing what to call her, of feeling like she's missing something vital that only we can provide.

I tap on the first website that pops up and scroll through the names until one catches my eye. In my chest, something clicks into place, the last puzzle piece on a project I've been working on for nine long months.

My eyes lift to Beau, still rocking our daughter, humming a tune I would recognize anywhere. It's the song we danced to at our wedding. There's something poetic about him humming it now. A new beginning for us.

"Beau?" I ask.

He looks up at me, still swaying. His eyes are tired but bright, so full of love I think my chest might crack open. He looks like every dream I've ever had come true.

"What about Nova? It means new."

EPILOGUE
ELSIE
JUNE
NINE MONTHS LATER

In theory, a date night sounds like a beautiful thing. In reality, it means I have to pump bottles for the Jenningses to give Nova, which I *hate* doing because it's so much more difficult than just feeding her. It also means we will have to pick her back up later tonight, and she will definitely wake up and it will be impossible to get back to sleep because she's teething and has been constantly uncomfortable for the last month.

Dating was easier than I expected the first six months of Nova's life. Lottie and Clint were always happy to have extra time with her and we would keep date nights short enough to be between feedings. But for the last couple months, she's been in a growth spurt and constantly hungry. And teething, which has made her in so much pain. It's been hard on all of us.

Which is why Beau suggested a date night. Something for just us. And I'm excited, I truly am, but I'm also tired. And a night rotting on the couch sounds more appetizing than getting dressed up and going out.

My phone vibrates with a text right after I put Nova down in her playpen so I can get ready. It's from Beau.

Beau: Wear that blue dress tonight.

He's talking about the one Jade wore to my baby shower, the one I would have killed to fit into at the time. I dig around for it in the closet and hold it up to myself in front of the mirror. It's going to be tighter than it was before, especially since my activity level has been way lower for the past nine months.

When I came back from maternity leave three months ago, I told Tonya I'd do it—I'd take over the studio. I wasn't sure if I was capable before, but if motherhood has taught me anything, it's that my abilities are limitless. We've been transitioning over ownership, and she's been showing me the ropes. It means teaching fewer classes, but I'm not interested in giving that up completely, so we're in the process of hiring a few more teachers to help with my workload.

It's been good. Hard, but good.

I stare at my reflection in the mirror for a moment, my free hand smoothing over the soft fabric. I've been working at the studio nonstop for the last three months, usually bringing Nova with me, and I can't remember the last time I did something for myself. The last time I got dressed up in something other than workout clothes or jeans and a T-shirt and felt beautiful.

Maybe a date night is *exactly* what I need.

I take my time curling my hair and applying my makeup, pausing every few minutes to help Nova with something, and when I'm finished, I look at myself again. The dress falls against my skin, settling over my curves. My hair falls over my shoulders in a sheet. My perfume, carefully applied to my pulse points, makes me smell like something other than *baby* for the first time in months.

Taking out my phone, I snap a photo and send it to Beau. He responds immediately.

Beau: I can't take you out like that. Everyone on the premises will be drooling over you.

I smother a smile and respond.

Elsie: I'm only interested in what you think of how I look.

Beau: I can send you a VERY detailed message when I'm not standing next to my father.

Beau: Also, I got held up here. Want to just meet me at the ranch?

I respond, telling him I'll be there soon, and pack Nova and her diaper bag into the car. She babbles the whole way there, bringing a smile to my face. When she's not teething, she's such a happy baby. She reminds me so much of Beau. She has my features, but his temperament. When she smiles her gummy smile at me, I swear sometimes it's like looking right at him. She may look like me, but there's a glimmer behind her eyes that's all Beau.

The ride to the ranch is quick, the windows down. There's nothing like summer in Montana. I remember sitting on our apartment balcony in Utah, watching the sunset on rare nights I made it home from the studio before dark, thinking about how they never felt quite right. The colors were there, the blues and pinks and golds, but the atmosphere was wrong. The air didn't carry the smell of larkspurs and honeysuckle, and the mountains were all wrong. *This* is where I was always meant to be.

I turn down the long dirt road to Lucky Stars and pull beneath the familiar sign, the rusted metal stars and lasso seeming to wink at me in the sunshine. The sight of it has always made me feel like I'm home, but it means something even more special to me now. When we told the Jenningses the name we had picked out, Clint called her our little lucky star, and they haven't stopped since.

I take a turn for the stables instead of heading toward the main house, since it's where Beau told me he'd be. We pull up in a cloud of dust a moment later. "Nova, you ready to see

Dada?" She's been saying it lately, and every time, it makes my heart swell in my chest, full to bursting.

She does it now, repeating the word over and over again as I unclip her from her car seat, grinning at her tiny face. She blinks at me with wide blue eyes and smiles back. I smooth a hand over her pale fuzzy hair and press a kiss to the same spot on her cheek that I always do—her deep dimple.

Her little body curls into mine as I pick her up, and I breathe in the scent of her—lavender soap and baby powder.

"Dada," she chants again.

I smile. "Yeah, Nova girl. Let's go find Dada."

But when I look up, I see what she did when I was focused on her. Beau standing in the huge doorway to the stables, one hand tucked in the pocket of suit pants that hug him in all the right places, a jacket draped over his shoulder, hanging onto a single finger on this other hand.

I blink at him, confused. "You're all dressed up."

He grins, something slow and seductive that makes honey slide down my spine and settle somewhere in my stomach. "I have a hot date tonight."

I look him over, my eyes hitting on all my favorite places. His thick thighs, broad, muscular shoulders, the mustache that I have *really* grown to love. His hair that is never quite styled. "I think *I'm* the one with a hot date."

He comes closer, moving slow enough that I can feel each step like a tether tied between us, tugging on my belly button. When he's close enough to touch, he leans down and kisses our daughter right where I did a moment ago before standing back to his full height, his body blocking out the bright summer sunshine enough so that I can only see him.

Sometimes I still can't believe he's mine. That he's mine *again*. That he took me back and that we somehow made it work after everything that happened. That we put ourselves back together and made something new.

His eyes are soft as he watches me, and I know he's seeing every thought in my mind. Before, that would have scared me—terrified me—but I like that he can read me like this now, that he sees what I need sometimes before I do. That he pushes me to take it before I get to a point where I fall apart again. Sometimes I wonder if he would have been able to do the same back then if I'd let him. Other times, when I'm watching him rock Nova back to sleep in the middle of the night or play with her on a blanket in the backyard, I'm glad I didn't, that we went through what we did, when we did, because otherwise, our life wouldn't look like it does now.

"I had an idea," he says, voice a rough scrape against my skin.

"What's that?"

He holds my gaze for a beat, and in his, I see a kaleidoscope of emotions—ones as familiar to me as my own—love, admiration, hope, longing, disbelief, contentment, and something else that isn't quite tangible enough to describe.

"Let's get married."

A laugh slips out of me.

In my arms, Nova mimics it. Beau's gaze settles on her, tender, before lifting back up to mine.

"We're already married."

A smile blooms over his face like a sunflower tilting toward the sun. "Let's get married again." He pauses for a moment, watching me. Watching as the matching smile lifts my lips. "Right now."

My jaw drops open. "What?"

His grin turns sly. "Everyone is already at the big house waiting on us."

I spin in the direction of the big house, like I'm able to see it from here, but, of course, I can't, not over the rolling hills dotted with cattle and horses. "You're not serious."

His hand finds mine, and I feel as he slips something warm onto my finger. I look down at it, my shock deepening. It's my wedding ring, the one we had to coax off my finger when my hands started swelling during pregnancy. We put it with my engagement ring in a jewelry dish on our dresser and didn't think about it again until we got home from the hospital. But somehow, it had gone missing. We tore the house apart looking for it, but never found it, so I've just been wearing my engagement ring alone since then.

"Something old," he says, and I can hear the smile in his voice. He drops my hand and palms my hip. "Something blue."

When he meets my eyes again, his are glowing.

"Where did you find it?" I ask.

A laugh rumbles from his chest. "In Nova's toy box, of all places. A few months ago," he tells me, his thumb moving back and forth across my hip, gliding against the fabric in a way that feels distracting. "But I was saving it for this."

"You planned all this months ago?"

His chin dips in a nod. "I planned it before Nova was even born."

Tears prick at the backs of my eyes, and I fight to blink them away, but his palm finds my face, thumb swiping away the stray tear. "I've got a pair of earrings in my pocket from my mom. She wore them on her wedding day. She wanted them to be your something old."

My throat feels thick. I'm constantly in awe of the way the Jenningses love. Of the way they love *me* when I treated them so badly. When I asked Beau to leave and froze them out. But they welcomed me back with open arms. I've never experienced love the way they give it.

I push past the lump in my throat and ask, "What's the something new?"

A slow smile crests over Beau's face like the sun breaking over the mountains in the morning, lighting the world up in a new day. "I thought that was obvious," he says. "It's Nova."

AUTHOR'S NOTE

Eight months before I began writing this book, my first pregnancy ended in miscarriage. My story is very different from Elsie and Beau's, and while the two of them and their tumultuous marriage had been in the back of my mind for years, the miscarriage element became something I knew I wanted to include in their story. When I started writing, I never had any idea I would end up pregnant again and that I would get to go on this journey with them. For so many reasons, this book has taken over my whole heart. It's all my mushiest pieces on four hundred pieces of paper. I hope their story—one of grief, hope, tenderness, love, passion, and fresh starts—finds the right people. If you see yourself on any of these pages, I hope you know you're loved, and that things will get better. I hope this story brings you a little bit of peace and hope wherever you are.

ACKNOWLEDGEMENTS

As always, I have many people to thank. And as always, they will pretty much be the same as the last book because I have the greatest and steadiest support system.

To my cover designer and editors, thank you for bringing my vision and words to life. Thank you for polishing them into something beautiful.

To my agent, Dani, thank you for championing this book from the very start and working hard to get it into as many hands as possible. You're taking my stories to places I couldn't have even imagined, and I think it's so dang cool.

To my best friends, Kelsey, Juliana, and Jamie, I couldn't do any of this without you. Writing and life would be much bleaker without you in it.

To my readers, I owe all of this to you. I wouldn't be where I am today without your constant support. You make all my dreams come true, and if I think about it for too long, I will really start crying.

To my husband and the little baby in my stomach that is currently kicking my laptop, I'm so thankful to call you mine.

And lastly, to my Savior, for giving me this beautiful, beautiful life.

ABOUT THE AUTHOR

Madison Wright is a hopeless romantic living her own happily ever after in Nashville. After falling in love with reading at a young age, she always dreamed of becoming an author. She writes romances that feel cozy and always feature a happily-ever-after.

She's a big fan of sunshine, pastries, and any book with a love story. When she's not reading or writing, she can be found exploring her city with her husband and dog.

To keep up to date, follow on socials @authormadisonwright, join her newsletter, or go to her website www.authormadisonwright.com.

Printed in Dunstable, United Kingdom